Table of Contents

The Families	vii
Chapter 1: Roaring River Woman (1920)	1
Chapter 2: Born of Ache (1930)	42
Chapter 3: Mother's Constitutional (1936)	77
Chapter 4: The Relief (1937)	103
Chapter 5: The Terrible Twinning (1938)	138
Chapter 6: A Seven Year Ache (1939, Spring)	168
Chapter 7: Six Men For Every Girl (1939, Fall)	205
Author's Note: The Reality of Eugenics in Canada	257
Acknowledgements	259

The Families

WORKMAN FAMILY
JAMES (1890-1917) AND JOSEPHINE WORKMAN (NEE FISHER) M. 1906

+ Kenneth James b. 1906
+ Rose Josephine b. 1910
+ Kathleen b. 1913
+ Carleen Margery b. 1914

LABEAU FAMILY
ALBERT AND JOSEPHINE LABEAU M. 1919

+ Eileen b. 1920
+ Albert Jr. b. 1921
+ Stillborn twin boys b. 1922
+ Twins Pansy and Tansy b. 1923
+ Beatrice b. 1924
+ Stillborn girl 1925
+ Lily b. 1926
+ Valentine "Vallee" b. 1929

KIRK FAMILY
CHARLES AND ELVIE KIRK (NEE KELVEY) M. 1908

+ Culain b. 1910
+ Crofter b. 1913
+ Christian b. 1916
+ Faith b. 1918
+ Hope b. 1920
+ Trooper Roaring Kirk b. 1923
+ Charity 1925 (stillborn)
+ Conan b. 1928
+ Grace b. 1930
+ Calhoun b. 1932

KELVEY FAMILY
MITCH AND ROSIE KELVEY (NEE WORKMAN) M. 1924

Petunia Rose b. 1924
Margery Josephine b. 1926
Mitchell Kenneth b. 1928
James Workman Kelvey b. 1929

ROSIE AND CULAIN KIRK

Carly Carleen Kelvey b. 1933
Cathy Kathleen Kelvey b. 1936
Charlotte Eileen Kelvey b. 1938

ROSIE AND OTHER

April Hope Kelvey b. 1940

Chapter 1

Roaring River Woman

(1920)

My momma ain't no girlie-woman. My big brother Kenny says that back east in Ontario, even before we come out here to the homestead, Momma was already famous for two things.

Number one, for being a white woman that married my poppa, my real daddy, who was not white, strictly speaking. Kenny says my poppa's daddy was a slave down south in United States of 'Merica, and he got away, come up to Canada on some sort of railroad they got underground. But my poppa favoured his momma's looks, Granny Workman, and she was Irish just like Momma's folks. So if people didn't know us, then they would never guess about Poppa's mulatto blood. Problem was, all the folks back there did know us and I guess they did not like the fact of who we was. Why, Momma's own family turned aside of her after she married Poppa. That's why we never known them.

Number two, for being the woman that took the bull by the horns. That's kind of a saying folks use sometimes, I know, taking the bull by the horns. But I'm saying it exact. Momma honestly did take a real bull by its horns and make it heed. This was back when Kenny was but a little gaffer and Momma and Poppa was working labour for some farmer. Momma herself was just a young girl back then. A slip of a girl, Kenny says. Why, even today, Momma ain't no more than four foot eleven.

Anyways, that day Momma was working with the women up in the yard and my poppa was down in the corral with the men, mending post. They'd blocked the bull safe back in the chute, but somehow he got out and come tearing into the corral, surprised the men, and drove my poppa face down right into the dirt. Had him pinned there, gouging and stomping at him, trying to kill him. The men was all yelling and heaving rocks, darting in front of him, whacking his backside with buckets and boards.

That bull did not care. He was too busy mashing Poppa into the ground to take mind of three or four men. Puny things they were to him, like flies at a picnic. He was a mad, careening bull, for God's sake! Over three thousand pounds! Poppa was a goner, Kenny says, weren't nothing no one could do about it.

But she came, my momma, peeling down from the house, howling like a hurricane, yelling my poppa's name. "James! James!" she was screaming, skirts a sailing and long braids flying. Threw herself between the wood rails and come up eye to eye with that bull. Bull was so startled, he too just gawked at her, same as the men.

But she grabbed him square, right by each horn, stood firm, cursing and shaking and going purple in the face. Teeth all gritted, lip curled, some sort of angry animal sound coming out of her. "Git off him, you!" she told the bull. "Git off!" She wrestled that huge head up to her level. Bull just stood there mesmerized, getting stared down by Momma, huffing steam and slobber, slowly easing his weight off Poppa.

I guess the men stopped gaping and hauled Poppa out from under there. Nobody knows to this day how Momma got out herself, but Kenny says that by the time they was dragging Poppa under the rail to safety, Momma was already in front of them, hollering him back to life. "James! James! Don't you leave me, damn you!" That's what she told him. "You hear me, James? You ain't leavin'!"

He did leave us though. Not that year and not by his choosing, but he was called to the Great War and had to go, and never did come home again.

Kenny says Poppa died at the Battle of Vimy Ridge. I don't really know too much about battles and wars, all them far off places and years you got to memorize for school. I just know I miss my poppa, and it aches right here in my chest, wishing he weren't took from us.

I think Momma misses him too, though she don't say so. Probably don't want to hurt Albert's feelings, her new husband, my step-daddy. Sometimes I ask her though, about back east and our life before. Things about my poppa and who our people was. Whether they might maybe take us back again someday.

Momma says ain't no use remembering back east. She says what we got now is each other and Manitoba, and we got to go on. That's all there is, Momma says, just each other and hard work and whatever's ahead of us.

* * *

It's our second year on the homestead, walking to the Roaring River schoolhouse, when me and my little sister Carleen first come upon the big animal. Carleen had to be six that year, making me ten, and we're about a mile down the mucky trail, doing our best to keep out of the mud and up on the skinny ledge of grass against the bush line. We're getting clawed by twigs and brambles, and just when we come around the bend, there it is, right in our path. Black, with shaggy, dirty fur and a long snout. It's full the size of our cow Bossy but squat to the ground, tearing and eating at a log there, making a low, thick grunting noise.

What do I do? Do I keep goin'? The animal don't seem to be taking no mind of us. Yet my heart is beating a mile a minute. It's so big! And got them mean-looking claws.

We'd been begging Momma all week to let us walk the two miles down trail to school and she finally gave in. "God knows yuz are drivin' me crazy with yur pesterin'," she said this morning at the table. "But Rosie, don't you git off that path. This here is Manitoba we're in now, it ain't settled like it was back east. There's wild animals out here, coyotes and wolves and God knows what. And you come straight back after, ya hear?"

"Hurray!" me and Carleen was singing. We get to learn reading and all, hold the actual books in our hand, and then we got twenty other children to play with at the dinner hour, tag or ball or Duck, Duck, Goose. We ran and got our duds on. Momma handed me our lard pail with the bread and butter sandwiches and off we went, not thinking nothing but that we get to go to school. We didn't never think about no big animal on the trail.

"Rosie?" my little sister is whimpering, eyeing the beast. I got her by the hand and she kind of moves over behind me there, up in the pussy willows.

The animal don't even seem to see us, just keeps ripping that log to shreds, huffing away, eating at it. Yet, I'm scared to go by. It's so awful big, got a horrible smell to it like a rotting carcass, and look at them claws—like the prongs on a pitchfork!

So I tell Carleen we better go back to the homestead. "Aaaw!" she groans. Yet she starts backing up quick enough, clinging to my hand.

We back ourselves up a bunch of steps till we get around the bend, then we turn and head for home, but it's a good mile on a uphill rise. At times, I swear I hear movement back behind us there, so I hold tight to my little sister and we hurry along. I keep looking back, afraid it's after us, and we're both sweating good by the time our homestead clearing comes into view.

I see Momma in the garden spot, chopping at that big ash stump, trying to drag it out of the ground. And that's exactly when I hear a big crack behind me, like a log being snapped in two. I just know the big animal is coming for us! I go all skittery, yelling and screeching, running to Momma for all I'm worth.

Momma looks up, sees us running scared, grabs the axe at the base of the head, jumps to the grass, and comes pelting towards us. "What is it?" she's yelling, face all tight screwed up. "What is it? What is it?" Her muddy boots must be sucking on her, as she kicks them into the air while she runs, boots and muck flying.

I'm screeching about the big animal, Carleen bawling loud back behind me, and I run right into Momma's open arms. She grabs onto Carleen too, pushing us both behind her, and stands forward with her chin out, axe held ready, her other fist balled up. I'm breathing hard, holding fast to Momma, Carleen sobbing into her skirts.

"Are ya hurt? Are ya hurt?" Momma demands, still glaring at the entrance to the trail. Carleen shakes her head, clinging onto Momma's hips.

Momma bobs her head out and back, peering down the trail. Just trees and more trees, that's all I can see now. No big animal after all.

Momma turns to me. "Now, Rosie, speak slow," she commands, my chin in her hand, "and tell me agin. What did ya see?"

"We dit'n know what to do!" I plead, all desperate like. I try to describe the big animal and where we seen it. I say we was scared and thought we best come back.

"What kind of animal?" she demands. "Did it chase ya?"

"I guess not," I tell her, squinting at the trail. "I don't know. I thought I heard it." I try to describe the animal. A big animal, full as long as the trail is wide but short to the ground. Near big as a cow, and a lot bigger than Scrappy, that old mutt that showed up here and adopted us. Black and bushy-looking with sharp claws, I tell her, and a bad smell like dead things.

"Don't be mad, Momma," Carleen begs, gazing up with her dark tragic eyes. "We twied to go to school."

"No, no," Momma clucks. "You done right."

Albert was down in the Two—that's the two acres we're supposed to have in crop this year if we don't want to lose the homestead—and he comes riding up, my big brother Kenny jogging along on foot.

Momma explains what we told her. "Musta bin a bear," she says. "I never seen one back east but they live out west here. Bin known to attack people but usually they don't—long as they got plenty else to eat."

She says Kenny will have to walk us to the schoolhouse the next little while, just in case, and us children cannot go alone to get water from the river. That's a place that draws all kinds of beast. Then she tells us that if we're ever on our own and we see a big animal like that, we should just do what we done. Give it room, steer clear, and come back home.

"But stay together!" she says, catching my eye. "You understand me, Rosie? Don't you never leave yur little sister behind."

"I won't, Momma," I tell her, slipping my arm over Carleen's shoulder. Kenny has went down the trail a ways to check. He returns saying there's no tracks nor nothing. He comes and squeezes us girls both together, so we hug onto him and start turning towards the house.

"Or, here's a good trick," Daddy Albert pipes up. We all startle and turn his way. He says a man in town told him that bears is just dumb animals, easily fooled. He says the man told him that when a bear comes after you, you should just lay down and stay still, play dead. Trick them, you see? They don't know what you are—might be a log or something—so they won't bother with you. "So that's what I say ya should try if ya see that animal agin," he advises me and Carleen. "Jist lay down and play dead."

We gawk at him. He's contradicting Momma. We look from her to him and back again, but Momma just purses her lips and gives a blink.

"Huh!" Kenny says, with kind of a sneer, and spits out the side of his mouth.

Daddy Albert collects up Clyde's reins, happy as a lark, and goes strolling down to the river to get a drink.

We watch him go and then I look back to Momma. "Should we... what do we do then, Momma?"

She studies Daddy Albert's back, a little consternated I think, and shakes her head. "Animals ain't stupid," she tells us, quiet. "Only stupid animal I know of is people. Every animal wants to live and will take food where they find it. Now, if ya come between a female and its young, that's a differnt thing. Any female will kill if they hafta, to pertect their young, like. But as to jist comin' upon a wild animal, mindin' its own bizness, well I say keep yer head about ya, walk away, and ya should be alright."

I nod and breathe deep, relieved for knowing what the answer is.

"But like I said, if it's comin' after yuz, stick together. And if it was to attack, well then, fight like hell. Ya never wanna act like easy food."

She starts back for the garden, us children following along. Kenny swings Carleen up in his arms and she giggles. He's got his other arm over my shoulder and I got my arm around his waist. "Now come help me with those damn ash roots, you girls," Momma says, "since yuz ain't makin' it to the schoolhouse today anyways."

Kenny leaves us at the garden spot and heads back out to the field. Momma grabs up her muddy boots where she flung them and starts scraping off the muck with a poplar twig. "Playin' dead?" she's muttering to herself. "What queer kinda thinkin' is that? Ya start playin' dead out here in the bush and the next thing ya know, you will be dead."

* * *

Well, our Saturday in town has turned out a bust. It's been rainy and wet the entire month of May but we can't wait no more to get the seed in the ground. So Daddy Albert and Kenny had to go into town today for seed and supplies. Momma was staying back as Carleen was fevered and phlegmy again, and Momma wanted to get the eyes dug out of them old seed potatoes anyways. But I wanted to go along on the buckboard and Momma said I could. We was hoping them clouds floating high up would just blow away. God knows them fields is pure muck already.

But no. We was longer than we hoped getting supplies and once we're heading out the highway, the sky opens. There's no trees nearby for shelter so Kenny puts me on the floor down under the wood seat with a old blanket around me and seed bags stacked in front to block the rain a little. Him and Albert are sitting up on the seat, taking the brunt of it. But it's coming down in sheets and then in buckets and we are wet to the bone.

At the turn onto Pretty Valley Road, there's a lot with some overhanging trees and we pull in under there until the rain lets up. Kenny fetches dry wood from under some deadfall and builds a fire in a little stand of poplars, then we all go to wringing ourselves out. Kenny takes some saplings and fashions a wrack for me to put my sweater and stockings on and leans it towards the heat. The men have their hats and overgear slung onto the little bushes all around too, so we just sit in our circle there, leaning against different trees, waiting for things to dry.

I watch my brother where he's slouched in against his tree. At fourteen, Kenny is lanky-framed and long as a man, his pant legs grown too short for him. His suspenders sag when he bends, though, his chest not yet filled out. He has curly black hair and dark features like me. Momma tells folks that her first husband, us Workman children's father, was what you call Black Irish and we got our looks from him. She tells us that anything more than that is nobody's business but our own.

My stomach growls. We tried munching on the bread and jam Momma packed up for us, but everything has got soggy. Then I remember them lollipops Daddy Albert bought in town for me and my sister Carleen. I leave the golden one in the paper and take mine out—it's red, the best of all—and I go to licking it.

Daddy Albert is shivering, back hunched stiffly against his tree, bits of dirty blond hair matted down here and there on his bald spots. But he smiles over at me, the big gap in his teeth barely showing.

"Strawberry for Rosie, right, Sweet Cheeks?" he grins. "Butterscotch for Carleen."

"Yup!" I grin back. "Thank you, Daddy." Kenny frowns and looks away. I correct myself. "Uh, Daddy Albert, I mean."

When Momma and Albert got together, he said right away that us children should call him Daddy. I'd been aching for a daddy of my own ever since I could remember. But Kenny had argued back right off that Albert was *not* our daddy, we had but one daddy, and Albert couldn't hold a candle to him. It was a terrible row, Kenny so angry, and Momma very consternated. That was the start of the new family.

My feelings about Daddy Albert is pretty mixed up. He always been nice to me and there ain't a whole lot of niceness in my life. Like two summers ago, on the train coming out here, I was only eight, kind of scared and shy, yet bored and whiny on the long, long trip. Momma tired of my complaints and questions, but yet, Daddy Albert didn't. He played cards and games with me and told stories about his boyhood in the Mohawk territories, his adventures working the ships on Lake Ontario and all.

Still, I feel wrong to like Daddy Albert, as if I'm not being loyal to my own poppa, or to Kenny, who purely hates him.

We was full of hope, all that long, hard trip. Posters at the town hall back east had showed nice little farm houses, rich fields, plump cattle. "Come West for the Good Life," they said. "Good Land Free in the Swan River Valley. Homesteads for the Having."

When we stepped down on the platform in Swan River, Manitoba, the Homestead Agent was there to meet us, and after Daddy Albert signed his book, he read aloud from some official papers. It turned out there was all these *Improvements* we had to do. Improvements, he called them. Had to have a well dug, a house built, two acres of land cleared and in crops. We had two years to make them improvements, and if we didn't, we would lose the homestead.

Momma blinked. "But... but..." she stammered. "We *own the land*. It's ours now, ain't it? We paid everthin' we had to get here."

"You *signed for* the land," the man corrected. "You get to live on it and work it." He was smirking like all get out. "But Gov'ment of Canada *owns the land*. Homestead is yurs, only if you can prove you deserve it. Prove yur the type we want here in the Swan River Valley. Hard-workin'. Worthy. God-fearin'."

Momma sat quiet and vexed all the long, slow wagon ride through the valley with its farms and golden fields, then up into the hills. Twelve miles we rode, fifteen miles, and the farther we went, the wilder the land. We crossed narrow bridges over a crashing, wild river that, each time I asked, the man said was the Roaring River. Two, three, four times we crossed the Roaring, rolling and thrashing its way along, till we turned off the main dirt road and went bumping and jolting up this skinny mountain trail through dense brush. Finally, the wagon moaned to a stop. "Here's yur homestead," the man said.

Carleen was whiny coming out of sleep, scratching at the welts of bug bites on her arms. I was trying to calm her, but I lifted my head high as I could, trying to see. Where was the homestead, the house and garden spot, the little white fence? All I seen was heavy bush. Momma slid herself off the wagon, all four foot eleven of her. Trees and more trees, that's all there was, far as the eye could see.

"My God!" she said that day. "It's the end of the world."

But Momma just dug in and got to work. She took our wagon box, turned it over, and made a lean-to for us to sleep in while they got a little shack threw together and a shed for the animals. Lord, lord, the bugs and the heat and the work we done scrubbing that wild, wild land.

Well, it's time to hitch up Clyde and get going, but now them two are fighting again. Kenny says the timber is loaded too far back on the buckboard, it'll tip going uphill, but Daddy don't want to do all the work of reloading it. He says it'll be fine. Kenny says he don't think so and they natter back and forth. Kenny finally grits his teeth and hitches up Clyde and we head out. But the dirt road is mucky and miserable, small streams of water running down as we come up. Terrible slow going.

It's getting dusk already and we're all tuckered out, especially Clyde, by the time we start our last steep trail from the road. The wagon's slipping and creaking and I'm asking myself why I ever wanted to go to town anyways. We've got the seed bags and a bucket of nails at the front for balance, but that timber is weighing us to the rear. On some of the steeper parts, it feels like the front wheels is near lifting off the ground.

"That's what I thought," Kenny says, glaring at the back of Daddy Albert. "If she starts to tip backwards, Rose," he tells me, "you jump off and to the side." I say I will.

This heavy rig is chewing up what's left of the trail, our wheels weaving and crossing back on theirselves in the muddy ruts. We're sliding this way and that—pretty scary—the daylight fading, and then Clyde gets so mired down, he can't even move. The men get off and try to drive him out of there. They're slipping around too, Daddy Albert yanking Clyde by his halter and Kenny heaving against the back of the rig. I call, "Kenny, you mind if that timber slides off, jump aside!" He says he will and then Clyde gives a great heave and we creak forwards.

We're only a few hundred feet from the yard when we get bogged again. Daddy Albert jumps down and grabs Clyde rough by the bridle, cussing a blue streak, which only scares Clyde, making him pull his head up and start backing away. Daddy's slipping and sliding and covered in mud, and it's starting to rain again. Kenny yells up to Daddy, saying he'll lead Clyde now, let him try. But Daddy only curses harder, slapping and punching at Clyde's withers. Poor Clyde just keeps yanking his head back and can't budge a inch.

Daddy comes stomping back and grabs the whip where it's fastened on the outside of the wagon box, Kenny yelling that he can get us out, no need for the whip. Daddy spins around to go back at Clyde, slips, and falls with a great splash right on his arse in the muddy gruel.

Well, my Lord, he's in a rage! Flailing and screeching, he clambers out of the rut, grabs Clyde's halter rough, and starts whipping on him. Clyde goes terrified and rears back, screaming, the wagon swinging sideways, stuck deeper and deeper, and I'm holding onto the seat for dear life. Half the lumber goes sliding off the back, just missing Kenny's head as he dives for the bushes.

"Ken! Kenny!" I'm yelling. "Kenny, is ya hurt?"

He untangles hisself from the hawthorn brush and stands, fists on his hips. "I'm okay, Rose," he says. But I can see his black eyes slit at Daddy's back, where he's hollering and wrestling with Clyde like a mad man. Kenny sets his jaw, goes up there, and takes hold of the bridle. "No more!" he tells Daddy, taking firm hold of his shoulders and standing him aside. "Now you stand there and let *me* try!" Daddy huffs and steams, fists clutched, jaw tight, but stands where he's been put.

My knuckles have gone pure white, but I watch Kenny as he goes carefully around the rig, squatting here and there, figuring out where it's bogged and where it's clear. Then he moves to Clyde, quiet and sure, talks to him calm-like, telling him he's a good boy and we'll get this done. Clyde is calmer now, not so scared like he was, and whinnies softly back. Kenny takes ahold of the reins and helps him get straightened around and aimed forward.

Daddy Albert stands by the bush, sulky and shivering, arms crossed.

"Let's go home now, Clyde," Kenny tells the big horse. "Hey? Woun'cha like to get into yur warm shed and outta this rain? Have some nice oats for supper? Hey?" I grab onto the seat. Kenny drives forward, Clyde heaving and heaving good, Kenny right there with him, and they drag the rig free. I let out a whoop.

"Good boy, Clyde." Kenny's laughing. "Good, strong boy," he says, patting the big fellow. "Okay," he says to Daddy and me. "Let's get this lumber loaded back on."

"Do it yurself," Daddy screeches, "if yur so damn smart!" He goes stomping up the trail and into the yard. We watch him go.

"Huh!" Kenny says, and spits out the side of his mouth.

So then me and Kenny has to reload everything by ourselves. Dusk has fallen, though the rain's let up, and I keep glancing into the darkness behind me, remembering that big animal, my back crawling for how it could come up on us, sudden-like. But we do finally get Clyde under cover and took care of.

Momma comes out to the shed in a bit. I know she's tender-hearted for my brother and I watch her watching him, as he's scooping up feed from the bag on the back wall. "James!" she calls out to him. "Kenny, I mean," shaking her head. "Kenneth James. Come here, son." When he's done with the feedbag, Kenny comes over and tells Momma about Old Albert loading the timber too far back and not listening to reason. Old Albert, that's what Kenny calls him. Then how he acted like a child when Clyde got bogged and Kenny had to get him out.

Momma nods and stands quiet. "Hurt his pride, I guess," she replies. "Albert, I mean. Musta hurt his pride to be taught by a boy."

"Well it should!" Kenny huffs, crossing his arms. "Should hurt his pride to *hafta be* taught by a boy. The man's a idiot."

"Mm-hm," Momma responds, thoughtful. "But Ken, that idiot, as ya say, is the one with his name on the land we're all livin' on here."

Kenny comes to a stand and pays attention.

"Son," Momma tells him, "I know. I know it can be... exasperatin'. I know he's differnt then us, got his strange ways. But son, a boy has got to be able to work with the men. And if you and him don't learn to work together, we're gonna lose this homestead. Our last chance. Do ya understand? We'll lose everthin' if you don't learn to get along."

Kenny studies her a minute, says, "Alright Mother," and goes back to work.

Momma says there's pigs' feet in the pot, waiting for us when we're done, and she goes in. My stomach is grumbling something awful and I'm shivering, what with my soggy clothes and the menacing bush at the black edge of the yard. But I stay with Kenny and we fumble our way around in the dark for another hour, getting the chores finished. I don't care, I ain't leaving my brother to do it alone.

* * *

I wake in the pitch black night. Something big is moving around out there, huffing and growling. There's been noises in the night before, and in the morning, we find tracks. Deer, elk, moose. A raccoon crawled in under the floor of our shack once and got stuck, made a terrible racket trying to get out. There's coyotes that howl and yip somewheres way out on the mountainside too, making Scrappy try to howl back at them.

This is different. Scary. I can hear Clyde and our cow Bossy out in their shed, shuffling and pawing and making their worried sounds.

Whatever it is, I can hear it sniffing and lumbering outside these flimsy walls, with low, thick, huffing grunts and growls. There's a loud thump on the east wall, making the whole little house tremble. I grab Carleen and dive for the corner, holding her tight. "Momma?" I call into the blackness.

But then I hear her, over where the kitchen is. She's grabbed the iron pan from the hook on the wall, banging and rattling it with the wooden spoon. "Git outta here!" she's yelling loud. Over near her somewheres, I hear my big brother stomping hard, bashing the broom on the inside of the door. "Git outta here!" they're both yelling. "Go on, git outta here!"

Eventually, we don't hear nothing else. The barn animals have quieted. Momma lights the coal oil lantern but keeps it turned low. We wait awhile longer and then Kenny takes that poplar club of his and goes in the dark to check the animals, Daddy Albert standing on the top step with the lantern held high. Kenny returns and says there's some gouging on the door frame, like from claws, but the animals is okay, it didn't get in.

We go back to bed. But once I'm awake, how do I get to sleep again? Me and Carleen is bunched up together here on the cot in the corner, and it gets so terrible hot at night. Yet, we dasn't kick off the wool blanket or we'll wake covered in bites from mosquitos and black flies and whatever else wants to feast on us.

I wish I could sleep and have a nice dream. When Momma and us children was back east, waiting for Poppa to come home from the war, I would lay awake at night, aching for him. Well, I couldn't actually remember him, not really, being so little when he left, but I would try to imagine him. Momma always said that Kenny is Poppa's spitting image, so when I imagined Poppa, he'd be just like Kenny... except bigger and older and darker. Black hair, all wavy and thick. Face so brown and good, big smile, teeth white like pearl, eyes black as night.

And Kenny said that Poppa used to rock us children when we was babies, and sing to us. Each one had their own special song and mine was *The Wild Irish Rose*. So in my dreams, Poppa would be holding me and rocking me, singing my song, his voice as deep as Lake Ontario, warm as milk fresh from the cow.

I do remember that awful day by the old stone well, me about four years old, with Momma, getting water. A man bringing a letter and reading it to her—on account of she ain't much for reading. And when he read out the start of it, "To the widow of James Workman," or some such words, Momma half-fell, groping and grasping at the stone like her legs had gone rubber. Her face was grey, and I remember the fear shivering my back, cold fear. Because if Momma went down, what would happen to me?

"What Momma?" I kept wailing. Felt like bees buzzing in my brain. "What Momma? What it means?"

It meant everything.

But there we was, Momma a widow, scorned by her family, with Kenny and me and our sister Kathleen and baby Carleen, who Poppa never knew, with nothing and nobody in this world to help us. War widows at that time was a dime a dozen, Kenny says. We was living in some old saggy shack in the bush, wind blowing through the cracks, us children always hungry and fevered. And then my sister Kathleen, five years old, she went and died on us. Had the consumption, Kenny says, but it was the want that killed her. Want and hunger and being poor.

So then Momma said, "No more! I am not buryin' another child." She said we was leaving, going where nobody knew us, starting over, homesteading in the Northwest. Course, only a man could hold title to land, so that's when she found Daddy Albert and, lucky thing, he stepped up and offered his hand. She had her little widow's pension, thirty-eight dollars, seemed a lot at the time, and she put it all into tools and implements, the advance on the livestock, and train tickets and grub. Momma married Daddy Albert and we come out west on the train.

Carleen rolls over, flinging her arm onto my shoulder, face shoved into mine. She's too hot, as usual, so I try rolling over towards the wall. But with the feather tick being so old and worn, our cot is more like a hammock, and no matter how I try to get some space, we always roll down into the middle together.

"Carleen!" I mutter, shoving back at her, but it's in vain. Sometimes I wish I didn't even have a sister.

Little birds is singing in the trees, with their *cheep, cheep, cheer up*, making me yawn, the poplars sighing and whispering their morning's-coming song. There's shades of light at the small window and I can make out the black shape of the iron stove, and Kenny, curled up in his bedroll under the window. The big lump on the other wall is Momma's bed, where there's her and Daddy Albert and my new baby sister, Eileen.

My poppa... My poppa, dark and strong like my brother, holding me in his arms, singing to me... *My wild Irish rose, sweetest flower that grows...*

Squawk! The grate of the iron stove gets dragged over, startling me awake. Momma's up, loading the wood in. There's light in the room and Kenny comes in through the door with two pails of water from the river. I sigh and get my legs over the side of the bed, sitting there for a minute, yawning and trying to wake up. Another day and work needs doing.

Kenny tells Momma them tracks had four claws on the ends of long finger-toes and was bigger than his hand. They was stamped deep in the dirt, he says, whatever it was must have been very heavy. Probably five hundred pounds and then some.

"The big animal," Momma says. She says she don't want us children going down the trail to the outhouse after dark no more. Either we got to go before dusk or else we got to use the chamber pail in the corner.

I say, "Okay Momma."

"And don't go down to the river alone, ya hear?"

"No, Momma," I agree.

Daddy Albert is up at the table. He yells over, all friendly-like, "Good morning, Rosie Sweet Cheeks! Up 'n at 'em!"

Rosie Sweet Cheeks. That's what he likes to call me, a pet name, I guess you'd say. But Kenny don't like it, I can tell, so I don't like it neither.

"Don't call me that," I respond, head shaking. Then I heave myself up into the day and go help Momma with the breakfast.

*   *   *

Right after our porridge one day, me and Momma gets a bunch of water brought up from the river, get out the lye soap, the tub, and scrub board, and get at them clothes. But then here comes the men from the Homestead department, driving their Sunday buggy into our yard. They don't even come up to the house, just go shifting and snooping around the shed and the yard and the garden spot. The one fellow is pointing and sneering at our stuff, the other one scratching away in his tally book, the two of them muttering back and forth.

"Two-year mark is comin' up," Momma tells me low. "They's checkin' up on us, for the 'mprovements, like."

"Already?" I ask. Our improvements are not made. That animal shed still needs a lot of shoring up and the two acres is riddled with roots and gnarls, though we did clear the trees and we've planted seed. But the seed has come in patchy and what grain there is, is only a few inches high. We ain't sure why. Is it because we left them wet bags sitting in the shed for a week while it rained and they got blighted? Or is it like Momma says, that seed was bad when we bought it?

And of course, the well is still not dug. Daddy Albert had said he knew how to witch the water and he took hold of a big red willow branch that pointed right to a spot near the house. But we dug and dug and there weren't no water. Daddy Albert gave up and said we'd have to get it done after harvest. That turned into another argument with Kenny of course, and Momma had to go get them straightened out.

"They won't actually kick us off the land, will they?" I ask her now. "We got nowheres else to go. Momma?"

She don't answer. Just goes into the house, makes a nice big pot of Red Rose tea, and pours a couple cups with fresh cream. She puts some biscuits on our only China plate, and we take it out to the Homestead men. But they look down their nose at Momma's offering, sneering their turndown the way a person might say no to dog shit on a stick. They turn on their heels and march around back of the house, like we ain't even there.

"Huh!" Momma snorts. "Gonna be like that, is it?" We eat the biscuits ourselves and don't make no more tries at being cordial.

In a while, we see they have shuffled out to the Two, where Daddy Albert and Kenny is dragging deadfall to a burning pile. Next time we look, that black buggy is gone. We finish hanging the dresses and bloomers on the line, Momma puts baby Eileen in her cradle, I take Carleen by the hand, and we walk out there.

We can hear them arguing way off. "You done it on purpose!" Daddy Albert is shrieking into Kenny's face as we come up. "You done it on purpose, jist to spite me!" Near as I can make out, Kenny had Clyde dragging a big stump out to the pile and almost run over Albert's foot, where he was having a sit-down over by the tree line.

"For Christ Sake!" Momma yells. "Albert! Could ya take a break from yur bickerin' long enough to tell me what the hell the Homestead men had to say?"

He slits his eyes at Momma, all peevish. But when she raises her brows and gives him her full look, he changes his tune. He says they wasn't happy. Didn't look like much of a crop, they said, and they wanted a full barn for the animals, not just the shed we got going. And we better get that well in, that's a solid rule.

"Shit!" Momma says. "Even if we do somehow get it all done by fall, where does the money come from to buy flour and such for the winter? And cloth to make warm clothes for the childern? They damn near froze last year, and it's them chills that brings on the fevers."

"Mother," Kenny says. We look towards him but he just stands there. Then he clears his throat and says, "Mother. That Mandy Mine up north there is callin' for teamsters. The horses haul the copper ore the thirty miles out to Sturgeon Landing where they can barge it down to The Pas for the train to B.C. And they need men to drive the teams. I'm good with horses, I could go."

"No!" she tells him. "We need ya here to help with the land."

"Crop's already planted, Mother, such as it is," he says. "And it's good money up north, real good money. Tommy Mares is makin' ten dollars a week up there. Mother, they're jist cryin' for men and Tommy would speak up for me. Then I could send yuz money to get whatever ya need!"

"Uh-uh!" I tell him, head shaking. "No, Kenny."

"No!" Momma frowns. "We... We don't need that. We'll find the money somewheres."

"Like where, Mother?" Kenny speaks up. It ain't like him to argue with Momma. "Shovelin' shit outta barns for a bed in some farmer's bunk house? There ain't no money to be made around here."

Momma blinks, brows knit.

Daddy Albert pipes up. "Well, God knows he'd be more help sendin' money from up north than he is here at home, drivin' the team over top o' my feet."

Kenny ignores him. "Mother," he says, "I'd send yuz money when I could. Money to buy food and cloth, more lumber for shorin' up the buildings, better tools to dig the well, good seed for next year."

Momma looks away, lips pursed, head shaking. "No," she says.

I'm starting to breathe again, Momma ain't going to let him go. But then Kenny goes over and takes hold of her sleeve. "Mother," he tells her, like the teacher explaining how to add, step by step, "we need the money. And I can make the money up north. And I'm strong and I'm old enough and—"

"No!" she says, yanking her arm away, jaw set. "We do not need that!" She turns on her heels and goes sweeping away towards the house.

"Kenny!" I yell up at him, all mad, hands on my hips. "You ain't leavin'!" His eyes come down to me, but he says nothing, and it's like he doesn't see me. "Do not say that, Ken!" I tell him. Then I take firm hold of Carleen and go running fast, dragging her along, to catch up with Momma.

"No..." she's muttering to herself all the way to the house. "No... we *do not* need the money that bad!"

But all day long, I'm distractible and making mistakes, scraping my knuckles to bleeding on the washboard, dropping clean things in the dirt under the clothesline, all because of Kenny and his foolish talk about going away.

* * *

We got some jumper meat that one of the neighbours was trying to get rid of, shot out of season. It smelled a bit bad by the time it got here so Momma cooked it up in a stew with onions and turnips to hide the taste. But now Carleen is throwing up in the night, and I guess it gave me the trots. I got pain in my guts, I really need the outhouse, and Daddy Albert has gone and left the chamber pail outside again.

I hold it as long as I can, praying for dawn to come, but I'm desperate. So I feel my way to the table and light the lantern low, get on my dungarees, and start heading for the door. I know Scrappy's out there and he'll go down the trail with me, but I'm shaking just thinking about the heavy dark, being alone out there, and all the animals, especially them big tracks with the four finger-toes we seen before.

But now Kenny has crawled out of his bedroll, put on his pants, and is taking hold of the lantern. "Kenny?" I ask, all hopeful, "Is ya comin' with me?"

"Don't want no wild critters chippin' their teeth on my sister's tough little hide," he says. He tries to turn his face aside, but I can see him grinning. "That would be cruelty to dumb animals."

I throw my arms around him. "Aw Kenny," I tell him. "I jist love ya!"

He goes with me and waits down the trail aways, one hand with the lantern up and the other holding onto that poplar club he has, just in case. I ain't scared no more though and get cleared out in a hurry.

Walking back up the path, I sigh. "I won't be able to sleep now, that I know for sure."

"Well, Sissy," he says, "there's a full moon has cleared the clouds and a little breeze to keep the bugs off. I s'pose we could sit out on the step awhiles." So we sit on the doorstep, looking out over the dark, familiar yard, watching the line of willows way out by the fields, dancing and nodding like graceful ghosts.

I snuggle into my brother's arm. "Kenny?" I ask.

And he says, "Mm-hm?"

"Do you amember back east b'fore the war? Do you amember our Poppa?"

Again, he says, "Mm-hm." And the trees go on swaying and sighing their pretty songs.

"Was he strong and good, Ken?" I ask.

"Yes he was." Me and Kenny sit together on the step, enjoying the night and the breeze and the beautiful Manitoba land, thinking about our poppa.

"Dy'ever miss him, Ken? Even though yur near a man. Dy'ever… long for Poppa? Wish we had him back agin?"

"Every day," my brother says softly. "Rose, I miss him every day."

Europe, that's where my poppa fell. I can't get the idea of Europe to fit in my brain, it's so awful far across the big, big sea. But I seen a picture once in a school book of this rolling hillside with red flowers in waving grasses. "Victory in Europe," the words underneath said. I try to hold that picture in my mind. Europe, somewheres ever so far from here, and my poppa laying peaceful in the ground. I hope there's them pretty flowers where he is.

After a long while, there seems to be some pink in the sky over the willows and Kenny gives me a squeeze. "Come on, Sissy," he tells me. "We better go inside." I nod my head and have a big yawn to go with it.

We open up the cabin door and go in, trying to be quiet so's not to wake up my sisters, but then there's a big "Boo!" right by my head and I scream. It's Daddy Albert behind me, grabbing my sides to try to tickle me, and he's laughing away. "Ha-ha, ya should of seen how ya jumped. Ha-ha-ha!"

"Oh my Gawd!" I tell him.

Kenny glares at Daddy Albert, sternly tells him it ain't funny to scare people, and says he's going to wake the baby. Albert argues back and Kenny shakes his head, cursing to hisself, and goes outside again. The baby's fussing now and Momma brings her out. "What the hell?" she says, not looking very pleased.

"Sorry, sorry!" Daddy Albert tells her. "Jist teasin' Rosie. Dit'n mean to wake yuz up." He holds out his hands to Momma. "Here, Josie," he says, "I'll take 'er." So Momma hands Eileen over and goes to get dressed. Daddy Albert sits on one of the kitchen chairs then drags another chair over and wedges his heel into it so my baby sister can lay back on his leg and see him.

He's chirping and cooing away to her. "Eileen," he says, "Eily-Isle," his face just glowing. "Daddy's baby girl, eh? Daddy's beautiful baby, Eileen." I come over to see and Eileen is gazing right into his eyes, little fists waving, lips in a "O" shape like she's trying to talk. Makes me smile too, just for a minute, and I forget to be exasperated with him.

"Eileen," I tell her over his shoulder, smiling big and catching her eye. "Eileen. Eileen. Eily-Isle." She looks right at me, eyes big and bright, like I'm amazing.

"Yes! Yes, that's yur sister," Daddy Albert tells her, nodding away. "That's yur sister, Rosie Sweet Cheeks." She gawks at me as if she understands, then breaks into her sunny smile again. Me and Daddy Albert are both grinning away.

Rosie Sweet Cheeks. There's that name again. I know it bothers Kenny so I've taken to saying, "Don't call me that," every time he uses it. But this time, I decide to let it pass.

I know he's always making mistakes and he sure does aggravate my brother. But like Momma says, it's only thanks to him that we come here at all. And I think he's glad to be part of our family. He was a old man already when Momma met him, like about forty-something, maybe that's why he don't really know how to get along with us older children. But he really loves my baby sister, that's for sure. Sometimes I can get myself to hate him, but times like this, it's hard.

* * *

One Monday afternoon, there's a lot of bickering and arguing going on out in the field. At one point, Kenny even takes a run at Daddy Albert, who throws him to the ground. Kenny gets up and stomps away into the bush. At supper, it's all silent glares. Kenny gets up first, saying he's going to try to patch up the front of the animal shed. ". . . which was put in crooked last year," he says in Daddy Albert's direction.

"Not my fault," Daddy Albert announces to the air. "Boards had a bow to 'em."

Momma starts the dishes while I sit on the end of the bed and show Carleen how to make a clothespin dolly by wrapping red yarn around the top for hair. We play Mommas for awhile, then I go sit on the porch steps and watch Kenny working on the shed. He's tied off a makeshift corral for Clyde and Bossy and threw down feed for them, and now he's knocking out the door frame. He has a bunch of 4x4 blocks stacked inside the doorway and some rough 2x4 boards leaning on the building. Eventually, he comes over to where I am, saying he'll get a sealer of water from the house and come sit with me.

While he's gone, Daddy Albert comes out of the bush trail. He sees Bossy, unties her, and takes her over to the shed to try and put her in. She can't get through the doorway, of course, because of the 4x4 blocks inside, and I think she's also spooked by the boards leaning on the outside wall. So she just stands there.

Albert slaps her rear end. "Get in there!" he tells her. "Get in, damn cow!" Bossy tries to step forward but she can't, so then she steps back again.

"She can't go through," I call over to him.

"What?" he says, starting to get frustrated.

Kenny comes out. "The blocks are in her way," he says, "she can't get through."

"Mind yur own damn bizness!" Albert hollers at him, spinning around. "You think I don't know how to put a cow in the barn? Get in there!" he yells at Bossy, slapping her rump. "Get in, damn you!" He pushes and shoves at her rear end, which don't do nothing. "If you don't like the way I do things," he yells over his shoulder at my brother, "then go live somewheres else!" He goes stomping over to the wagon and grabs the whip. "Why don't ya just go north like ya said?"

Kenny's jaw flinches and he stares straight ahead.

"He *ain't* goin'," I tell Albert. "Momma said!"

"Nobody needs him here anyways!" Albert rants, tromping back to Bossy. "This is my fam'ly! Not his. This is my home! And there ain't room for but one man in it!"

Kenny sits very still on the step, looking out. I rub his arm. "He don't mean it, Ken," I tell him. "He's jist mad." Kenny takes the last swallow from the jar and pats my hand. Then he stands, turns calmly, and goes into the house.

Daddy Albert starts whipping Bossy, which I don't like, so I go in too. But as I'm coming through the porch, I notice something tucked in behind the wood box, the satchel Kenny carried his things in when we moved here. Seems to be packed up to go somewheres. I step into the kitchen doorway.

"Yes I am, Mother," Kenny is saying to Momma. "I'm gonna walk out to Mares's place tonight. There's a boss down from Mandy Mine will be drivin' by at dawn, takin' as many men as can cram into the back of a half-ton truck. And I'm gonna be one of 'em."

"Kenny," Momma tells him, taking him by the arms, "we will find the money somewheres. You don't hafta go."

"Yes, Mother," he says. "I do hafta go."

"No, you don't," she argues back. We can hear Albert screeching and squawking at poor old Bossy outside.

"I do hafta go, Mother, because I'm tellin' ya, if I don't, I am gonna kill that man."

"No," Momma tells him. "Ken, no. Why? You ain't old enough."

"It's time for me to go. I'm fourteen years old and I can work like a man. I know I can do it. And I'll be able to help yuz better from up there than from here. I promise you, Mother, I will always help yuz, no matter where I am."

"Kenny, no!" I tell him, starting to bawl. "Don't leave us, Ken!"

He comes and puts his arms around me, trying to make me feel better. Out the window behind him, Daddy Albert is whipping Bossy over and over, around her eyes and on her tender pink nose. She winces and bawls, then scrunches her eyes closed and hunkers down to take the beating.

"Son," Momma is saying to Kenny's back, "don't go! Stay! I'll make him treat ya better. Ken, stay and help us. Please! Help yur father."

I look up at my brother's face. "My father," he is saying, Adam's apple working, "died at Vimy Ridge." He turns and looks at Momma, eyes dark and deep with truth. "He is buried somewheres, far from this God-forsaken place."

Momma's eyes, gone glassy, travel down to a knotted hole in the rough floor, and she stands, shaking her head. Kenny goes and puts his arms around her, talking gentle-like in her hair.

Where I stand is on his way to the door, and as he reaches me, I cling on for dear life, burying my head in his chest, pleading as hard as I can. "Don't go, Kenny! Don't leave us!" I just know I can make him stay. He rocks me and pats my hair, giving me hope. But then he takes hold of my arms, unwraps them from his waist, kisses my head, and calls me Rosie Sweet Cheeks. "No, Kenny," I say, my voice gone weak.

But he steps past me, picks up his bundle from the porch, and reaches the outside door. It squeaks softly open, he goes through, and it shuffles quietly back against the faded wooden frame.

* * *

The Rock Island rooster crows and we got to get up. It's been so hot all August, just stifling here in the house, and Carleen is fevered again as usual. She's like a hot little stove, moaning and thrashing all night. "Git over!" I kept telling her, but she wouldn't. Momma got up and doctored her, but I took my blanket and went to sleep under the window against the cool wood wall in Kenny's old spot. Momma lights the fire in the woodstove now and puts the tea and porridge water on, then she goes back to nursing baby Eileen. I get up and go down the trail to the outhouse.

I miss my brother Kenny so much. Momma got a letter not a month after he left, and Mr. Coleman at the Post Office read her how he was doing good and not to worry. Sure enough, Tommy Mares had got him on with the teamsters, and he was driving a pair of big blacks named Bull and Bennett. With the money bills that was shoved in there, Momma bought lumber for shoring up the well, soon as Old Albert gets it dug, and she bought a flat of sealer jars for the canning and a clutch of big chickens for eggs over the winter. So, as long as they don't kick us off the land, we got a chance.

I'm keeping a eye out for old Scrappy. He was barking away out in the bush a few nights back but we ain't seen him since. I always stand in the yard in the mornings calling, "Scrappy, here boy, here boy. Where are ya, Scrappy? Come on home."

Momma says I might as well save my breath. She says he's a male and was always answering them coyotes with their *yip-yipping* out in the bush. He probably got a girlfriend over there and will come back when she's finished her heat. Either that or they ate him up. Anyways, Momma says, we got work to do.

We have our porridge, though Carleen don't take none. She looks mighty peaked and seems groggy so Momma tells her to go lay down then. My baby sister Eileen is fussy too and Momma says she's awful hot. Momma yells at Albert to get up and eat so's he can get out there and dig that damn well.

"What's the point?" he grouses from the bed. "We're jist gonna lose it anyways!"

"We'll lose it for sure if we don't get the damn work done," she tells him. "Can't give up before ya even finish tryin'."

Momma don't have much patience for that man no more. They argue lots and she told him to his face she blames him for driving Kenny out.

I ain't having my old problem of finding it hard to hate him neither. Sometimes when Momma sends me to pick berries or fetch wood, he comes and tries to help me.

"Ain't ya s'posed ta be diggin' the well?" I huff. "Jist git away from me and do yur own damn work."

I do get lonely though, and bone weary of this sweaty, dirty work that never ends. But I do not care. If it wasn't for him, my brother would still be here.

Well, them vegetables ain't picking theirselves, I suppose, so me and Momma heads out to the garden. Momma is worried about baby Eileen and don't want to leave her in the cradle, she's so hot and all. So we take her with us. Momma slings a sheet from the poplar branch nearby to make a little hammock, and I stand there rocking her for a bit till she falls asleep.

We get lots of work done. All them beans is picked and we dig out a bunch more potatoes for the root cellar. Then we sit on the ground beneath the tree, snapping beans into pails. Eileen's awake and smiling, her head ain't so hot now, and I sit with her on the grass, taking some corn silk and making a skirt for a corn cob dolly. A breeze is blowing gentle from the east, a meadow lark calling out clear and pretty from a nearby willow.

"Rosie," Momma says, "go get us a big sealer jar of drinkin' water from the house and check on yur sister Carleen."

I go run up to the house, through the door, and to my sister on the cot. "Git up, Carleen," I say, giving her a shake. She don't move. I shake her again. "Carleen?" Her arm feels cold, the skin somehow wrong. I stand back and cock my head. "Carleen?"

That's when the buzzing starts and everything goes strange on me. I come out through the porch, things moving unnatural slow, and it's like I can just see the steps in front of me, then the path to the garden. Like it's not really me at all, just a dream of me moving through the world.

Then I'm at Momma, where she's bent over, scooping up leaves and corn silk for the burning barrel. I stand looking at her hair, thinking it's actually the colour of straw. Baby Eileen starts fussing in her swing and I watch, as if I'm far off and it's someone else who's watching. Momma picks Eileen up to change her diaper in the grass. "How's our Carleen doin'?" she asks, busy with the baby.

"Carly won't wake up," I hear myself say over the buzzing. Feels like something terrible is happening, something more than I can understand.

The dream of me watches Momma take Eileen's two ankles between her fingers and lift while she slides the clean diaper under. "Needs more sleep I guess," she says, bringing up the flap between the legs. She folds in the left side and the right, then fastens it all with the one big pin.

"Now where's that water you was s'posta bring?" she asks, looking up. "Jesus, Rose!" she yells. "You's all blanched. Is you sick now too?"

"Carly won't wake up." I hear the words coming out of me in a quivery voice.

"What d'ya mean?" Momma frowns. "Is she hot?"

My head shakes itself from side to side. "She won't wake up," I tell her again. "She won't... wake up."

"Won't wake up?" Momma repeats, looking full at me, alarm beginning in her.

"She won't wake up," I tell her, a heaving in my chest that must be crying. "Momma..." I try to say to her, holding out my hands, trying to reach her across the terrible thing that's happening. "Momma…" I plead. "Momma, Carly won't wake up…"

She gawks, jaw dropped, then leaps up and shoves Eileen onto me, races to the house, and crashes through the door. I bring my baby sister and trail her in there. And there is calling and pleading and thrashing. There is roaring and cursing and weeping. But Carleen Margie won't wake up.

* * *

I wasn't a very good sister. I go sit at the little grave they dug by the treeline and I tell Carleen I'm sorry. I shouldn't have shoved her away in the night, I shouldn't have left her alone in the bed when she was sick. It's just that she had so many fevers, we had no way of knowing this was a killing one.

Momma didn't even know. "I never seen it." That's what she kept saying at the funeral when our neighbour folks come up. "I shoulda seen it. But I never seen it." Now she don't seem herself.

I tell my sister I'm sorry though, and I tell her it's so terrible lonely here with her gone. And Kenny gone. And Momma so still and sad.

I feel the pangs in my stomach again as all the food left over from the funeral has run out or gone bad and Momma don't seem to want to cook nothing. I seem to remember there's a spot just down the trail where we found hazelnuts last year, and cranberries too. I wonder if they're ready. I go as far into the bushes as I dare—don't want to get lost—but I don't see nothing but burrs and deadfall. I start working my way back out to the trail, but just when I'm coming up to our clearing, there's a gust of wind and I smell it. Something rotted and dead in the tall grass. I peer in. It's a animal of some sort, all tore apart.

One leg over there, all chewed up, the other dangling from the carcass. Black and white markings. A dog? Scrappy! Poor old Scrappy!

I start screeching, "Oh, Scrappy! Oh, Scrappy!" as I back up towards the house, and Old Albert comes running. "Look what them coyotes done to Scrappy!" I point. "They kilt him! Kilt him bad!"

He squats down and squints closer. "Ain't no coyotes done that," he says. "Bones is bit right through, and see there? That big pile of poop left behind? That's the big animal left that. To show its might."

I want my Momma.

I go run to Momma and tell her how we found Scrappy. I tell her the big animal done it, I tell her we got to get him. I want my momma to roar and rage, I want her to take care of me and hug me up, and I want her to tell me how to think about this. I want her to say she's going to kill that big animal. Kill him bad.

But she just sits at the table, baby Eileen nuzzling at her. Just sits there shaking her head and don't say nothing.

In the night, I dream I'm lost in the woods. There's coyotes howling way off and I can hear bushes shuffling and a log snap nearby. The big animal is coming for me. I run and I run and I scream for my momma but I can't find my way out.

* * *

Mornings is cold in this rickety shack now that it's fall. I'm shivering on my lonesome cot. Old Albert is snoring away but it looks like Momma might be awake. I get up and say "Momma?" but she just lays there staring at the wall. Someone needs to light the stove. So I go over, get the tinder and wood in, and I light it up. Momma has rolled over to the wall again. Eileen's fussing so I go get her and carry her around on my hip while I get the porridge water on.

Eventually, Albert goes out to feed the animals. But Momma just sits at the table. She nurses Eileen when I hand her down. I tell her we're running out of potatoes so I guess we'll need to dig some more. I tell her there's some sort of bug on the corn stalks and she says she'll have a look. Then she pours another cup of the tea that's already cold and just sits gazing out the window.

The church buggy comes up the road. The Homestead men wave their papers and say their words. Improvements are not made, conditions are not met, we have to move on. "Do you understand?" they say loudly to Momma at the table, as if she's deaf. "You got to get out!"

"We lost the little girl," Old Albert whimpers. "We got hard times."

"Well, that's unfortunate," the man says, "you have my condolences. But you still got to leave. We got new folks on the way, new homesteaders to give it a go. Maybe they'll do better'n you done, work harder. They'll be comin' on the train in a week, you got to be gone by then."

I watch the church buggy rattle down the trail and I ask Momma what we're going to do. She says we'll start loading the wagon box. But when I ask where we're going, she just shakes her head. Eileen cries steady in the night and when we get up, I tell Momma there's no more sugar for the tea. And we're out of bread again. Can she bake some bread? She says she will.

I dream the big animal again. All that same terror. But when it catches me, I don't fight. It takes me in its horrible grip, squeezing me, squeezing the life from me. I'm dying. And I just wrap my arms around it too, holding hard and strong, returning the hug with all my heart. I just stop my struggle and let all this come to a end.

* * *

Mrs. Mares comes into the yard, one of the women that come up for Carleen's funeral. She's a very big woman, a three hundred pounder, Old Albert says, and she has a whole gaggle of little girls at her hips. Norma is the one my age. Momma comes out and stands on the step and Mrs. Mares says there's a old bunk house at the end of her property. She says we are welcome to stay there till we can get ourselves straight.

"I..." Momma hesitates. "I can pay ya when my son sends money."

"Oh no, jist yur own grub, that's all you'll need. We're neighbours, after all," the woman says. "Out here in the west, we're all far from fam'ly. So us neighbours got to be fam'ly to one another."

Momma nods and goes inside. But she don't make no bread. Just goes to sleep while there's still grey in the room and don't get back up. I try to make stew for myself from the last of the turnips and beets. It's Gawd-awful but better than nothing.

I open my eyes and dawn is at the window. I sit up on the edge of the bed. Momma's just laying there, staring at the ceiling. I want to sleep too. But I ask Momma if she's going to make food today and she says yes, so I heave myself up and go put the porridge on.

There's no water in the pail for tea now. I've got to get some from the river. Sky's still grey above the eastern line of pink. I scoop up the water pails from the edge of the house and head down the trail through the high grasses. It's early, the air is still chilly.

The green growth is so thick this time of year that leaves and branches overhang the path and I have to stoop and duck my way along. The soft leaves brush and pat my arms as I go, encouraging like. Little birds are chirping in the bushes and the Roaring River sings as it rolls on by.

River's lower than it has been so I take the foot path and go further down river to where I can step out on a big flat rock and fill the pails.

Then I leave them standing and sit down on the moss bank in back of the trail. The chokecherry bush at the bend a few feet away hangs so heavy with black berries, it completely veils the path and all the world outside. Feels like I'm in a green cave now, middle of nowhere, seeing nothing but the river. Hearing nothing but its roar.

I don't know how to rouse my momma. Don't know how to wake her up.

Then, snap! Birds startle to wing. I hear something coming from up river, something big. Branches crack, brush grinds back, and the earth seems to tremble. *Momma! What do I do?*

I lean forward on the moss bank, eyes searching farther up the path. But that's away from the house. I don't want to go farther from the house. *Think! I gotta think.* I don't know what to do and it's coming! I stand.

A heavy crackling noise, chokecherry bushes swoosh open, and it's there. *God! God! The big animal!* Black. Head as tall as me. So wide and big he wipes out all behind him. His breath is thick and loud.

He sees me.

Oh Momma! Oh Momma!

He takes a step, weaves his head, huffing.

"Momma!" I whimper. *Where do I go? What do I do?*

He makes a sound like a growl or a grunt, so huge a sound that it numbs the world, freezing my brain, striking terror in my chest.

Oh God! Oh, Momma, what do I do?

He steps again, his rancid smell hits me and I step back. *Momma!*

He sniffs and grunts, seeming satisfied, and comes ambling straight for me. Calm. Deliberate. That smell I smell is death. *Oh God!*

"Git back!" she roars. Somehow, Momma's coming up from the river, face red and angry, skirts wet to the knee. "Git outta here!" she's hollering, throwing her hands up over her head. I gawk.

She clears the sand bank and is on the path between him and me, thrumming her arms up and down like heavy weapons. "Git outta here! Git back!"

The animal pauses, weaving his head.

Momma, not four feet from him, beats her arms like mighty wings, air singing like a drum.

"You ain't comin' here!" she's screeching, and I cower there behind her. "You ain't takin' my girl! You ain't killin' her! Now git outta here, you!"

The animal blinks his beady eyes.

"You ain't killin' us!" she screams in his face. Her fists, her arms, her legs so hard and huge, I think she could tear him to pieces. "We ain't layin' down! Now git outta here! Git!"

I'm half crying, staring up at the side of Momma's face. It almost ain't even her, that face. Twisted. Murderous. "You ain't killin' us!" she yells, neck stuck out a mile, fists like molten steel. "Raaaaa!" she roars, mouth ugly and snarling. "Raaaaa!" body taught and quaking.

The animal weaves and grunts, backing away like he ain't sure what kind of thing he's happened on here.

"That's right! Git!" my momma hollers. "You git outta here!"

He turns back the way he came and disappears, green swooshing shut behind him.

"Not you!" Momma yells at where he was. "Not the homestead men! Nor sickness! Nor death, death, death! We ain't layin' down! We ain't givin' up! You ain't killin' us!"

We can hear the noise of him getting farther and farther off in the distance.

The regular world eventually comes back into view. Momma takes ahold of my shoulders and gets my eyes to look at her, telling me it's over. I blink, nodding. Then she walks into the river and squats on the flat rock with her knees apart, scooping up handfuls of icy cold water, slapping it on her face, her arms, her neck. She slaps it up under her dress too, gasping and growling, the water so cool and good.

I cock my head. "Momma? Where did ya come from?"

"From the river here," she nods, "the Roaring."

A feeling come over her in the house there, she says, just felt in her guts that I needed her. Heard and seen the animal signs when she got to the river bank, figured I was trapped down the path. She went into the water to get around the bend to me before he could.

Momma says that when we get up to the yard, we'll start loading up the wagon box. We're going to stay down at Mrs. Mares's till we can get ourself straight. We stop and set down our pails. She slides her arm over my shoulder and we stand together looking out at the homestead. "You ready?" she asks.

That small house is fading already, the black dirt path well-beaten to the step. There's the crooked little animal shed. Rusty, old burning barrel, leaning off-kilter. A sad little excuse for a wood pile. And the long, dry grasses scratching and sighing all the way out to the tree line where my sister Carleen sleeps.

"We lost this," I say, resting my cheek on Momma's shoulder.

"Yes," she agrees, pursing her lips. "We worked so damn hard but we lost it anyways." She looks beyond the yard to the green, hazy distance. "But you still got yur momma, my girl," she says, "and she ain't givin' up." I tuck myself more snugly into her and she gives my shoulders a squeeze before launching into the work ahead. "Whatever else happens now," she tells me, "we are not givin' up. Gonna make it in Manitoba, or die tryin'."

From here, we can see the beginnings of the road, land sweeping out and falling gently towards the valley floor miles away. Not far down, Mrs. Mares's place is an open patch in the green, smoke already curling friendly from the house, with small golden fields nearby. A lark's call is sounding from the meadow, crisp and musical. There's a clean feel to everything now, like all that was burdensome has been lifted.

Clouds still float high up there, shadows moving over trees and fields, houses and barns, critters and their many weaving trails upon the land. Those dark shadows must cross the growing towns too, I suppose, and even the rail lines laid out to gleaming cities afar. But for today, the sun has topped the poplars, a glorious yellow sun lighting hill and valley and shining distant rail. Momma is back to herself and the day has begun.

Chapter 2

Born of Ache

(1930)

I was twenty years old by then, but already with the four children and a old-man husband growing irksome on me.

"Why the hell ain't there never no water in the pail here?" I says to Mitch one morning. "You ain't workin', there's no reason why you couldn't go to the well a couple times a day." He goes out the door with the pail, bitching that his arm stump is sore again and his own wife don't even care. "You get no pity from me," I say to nobody. "Arm ain't growin' back and mouths still needs feedin'."

After breakfast, I take my children and head down the road to Mother's to see if she heard anything in town yesterday about work that might be coming up. What with these past two dry years, crops so sparse, cash jobs would be the ticket for this summer, keep food on the table till gardens come in again in the fall.

Mother's twins, seven years old, come running out to meet us, one of them plopping my little Mitchell Ken on her hip, and the lot of the little girls, Mother's and mine, go take him to play horsees in the shade by the house. My oldest, Petunia, age five, comes in with me, leaning up against the cupboard. "Lily... I mean, Margie... I mean Beatrice!" Damn! I hate it when I get the names mixed up. "I mean, Petunia!" Now, where was I? "Petunia, put a couple scoops a black tea in the pot there and get the kettle on."

The twins had Mother's youngest little guy, Vallee—his name's Valentine but we just call him Vallee—here in the cradle on the bench, so I chuck his little chin and he smiles big. Huh, look at them blue eyes, just gorgeous. I'm sitting there with the tea made and my baby, James, on the tit when Mother comes through the door with a half-pail of fresh milk.

She sits down with a heavy sigh and Pet does a good job of pouring her some nice hot tea. "Looks like farmers ain't hirin'," she says. "That's what thur sayin'."

She says it's no wonder. When her and Old Albert was crossing the wood bridge to town, they seen the Roaring River weren't nearly up to flood level. And this at the height of spring, when normally there'd be water on the bridge floor. "Dry as hell last year," she says. "And not zac'ly Noah's damn ark the year before neither. Now another dry one."

Mother says we got to work like crazy this next month, make sure them fields is just right for the seeding. "That and pray for rain," she tells me. "Taxes is due agin in fall. Gotta be paid or we'll lose the farm. And if there ain't no other way to get that money but sale of crops, then crops we got to have."

I'm just thinking me and the kids will stay for dinner, going to offer to make some biscuits if she wants, when here comes Culain Kirk, trotting up the dirt road on Jonesy, his black gelding. We go out and he says his mom is having problems with her next baby. It ain't even due for a couple more months. So Mother goes to the back room to grab up her little sack of cloth and herbs and woman-things, leaving me there on the step.

Culain nods. "G'day there, Rosie Kelvey," he says.

"G'day, Culain Kirk," I say. I wish I'd had a minute to pin my hair up. "I hope... everthin's alright there with yur mom then."

"Yep," he says. "Hope so." He smiles, and we just kind of stand there, waiting. His brown hair looks so soft and full, got a gold sheen to it in this light.

"Dry year," I say, beckoning off to the world in general.

"Sure is," he says. For some reason, I feel a blush going up my throat.

Times like this, I feel I stick out like a sore thumb, even from our own family. Them's mulatto looks, Mother says, that I got from my poppa, my real daddy. My skin browns up deeper than all get-out soon as the first warm days of spring come around. And don't I tire of trying to get a comb through this thick black mop of curly hair? At least I kept my shape so far, wide in the hips and lots up top, I guess because I had my kids young and always have to work so hard. *Black beauty*, that's what Mitch used to call me, and it give me such a thrill. Back when we was close and I used to care what he thought of me.

Mother comes stomping out and swings her skirts over Jonesy's flank. "Rosie, yur in charge," she says, and off they trot up the dirt road.

I hope Elvie will fare alright. Culain's mom, Elvie Kirk, is Mitch's sister, my sister-in-law. A quiet little dove of a woman. This is the third time Mother has midwifed for her.

My mom is getting known for her midwifing out here in Roaring River district, ten miles south of Swan River. They got but the two doctors, Doc True and Doc Kilda, for all the towns in the whole valley, and a woman threatening miscarriage just ain't enough to send for one of them. The women got to help each other.

A Seven Year Ache

I'm used to taking over when Mother gets called away, so I just set to work making dinner for both families, Mother's seven children she's still got at home, and my four little ones. Albert's gone to the bush for the day so I ain't got to deal with him. Griping and moaning, that's about the worst that old man can do ever since Momma took him down to size over his screeching and yelling fits.

Well, Mother's older children have come up from the barn for water so then I send them out to get wood. "Mind that axe," I tell them. "Eileen's the oldest, she's the only one that gets to chop. The rest of yuz can collect and carry." I start getting things out to make the biscuits—flour, salt, baking powder, sugar, lard, eggs. I got my baby James napping and Mother's little Vallee down on the floor with my two middle ones. I got Petunia at the table washing dishes in the big pan and Mother's twins doing the drying and putting away. I'm organized.

Once I've got the batter mixed, I get Pansy, one of the twins, rolling out the dough while I run up the road to tell Mitch I'm staying at Mother's for the day. Mitch lost his arm in the Great War years ago and keeps hurting his stump. It's healing up good this time—no more gangrene like when he froze the tip two years ago—but it's paining him, and he starts grumbling about me not cooking nothing again.

I tell him it's his sister, Elvie, that needs Mother and I got to take over down there. He can come down and eat when it's ready. "Now ya don't even want Mother to help yur own sister!" I tell him.

I run back down, change the two babies' diapers and put my two-year old on the potty. I put James on the tit again and have a cup of tea, watching Pansy while she punches biscuits out of the rolled dough with a sealer lid.

Mother did not know she was having twins when them girls come along, but she was pukey sick and could barely get out of bed with the retching. That was when we was still living in that old shack at the end of Mares's. I was fourteen and, as it turned out, also expecting at the time but didn't know it yet. When it all come out later, I married Mitch and we built on another bedroom back behind Mother's for us and baby.

Old Albert was not working as usual, always laying around, claiming to be too sick to work. It was a bad winter, one or two chickens dead in the henhouse every week. By March, we was desperate, most of our flour gone. Even the potatoes was running low. So Mother took the .22 down off the wall and went out to see if she could shoot something.

She was gone for hours and a freak storm had blew up. North wind screaming at the windows, driving snow. I was crazy with worry, thought she might have died out there. Finally heard her stumble into the porch. I grabbed the broom to knock the snow off, and helped her to the bench by the wood stove. Gave her tea to warm her. And out from her coat she brought two frozen rabbits for us to fry. Every week was like that, just living from hand to mouth. Trying to get by till things would get better.

But Mother was never right all through that carrying. Pale and sweating and tore apart with pain many nights. Made sense to me later that the hurt was so strong, since there was the two babies inside her all along.

I wonder how things is going up at Elvie Kirk's place. This one will be Elvie's ninth child, I think. No, eighth, her eighth child, because she lost the second last one. A little girl they was going to call Charity. Elvie has the whole range of children, just like my mom. From little babies all the way up to Culain Kirk, who's twenty, same as me.

Babies sometimes die, that's just the way of it. Them twins of Mother's almost didn't make it, getting born. They come early when the Roaring River was in flood. Old Albert, dumb ass that he is, had buggered off with the wagon and got stuck in town. I'd had my Petunia just a few days earlier and was still weak myself, milk and tits hanging down like old Bossy. But my sister Eileen come screaming in that Mother had fell down coming back from the outhouse. I run out and she was just up on the one knee, sweating and moaning, grabbing her hard little belly. I could see the trail of blood on the path behind her.

I got her up and in bed. Bawling like a kid, I said, "Momma, don't you die on me."

Gritting her teeth and white like death, she took my face in her two hands and made me look in her eyes. "Rosie," she told me, "it's all on you now. You gotta help me. Cuz if you don't, then somebody's gonna die."

"Oh Momma!" I wailed.

But she just wedged her feet into the footboard, sitting up with her knees half-bent. "Now pull on my hands," she told me, "and don't you waste yur strength cryin'."

Well, I took both her hands and I pulled when she told me. I pulled and she heaved, I pulled and she heaved, and quicker than would be right, out come this little tiny girl, size of a kitten. Wailing strong though. I handed her to Mother, the cord still dangling, and Mother give her milk, and we was laughing and crying, and the children was coming in, trying to see the baby. I shooed them away, the afterbirth wasn't delivered yet.

I went to the kitchen to get the scissors from the boiling pot, and just then, she's yelling, "Rosie, God, God! There's another one comin'!"

"No!" I run in. "Where was there room for it?"

But I pulled and she heaved, I pulled and she heaved, and out it come, another tiny, tiny girl, pink and screaming. And both of them lived. No bigger than little cats, but both them girls lived, if you could believe it. Pansy and Tansy, she called them. Medicine flower names.

Well, Pansy has done a real nice job getting the biscuits in the pans. I've stoked up the flames in the summer stove under the tree and she slides them into the oven, closes the heavy iron door using a balled-up tea towel like I showed her, and goes jumping off to brag to the other children. "Me may bit-kit," she tells them. "Me-me, bit-kit in uffen."

Them girls has always talked their own queer language—they look like regular children, but they don't talk like regular children. That's alright, us in the family can usually figure out what they're saying. "Oh, biscuits!" Petunia replies politely. "You put them in the oven? Good for you, twin."

I get some spuds peeled and throw a bunch of chicken feet in a pot of water to boil before I sit down under the willow tree to try to quiet my James. But then Mother's little Vallee is screaming in the basket and my little Mitchell is eating dirt again, black goo running down his chin. So I get up and go whack him, take that big clot of gunk out of his mouth, and now he's screeching too.

Out at the road, I see Selma Fjordason, same age as me. Her and her beau is walking up the road together, big broad smiles on, holding hands and swinging them back and forth, all free and easy.

What am I doing? Barely twenty years old with four children and what kind of damn life is this?

I was only fourteen when I took up with Mitch. I was a willful girl by then though, already my full height. I was filled out real good too, and having periods like a woman. I was tired of being bossed around by Mother, tired of all the work and all the kids and having nothing, never, to show for it.

Why shouldn't I be the queen of my own castle? That's what I wondered. I was big enough and strong enough. I had it in my mind that I just had to get away somewheres. I had this longing, like a ache down in my guts, just to be out from under. To do what I wanted, to have my own man, my own house to be the boss of.

So I'd go over the meadow and spend time at Elvie Kirk's place. Culain and her other boys would be out in the fields with their dad, but her brother Mitch was always around. He had but the one arm left and was almost twice my age, closer to the age my own poppa would have been. I would get him to tell me about the Great War and the countryside in Europe and what it was like over there.

And then, the next time I had a row with Mother, I would run to Mitch.

The first time I run, Mother showed up mad as hell and whooped my ass all the way home. "You ain't leavin'!" she told me.

"Oh yes I am!" I told her back. Next time she looked away, off I sprung, like a jack rabbit through the bush.

She come got me again and beat me sore, but first chance I got, I was gone again. I was like that. You couldn't tell me nothing. Finally, when I told her I was expecting, she had to give up and let me marry Mitch. Be a woman in my own right.

Well, I got what I wanted and now here I am. I'm the mother, I'm the one in charge, but so what? Not even drinking age and up to my neck in children. With a weak little useless husband wearing on me.

Queen of my own shitpile. *La ti da.*

Well, I get the food on the table and the children all come crashing in. Those biscuits is just right. We have our dinner and then the big kids all head outside again for chores. I stay back with the little guys, get down on my knees and scrub the rough wood floor. Damn slivers.

Five years of married life and I think different now about what I'd want from a man. If I had it to do over, like. Mitch still wants his fun from me, I am his wife after all, and sometimes when he's begged and whimpered me into it, I'll crawl up onto him in the dark. But after he's snoring his way to happy dreams, I just lay there, staring up. Sometimes I wonder, what it would be like. . . To be. . . took over, I guess I'd say, by a man. A real man, strong, knowing how to do for a woman. What would it be like to be... pleasured by a man?

The past two years at harvest, me and Mother went travelling with the threshing crews. That's where some of the bigger farmers got the horses and machinery that the smaller farmers don't have, but there's lots more farm labourers for manpower. So they get all the men and horses and machines together and make up crews that go around from one farm to the next, harvesting. And the men get paid.

Well, of course Old Albert wouldn't go. He was always sick with something or other, so he claimed, lazy old bugger. And Mitch can never do nothing that takes two hands. But yet we needed the money.

So that first year, Mother says to me, "Rose, let's go see if we can sign on to cook for them. They'll need women too. Men that works hard has got to be fed." So we put Eileen and the men in charge of the children and hitched a ride into Swan. Sure enough, Maluks was looking to hire cooks.

Well, did we ever have fun! Getting up at four in the morning, making breakfast for thirty men. A hundred pancakes to start, eight dozen eggs to fry, plus bacon and sausages. All served on long tables set up by where the men was camped out. Soon as you finished breakfast dishes, you'd have to start getting ready for dinner at noon. And then supper. We baked six dozen loaves of bread a day and a dozen pies. Every single day.

And they worked hard, them men, right from dawn to dusk. But then, late in the evenings, even if they was pretty much bushed, they'd play music. There was always a couple guys with guitars, a couple fiddles, and somebody with a accordion. Playing old gospel songs, cowboy songs, hobo songs.

And then, at the end of each job, when that group of farmers' crops was all in, before you moved to the next camp, you'd get paid. So me and Mother got cash, actual cash money for our own! We put most of it aside to pay taxes, but my Lord, that was exciting. Getting that envelope with all those—whatever—sometimes five dollars or more!

Last year, a bunch of the Kirk brothers was on that crew too. My nephews by marriage, though they're all nearly my same age. They had so much fun teasing me, calling out from the tables, "Hey, Auntie Rosie, ain't there no more bread?" Buggers, pretending I was like a old auntie. "Oh Auntie Rosie," they'd say, "can you pass one a them pies over this way!"

That Culain Kirk would always get me laughing. And sometimes when they played the music at night, Culain would come sit beside me there on the log, people singing along or just sitting quiet in the night air. Sky full of stars, everything smelling so dark and free.

At the end of that job, I was at the cook tent, rushing around to get the clean-up done so's we could go get paid. The cook tent is right by the tree line, and you would just step out the back to throw your dishwater or whatever in the bush. So I was going to throw out this pan of water real quick, just lift the tarp, take three steps, throw the water, go back in. Right at that moment, though, young Preteau was driving a team of the big Clydes through that space behind the tent, just with the traces, no rig. But I didn't know that, and was stepping out right into their path. My God, them horses would have mowed me down.

But there was a yell, and I was being lifted right off the ground, this calm voice in my ear saying, "I got ya!" and I was whirled around and set down again back by the tent, safe as could be. It was Culain Kirk. He'd just picked me up light as you please and swung me around behind him.

That give me a shiver, I'll tell you, like a actual physical tingling going all up my spine. To have those two arms like that, just sweeping me up and taking me over, that man's voice, so tender and strong in my ear.

And yet, Culain is my husband's nephew. *My* nephew, I suppose you'd say.

Well, now I get a big tub of water, heat it on the summer stove outside and scrub a load of diapers on the washboard. I hang them on the line slung between the poplars. I've put the last four pigs' feet in the oven for supper, with some big chunks of fatty hide for the rind. I got the leftover potatoes smashed up and some turnips boiled, and by then the big kids are in my way, trying to peek into the pots.

"Git!" I tell them.

Perfect timing, that's when Jonesy comes trotting into the yard with Mother up behind Culain Kirk. She says Elvie Kirk should be alright for now. I guess she was having some blood show but Mother gave her strong nettle leaf tea and got her laying down and the flow seems to be stopping. Mother gave strict instructions to Elvie's girls, ten and twelve years old, that they is to do all their mother's work. "We'll try and hold that baby back long as we can. And jist hope for the best," Mother says, washing up in the wash basin under the willow.

Culain grabs the dipper and glugs down a nice drink from the pail. "Hey, gorgeous," he says to me, wiping his chin. "When ya gonna leave all this behind and run off with me?"

"Any day now!" I tease him back.

Culain ain't much taller than me, maybe five foot six, and of a stocky, muscular build. But he goes over, grabs the reins and the saddle horn in his hands, and swings hisself right up into the saddle. Easy-like, as if it ain't nothing. He pulls Jonesy back three quick steps, then goes jaunting away down the lane.

Me and Mother goes in and feeds both crews again, then I load up my four and head on up the gravel road towards me and Mitch's little shack. In Fjordasons' field, right by the ditch, there's four or five dogs. That young black curly-haired bitch is in heat, I guess, as one of the dogs is trying to mount her.

"They're hurtin' Trixie!" Petunia starts yelling, "Stop hurtin' Trixie!"

I giggle, though I'm trying not to, and I say, "They ain't hurtin' her, she likes it." Petunia stands at the edge of the road, pursing her lips, eyebrows still vexed. "Get outta there now, let's go," I say to her. "I'm tellin' ya, Trixie ain't gettin' hurt. She's jist testin' out the males to see which one she wants for a beau. Whichever one proves he's best, that's the one she'll take to be her mate."

A breeze is blowing at our backs, a hot breeze for spring. Hope we get lots of rain this year. We sure don't want to be in the same boat as before, wind up losing this farm for non-payment of taxes like we done with the other one. But if it will just rain, we'll work hard, the crops will come up, and we'll sell them and pay the taxes.

It's a new decade, as they say. The Roaring Twenties is gone with all their hard times, troubles, and bad losses. The thirties are here, a new day with new hope. The Purdy Thirties, that's what we'll call them. With a little luck and lots of rain, I just know we can turn things around.

* * *

Well, the third week of May has come and gone, and our seed is in the soil, dry as it may be. I walk down to Mother's with my two pails for water, but I can hardly get no water up, it's so low down in the well. And when my pails are finally full, there's a lot of muck and stones mixed in. I go tell Mother.

She says they been having the same, what with the dearth of rain. She says she'll have to tie a rope around Junior and lower him down there with a shovel, see if he can scoop down a bit lower to get at the water. When the rains come, the water level will rise again like proper.

I ask how her visit with Doc True went yesterday, the one with the twins. We known for a long time now that something ain't right with them girls. Most people can't understand the way they talk, though we know what they mean with their funny words and rhymes. And they ain't very smart. You try to learn them something, but then the next time, they still don't know it. So you can't leave them alone to do work like other children. Have to help them all the time, and watch they don't hurt theirselves. So Mother decided to ask Doc True what we should do. Like, is there a medicine that can cure them?

She says Doc just scratched his head, didn't rightly know of nothing. Said maybe Mother could take them to this big-shot doctor down in Brandon he heard of, supposed to be a expert on such things. She shows me the paper Doc wrote on.

"Dr. Ewe... Ewan Cameron," I sound out. "Ewan? Yeah, that's what it is. And Doc wrote a address here. See? It gives a street and number in Brandon. So's you can find him when ya get there."

Mother shakes her head. "And where in the world would we get the money for that?"

I think about my brother Kenny, where he's working up by Cold Lake there, setting up a copper mine. He's helped us out so much these past years, too much, really. By the third year me and Mitch was married, we had the two babies and another on the way, all jammed into that back room of the house at Mares's, and Mother and Albert with their six in the other two rooms. Then this place come open, with the two shacks, one at each end of the two acres. Mother sent Kenny a letter, asking would he be able to help us out buying it, and the very next month, we had the money and was packing up to move over.

I guess he was already courting Vera at that time, though we didn't know it till the following year when we got the wedding invite. Well, I wanted so bad to go, but he had only sent one train ticket, and Mother would have to be gone a week all told, so I stayed back and took charge here.

I figured Mother would return happy and full of stories, but wasn't she quiet and sad instead when she got off the train? There had been a terrible row at the wedding. Mother had held her tongue with Vera's frosty welcome and the many slights and backhanded compliments she had given. But then at the wedding supper, she just couldn't stay out of it when Vera insulted Kenny. He had asked his new wife to dance when she turned to her bridesmaid and said what was supposed to be a joke. She said, "Ugh, now I got to get pawed at by them dirty miners' hands!"

Mother pointed out that the work of them dirty miners' hands was what was paying for this fancy shindig, that ring on her finger, and the two-storey house he had bought her. "Jist cuz yur fam'ly's a bunch a high-muckety-mucks," she told the woman, "don't mean the rest of us jist gets it all on a silver platter! We gotta work for a livin'!"

Well, Vera did not take kindly to that, and they were off. Vera screeching, red-faced and mean, in Mother's face. Mother giving it right back to her. Kenny in the middle. My brother had to wind up getting Mother a room at the CN Hotel for the last night as Vera wouldn't have her in the house. That's how bad it was.

"Freeloaders," Mother said, eyes downcast, on the wagon ride home. "That's what she called us. Freeloaders, moochers, and scroungers. A chain around Kenny's neck, tryin' to suck him down with us to the bottom."

Ever since then, Mother don't want to ask Kenny for help. He still writes every month and Mother gets me to write him back. She says maybe someday when Vera has finished her mad, we'll go and visit. Or maybe they'll come to see us, 'specially now that they got the one baby and another on the way. But Mother says, "No more leanin' on Kenny. Let him make a life for hisself, raise a family, be happy. Stead of worryin' 'bout us."

So I just watch the twins, jumping around with the children in the yard. Wish we could help them somehow. But I don't mention Kenny. And neither does Mother.

The month of June turns out to be a scorcher, one heat wave after another. At first, it's just a good excuse to go swim in the muddy bend of the Roaring River or stay in the house playing cards. But pretty soon, it gets worrisome. The fields is thirsty, young plants drying out, stalks hanging limp. We can't do nothing for the crops, but we drag barrels of water all the way from the river and try to keep the gardens alive.

One evening, the sky clouds over, a light breeze ruffles the leaves, and it dribbles rain for a hour. I dream of a long, beautiful downpour, green leaves, peas and beans and corn hanging fat and ripe. But when I wake, the clouds have blown away, and it heats up so fast, the soil is dry by the time we finish breakfast. Like it never rained at all.

Then the grasshoppers come. For days, we chase them and stomp them and pluck them from the leaves, but there's more than we ever seen before. They're plastered on the clothes drying on the line, they're in our blankets when we try to sleep, and one morning when I wake, I see a big, fat, green one on my baby James's little forehead. Just like a insult to us, making it personal. I snatch that green bastard up and kill hell out of him.

What crops ain't been choked by the drought is half devoured, leaves pock-marked and torn. Old Albert goes out to the fields, trying to do something, I don't know what. But Mother and me and all the children is out picking off grasshoppers from the potatoes and beans and corn. We need the food or we'll not eat come winter. So cash be damned, paying taxes be damned, we cling to the gardens.

On the Thursday, I go over to Mother's, and she's back from her trip to Brandon with the twins. She had give it a lot of thought, how to help the girls, but yet, where's the money? So then she went up to the Orange Lodge, see if they could help out, and sure enough, they bought her and the girls tickets for the train to Brandon, and even give her a nice five-dollar bill for food while they was there.

We go in and she puts on water for tea, launching into the goings-on of her trip to see this bigwig doctor, Ewan Cameron. I guess he checked the girls over, did all his tests and such, and then he told Mother the girls was not right in the head, what they call *retarded*. They don't think right, he told her, they can't learn.

Well, we knew that. So Mother told him what we need to know is, how do you fix it? Like, what can we do for them?

And I guess he told her there ain't nothing you *can* do. "You just have to have them put away," he told her. He said there's a special place for damaged children in Brandon, a part of the Insane Asylum, where they're locked up and kept from doing harm.

Mother's jaw dropped. But she didn't want to be rude, so she said, "Oh well. I wout'n wanna do that."

So then he told her it's natural for mothers to be faint-hearted about such things, women being the weaker sex, tending to hysteria and tears. But never you mind, he told her. You might think about them at first, but time will pass and soon enough, they will just fade from your mind and cease to trouble your memory. "Just put them away and forget them," he told Mother.

Well, Mother just laughed in his face. "Put 'em away?" she told him. "What the hell kind of foolishness is you talkin'?" She got the girls right up out of them fancy leather chairs and away from that guy. She couldn't believe the nerve of the man. "These here is my little twins," she said to him. "They ain't some piece of ruint junk, to be threw on the scrap heap. These is childern here, people, jist like you or me. Right in the head or not. Retarded, or whatever you wanna call 'em."

"What? A doctor said that?" Doc True would never say such a thing.

The twins is sitting, one on each side of Mother, in their red plaid jumpers and white button-down blouses she sewed special for the trip. "How could I forget my own childern?" Mother scoffs. "And why would I wanta?"

The girls gaze up at her, wonderment and love dancing on their faces. "Who's gonna forget you? Hey?" she teases, squeezing them in at the sides. "Not yur mom, hey! Not yur old mom, that's for sure!" They jump and wiggle and laugh.

"Nee gudda get get get. Nee me Mommy!" one of them tells me excitedly. I think it's Tan. They both cuddle their heads into her.

"Yur mom is not forgettin' yuz, and neither is yur sister," I tell them, giving Tan's hand a little slap. "Nobody's forgettin' yuz!"

"Put 'em away, my arse!" Mother says, arms wide and full. "Whatever words them people wanna call 'em, they is still mine."

The next week, I'm down at Mother's, helping get her dozen loaves of bread into pans. Looks like we may be shed of the damn grasshoppers, must be past their cycle finally. McKay's fronted us more seed, just like half the farmers in Swan River Valley, and Old Albert and Junior has plowed and sowed again. If it will just rain for us now, maybe we might get some crop this year yet. If not, how the hell are we going to pay taxes?

Me and Mother has some hope for our beans and corn anyways, and the rutabagas and potatoes is hanging on. But all of a sudden like, the wind picks up and the sky goes dark and Mother says it's going to be bad, I better get back to my children. I run up the road and fight the wind to get my clothes off the line. At least it's gonna rain.

But it don't. It's a dust storm instead, a real bad one. Dirt and sand blowing through the cracks in our rickety walls, getting in our mouths and stinging our eyes, making us think we're living in a desert. I get the children down on the floor there behind the table. It blows for hours. After, I sweep up pailfulls of dirt and grit. It takes us days to find the chickens, them that survived. There's dunes like snow drifts in the south field, choking all them young plants. We spend days digging out any green thing left in the garden, bringing them water all the way from the river, now that the well is total dry, shoring up the sad little stalks, gentle and kind, willing them to live. *Please grow, please don't die.* Hoping against hope the skies will open.

"What are we gonna do, Mother?" I ask her quiet, when there's no children nearby. "I mean, what's gonna happen?" She just shakes her head and keeps on working.

One day, Mother takes a bunch of her kids and goes to town for flour. She was going to make bread that morning and there was some kind of black bugs in the flour bag. The farther down she went, the more bugs she found. Going to need another hundred-pound bag. We'll have to add it to our bill at McKay's. But where will we get the money to pay it off?

Just after midday, me and Mitch is trying to dig out that big rock at the edge of my garden. Can't get it to budge so I go down the road to Mother's, looking to borrow a spade. I duck into the cow shed and there's Eileen, down in the back stall.

"Eily-Isle!" I call out, picking my way through the piles of dung back to where she is. Looks like this barn ain't been cleaned in a year. I see there's mud or worse all up the backs of Eileen's pant legs and coating her arse. She's got the shit shovel in hand, cleaning out the cow stall.

"Hey, Sissy!" she smiles, using the back of one small, filthy hand to try and push the blond hair back off her pretty face. "Sorry if I stink," she giggles. "Fell right on my arse in the shit over there and now I'm wearin' it."

"Oh, ya jist smell like sugar ta me," I tell her as I give her a little squeeze around the waist. "Why the hell is it you doin' this work anyways?"

She goes back to her shovelling. "Junior's gone to town with Mother, and Dad ain't feelin' good today, so I jist let him take a lay-down. I told him, I'm near eleven years old now, no reason why I can't do the hard work. 'Sides, this really needs doin'. Bossy's got some sort of rot in her hooves, prob'ly cuz of swimmin' in shit."

"Hm!" I say. "Well, yur dad seems sick a awful lot. 'Specially when there's work needs doin'."

"Mmm, no," she mumbles. "Dad would do it if he could."

I don't say nothing more. Lazy bugger. Getting Eileen to do the work that should be his.

"He been spittin' blood lately," she says.

"It's jist from the dry heat," I explain. "My Mitchell's had nose bleeds from it."

"Mmm." She shrugs. "I don't think so..."

"Anyways," I say. "I jist come to get the spade."

"I think I seen it in the porch."

"Okay, I'll look there."

She's cleared most of the stall floor, scraping all the shit into a long pile. Now she shoves in under it, scooping up a big shovel full, and starts hauling the heavy mess towards the door.

"I can take that," I say.

"Git!" she tells me, swinging the handle back so I can't take it. I follow her out to the big pile of shit and dirty straw back behind the barn, where she heaves on her stinky load with a groan.

"Whew!" she says. "Hot work!" She wedges the shovel head deep into the base of the pile. "Think I'll come up with ya for a drink," she tells me, tucking that wisp of stray hair back behind her ear.

I hold out my arm so she can link hers in, and we go swinging on up to the house together. She's humming a little ditty and I smile over at her, just happy with her pretty face and her soft yellow hair and the sweetness of her. She's going to be a beauty, my sister. Is one already.

Reaching the end of the corral, she's still humming and so am I. She grins at me and we start singing the words together.

We will all have chicken and dumplings,
We will all have chicken and dumplings,
We will all have chicken and dumplings when she comes.

"Yeah, babe!" she yells at the end, and slaps my butt. I jump and laugh and she giggles like water burbling over stones. We're belting out "*We will hafta sleep with gramma*" for all we're worth by the time we reach the porch.

I see the spade there but I go into the kitchen for water first too, and there's Old Albert, sitting at the table, playing hisself a nice little game of solitaire... while Eileen is shovelling shit in the heat.

"Oh Daddy," Eileen says, hugging him around the shoulders, "I'm glad yur feelin' better."

I go over to the water pail and scoop up a dipperful. "Oh yes," I say loudly when I finish drinking. "But the work ain't done yet though. Hope he don't start feelin' worse agin."

My sister looks at me sideways and makes a little frown, but I just feel the gall rising up in me. I turn towards the table, leaning my back against the counter. "Well, ain't that how it works, old man?" I ask him. "When there's work needs doin', ya feel poorly. But when the work is done, ya feel better?"

He purses his lips and squints his eyes at the cards. "The laydown helped is all. I was jist gonna come outside when I was done here."

"Huh!" I mutter to myself. "Lazy old shit..."

"Rosie!" I look over at my sister and her face just seems so pained. "Please don't be mean to my daddy."

"Well... well, he..." But the wind has gone out of my sails. I guess if I had a dad, I wouldn't want me to tell him off neither. "I... I'll see ya later, Eileen," I tell her, trying to soften myself. "I got a date with a rock, ha ha," I say, starting to leave.

But she comes and walks me out to the yard. "Sissy, it... it's easy, ya know," she tells me. "Cleanin' the barn for daddy? I don't mind it."

I shake my head like it don't matter. "Oh yes, I know. Yur tough and strong."

Walking up the gravel road, I see a couple of Fjordason men in their field, that little dog, Trixie, sitting pretty, watching them work. Looks like they're digging a big stump out of the ground. They got a piece of timber shoved under it there like a wedge, and right while I'm watching, they both heave together, and out pops a big ball of root.

Why does me and Mother have such useless men?

Over across the dry meadow here, Fjordasons have let their bull in with the cows and he's got one of them mounted. She's standing still for him, so I guess she don't mind, though she's bawling away. I don't know if it's because she likes it or she don't like it.

Why did it have to be Mitch Kelvey I wanted? Just that he was there, I guess. All the boys my age was either in school or out in the fields, working. Mitch was always smiling sweet, wanting to hold my hand, and crazy to please me. I could get him to do whatever I said. So when I decided to get pregnant, solving the problem of how to get out from under Mother's rule, I knew he'd oblige me.

I'd seen things before, playing in the big field by Mares's when we lived over there. The young people would couple up in the tall grasses in the dusk, and one time, hiding up a poplar tree, munching stolen bread and honey, I seen Jake Mares with a girl, doing things in the grass below.

It made me curious. Why would touching down there make a girl buck and shake and roll her eyes back like that? And yet not want to stop?

I thought maybe that would happen when I come to Mitch at the woodpile that time and got him to go into the trees with me. Or would it hurt real bad? I didn't know. But I just started kissing and such and then I just… just did it. I just climbed on. It didn't matter that he was missing a arm. It made him less… less scary, I guess you'd say.

Mitch had no experience at all, even though he was so much older than me, and I just remember how proud I felt after, how old and smart, because I had done a big thing, just like I wanted. It didn't hurt that much really, even though I had to throw them bloody panties away after. And it didn't make me roll my eyes back and buck like a crazed thing, which was a relief. But kind of a letdown too, now that I think about it.

I'm coming into the yard already when I realize I've left the damn spade on the porch that I went there for. And right there at the edge of the garden, still, is that damn big rock. And Mitch, still struggling foolishly to budge it.

I sigh and purse my lips at him, and he leaves off and stands puffing. Then I get a idea and go grab the axe, cut down a little tree to use for a wedge the way them men up the road did. But the first time we try, Mitch pushes the tree at the wrong angle and gets my leg scraped up against the rock. Then, when we're both heaving together, he loses grip and the tree snaps back, barely missing my chin as it goes.

"Oh for Christ sake!" I tell him, and he says he'll hold harder next time, he's sure it'll work next time, just give him one more chance. But I tell him "No!" I tell him it ain't never going to work and I'm tired of this bullshit and, far as I'm concerned, that rock can stay there till Hell freezes over. I go limping up to the house, drag a stump over under the big willow, and sit there in the shade with my arms crossed till it's time to make supper.

* * *

The heat continues, unbearable. One day in July, I wake early from this dream, a dream of ache and longing, my summer nightgown clinging to me, wet all over. It's been a long time since I bothered with Mitch in the night, and longer still since I felt any interest in it.

I don't remember the whole dream, but Culain Kirk's gelding was there, proud and pawing at the ground beneath this huge willow tree, haunches glistening with clean rain. Except that, in the dream, he was a stallion, because I remember his thing, the male part I mean, hanging heavy. Dangling and growing how they do, the skin of it fine and healthy like well-oiled black leather.

I shake off the last of the dream, get out of bed, and go to the wood bin. No wood. I go outside to the wood pile to split some, still yawning, the wind blowing through my light nightdress. I catch a movement in the trees, so I wander over towards the trail and there's Culain Kirk, heading down the path from their place.

"Well, ain't you a sight for sore eyes," he says, grinning. I should maybe move over behind that little bush there, not being really dressed. But for some reason, I don't.

"Where you off to so early?" I ask. He says he's going to Howdles' to clear brush.

He's standing right in front of me, the dappled sunlight through the trees seeming to tussle his chestnut hair. He wears a light blue cotton shirt, the sleeves turned up above his elbows. A small burlap bag is cradled in the crook of his arm, probably his dinner.

I can see a hundred golden hairs sparkling like lake waves on his thick, tanned arm. I reach out my hand and touch them. I pet the hairs back along his arm, making them smooth and pretty. Over and over, I stroke them, and we just stand there together, the shade from the poplars dancing back and forth over us, me gently petting his thick, golden arm. Him motionless, blue eyes gazing, letting me.

He drops the package and lightly takes my wrist. He pulls me into his chest and then… I'm being kissed, the kiss I've wanted for oh so long. I can taste his mouth like sweet milk, and both his arms are around me, strong and gentle. I grab onto him, mouth so hungry, arms around his shoulders, trying to climb right into him. He hooks the bulge of his crotch into my groin and half-lifts me, walking me backwards. I stumble a step but he's got me and his kiss is opening me up, I hear myself moaning.

Somehow, I'm up against a big oak tree, my back and arse pressed tight into the trunk, and he's grinding hisself into my crotch and, my God, I can feel it, his thing, uncoiling thick and hot. I'm using him as a hoist, my legs out and open, my hands reaching down desperate, fighting the hem of my skirt, trying to claw it up.

Then I'm dropped, we're undone, and I'm slumped, half-fallen down the tree trunk. "What?… No… What?" I stare at him. He's looking up the path past my shoulder and I follow his gaze. It's Mitch. Just in his trousers, bare chest pale and scrawny, arm stump puckered up and raw.

Culain gapes at Mitch and blinks. "Sorry," he says, grabs up his lunch sack and goes hurrying down the path.

I stand up, gawking after him. Then I try to straighten myself. But Mitch comes and gets in front of me, face all caved in sad, searching my eyes.

He says my name, like a question. "Rosie? Rosie?" I shove by him on the trail, bumping his stump arm. "Rosie, yur my wife," he tells me, trailing me back to the house. "Don't be a bad girl, Rosie," he whimpers. "Don't be bad."

I'm still in a daze. I still want Culain Kirk, his strong arms, his hard body pressing into where I'm craving it. "Get away from me," I tell Mitch. "Don't talk to me, leave me alone."

He follows me into the kitchen like a lost dog. I put the kettle on the stove but there's still no wood for a damn fire. "Rosie?" he keeps repeating.

"Will ya get me some damn wood," I tell him, "so I can make the breakfast!"

"Rosie? Rosie?" Tears have made channels down his dry cheeks. "Rosie, please, yur my wife," he croaks. "Don't leave me, Rosie. Please don't leave me."

"Damn!" I shove him. "You... whining baby!" But it's harder than I meant to and he falls back, stump arm flung up, his side smashing the table, and he bounces, grabbing at air, feet flailing, and hits the floor with a crash.

"I know I'm yur God damn wife! That's the problem!" I want so much to kick him as he's sprawled out there, struggling and foolish. "Ya damn cry baby!" He's cowering and bawling like a kid, repeating my name over and over. "Coward!" I tell him.

"Don't you hurt my daddy!" Petunia's screeching, peeling out from the bedroom in her little shirt and panties. "Don't you hurt him!"

She flings herself at us and comes sliding onto Mitch's chest like a base runner into third. Black eyes flashing, little arms flung wide like a shield. "Don't you hurt my daddy! Don't you call my daddy names! My daddy ain't no coward! My daddy's a hero—he fought for the country in the Great War!"

"Huh! On the floor!" I tell them. "Some hero!"

Why they got to make me feel like shit?

I turn away, go out to the wood pile and split my own damn wood. I load up a big armful and go back inside. Petunia is sitting on the kitchen chair glaring, her feet dangling nowheres near the floor. Mitch comes out from behind the curtain with a faded checkered shirt on, still trying to hook the empty sleeve into his belt. I go over to the stove, just wanting a minute to try and settle these mixed-up feelings. But don't he come and stand behind me again. "Rosie? Rosie? Rosie?"

"I know I'm yur damn wife!" I tell him, loading the kindling in. "But that don't make me livestock. You don't own me!" I put in some bigger sticks. "I want to live, I want to do things," I tell him. "I'm young yet, you forget that. Yur a old man."

I strike a match from the Bluebird box to light the fire. *Shit!* I meant to start the little pot-bellied stove outside on the north wall. As if this damn place ain't hot enough already. But I got the fire all built now, so I just light it anyways.

"It's my biznus what I do in my life," I tell Mitch. "You don't rule me!" I take the poker and move the burner back over top. Then I turn and face him.

He looks so small and crooked, so much slashed away from the top half of him already. His head is bent, like he's praying, his bald spot showing, making me think now of that tenderest place on a baby's head. When he raises his eyes, I can see the walnut tone to them. And I almost see the man, so safe and good, that I once saw. The father of my children, a kind man who cared for me, a brave man who fought in the war... just like my own Poppa.

I cannot believe the words that came out of my mouth. I've gone crazy and am beyond all reason, and I need someone to take me in hand. Somewheres deep inside, I think I do want Mitch to rise up and make me stop. Settle me down and give me something solid to hold onto.

"Anything, Rosie, you can do anything ya want," he whimpers, everything in him sad and weak and aggravating to me. "Jist don't leave me, Rosie, that's all I ask. And you can do whatever else ya want."

* * *

The year looks to be a dud. It's August, but the gardens are in ruins, everything above ground brown and crackling, what ain't already blowed away. Even the potatoes and turnips are small and wrong-shaped. Mother's whole three acres of wheat is scorched, and still every day is mean and dry. How in the world are we going to pay the taxes?

It's six in the morning, there's nary a breeze nor hope of one. I'm laying on the cot there, baby James on the tit and Mitchell's little sweaty head pressed against my side, trying to get myself going when I hear Jonesy's hooves thrumming hard way up the road.

I spill all the kids off me and jump up, throw on a skirt and blouse, and run out to the road. I can see Jonesy standing at Mother's front stoop, reins flopped to the ground, dust still hanging in the air like a veil. As I go clipping up the road, I see Mother come out with Culain and swing onto Jonesy.

Elvie Kirk must have finally gone into labour. The fact the child waited till term after nearly being miscarried is a minor miracle.

"Come up, Rosie, case I need help," Mother yells as they go flying by. So I run in, tell Eileen to watch my kids, then go hoofing up the dirt road fast as I can.

I come into the Kirks' kitchen where the big girls and a little guy is sitting at the table eating Sunny Boy from bowls. I say hi and walk through to the bedrooms. One room's empty except for all the feather ticks on the floor. The small bedroom is crammed full with one big bed and the youngest little guy sleeping in a cradle tucked into the far corner. I come back and ask the girls where their mom is. Hope says she thought her mom was having a baby, but she don't know where. "Did they have to go to town?" I ask. She says she don't think so.

I go look out the door. I can see Charles Kirk and Culain and a couple other sons, probably Crofter and Christian, way down the field where there's a patch of corn, short but still living. Looks like they're trying to dig a trough out there from the little slough by the bush. I go around the side of the house. Nothing. I come back to the step, and that's when I see the women out in the summer kitchen. Must have been the only place there was room enough for us all, and not so stifling hot as in the house.

The willow trees on either side of the wall-less kitchen are lush enough, even this year, that their branches make a green ceiling high above, giving deep and welcome shade. The brown dirt is packed hard and flat like a real floor. On the south side is the iron stove, some wooden boxes stacked for cupboards, and a wash stand and basin. At the far end is a rope line, hung with kitchen rags, a big serge-coloured cotton towel, and a few of the children's clothes. On the north is a long table made from planks with rough legs and a couple benches alongside.

Standing in the centre is Elvie Kirk, absolutely silent. She is such a small, quiet woman, Elvie Kirk. Delicate, like a dove. You wouldn't think she'd be able to have all these children, let alone feed them. Her brown hair is in a bun at the nape of her neck, she wears a loose faded dress, daisy print, and no shoes. One arm sort of cradles the underside of her big tummy. Her eyes is shut but not squinted, kind of how a woman will close her eyes when she's trying to remember where she put something.

Mother is waiting a little to the side, hands clasped loose in front of her. Mother is short like Elvie but she's built more solid. Her dress bears the very same faded daisy pattern. There's a stillness here that I don't want to spoil, so I come in quiet and stand by my mom.

She turns and catches my eye, nodding for me to light up the stove and put water on to boil—to scald the tying-off string and scissors. We have a couple blankets stacked on the table, some cloth, herbs, and such in the basket on the bench.

The pains don't last long. Every couple minutes, Elvie closes her eyes and has one. In between, she just stands there, calm and looking away to the far fields. Once, Mother brings her a cup of water and she has a few sips.

Next time Elvie opens her eyes, Mother squats outside her knees and reaches a hand up inside the dress, checking things. Elvie shifts for her like a filly will let you check a shoe. Then Mother rises and steps away.

"The bag of waters is not broken," she says.

A pair of doves are cooing high up in the willows. Elvie makes a kind of small bending move with her knees, as though she might curtsy, but she doesn't. Then, I feel something ruffling my hair and I realize there's a cool breeze blowing.

"The breeze," I whisper, turning to Mother. But she don't hear me. She kind of lunges forward, taking one long step to Elvie and stoops, then Elvie opens up her curtsy and makes a little squeak, and there's my mom, holding something in her arms.

"Oh," Elvie says as she kind of bends towards Mother. And I jump and grab Elvie in case she might fall. I throw down one of the blankets on the dirt floor and help her lower herself to it. Coming from her is a long, thick cord, spongy. Bloody on the inside but pale and milky, like a pike's eyeball. It's attached to the something in Mother's arms, some powdery, watermelon-looking thing.

"Oh my God, it's in the caul," Mother says, "the waters are not broken."

Elvie is silent-laughing, big green eyes full of tears. "In the caul," Mother repeats a few times, coddling the strange thing in her lap. "Baby's in the caul, in the caul." She works her fingertips carefully into a spot near the top of the sack, there's gushes and spurts of water, and then she peels the bag back this way and that, revealing a baby.

"A little girl it is," Mother says, giving it gently over to Elvie, who hums and coos to the tender thing, face alight with happy tears, and we wrap them both in blankets. Mother cuts the cord, and as soon as the afterbirth is out, I go tell the children they have a sister. So they come and fuss over her and eventually we get Elvie walked into the house with all the children and the baby. We get them settled and give Elvie some nice hot tea with honey. Me and Mother stays for a few hours, watching over them and visiting. We make biscuits and stew for when the men come up from the fields.

Charles Kirk is amazed about the birth. He says they was always told that a baby born in the caul means very good luck. Mother says that's what they was always told too, good luck and the power of healing. They decide to name the baby Grace.

"Well, if this means good luck," I say, "maybe the heat's gonna let up now and we'll get lots of rain. And everthin' will be alright."

"Maybe," Charles Kirk says, frowning out the window like he don't think so.

"Don't ya think?" I ask them all. "Maybe this could mean the crops will be saved and we'll have a good harvest after all? That would be lucky, wout'n it?"

"Well, there's luck and then there's luck," Mother says. "I think the luck we're talkin' about is a bigger kinda luck." She watches on as Elvie gives milk to her little Grace. "More of a lifetime kinda thing… And as to the healin' power, it's the child carries that, and only with time would ya see its work."

Elvie purrs to the babe in her arms, green eyes tender, lips gentle. "Little baby Grace," Charles Kirk clucks to the tiny thing, stroking its cheek all gentle with his large, work-calloused finger. "Hey? Will ya bring us happiness and good fortune, wee girlie?"

Culain has took his bowl of stew outside somewheres to eat, and I ain't seen him since. The men go back to the field and Mother starts packing up her things to head home, saying she'll come back and check on them again after supper. I get up and put some water on to heat for dishes. I tell Mother I'll stay and help out a little longer, I'll be down in awhile. So she goes.

Soon, Culain comes in, saying he has to take a trip down past my place, did I want a ride?

"Oh, well sure," I say, like I'm surprised, "since yur goin' there anyways."

He saddles up Jonesy, swings hisself up and I climb on behind.

"You better hold on tight!" he shouts back over his shoulder. "Cuz once I give Jonesy his head, there's no reinin' him in!" And we fly.

As soon as I get home, I start getting ready. I set up the washboard, get the lye soap out, and heat up lots of water. I wash my bedding and hang it on the clothes line. I wash my good town dress and some under things and hang them too.

I take down Mitch's things that are already dry. Maluk is digging a water line to try and save his oats, and he said in town yesterday that he would take on Mitch for chores, a couple days at least. I fold up Mitch's things and put them in a sack for him.

I even get down on my knees and wash the bedroom floor.

Then I walk my four kids down to Mother's. The older three go to play in the trees with the twins and I hand James over to Eileen. I tell her to just rock him to sleep tonight, he'll be fine. I'll be down to get them in the morning. "I have just *got to* catch up on my sleep tonight," I tell her.

On my way back through the yard, I bring in my bedding from the line. Mitch is standing on the step as I go by with the bundle in my arms. He says he sees Maluk's rig coming up the road far off, and I tell him his pack is on the table.

The sheet smells like clover and fresh breezes. I fling it into the air above the bed and it flutters down, but it's a little turned under at the far end. So I crack it out twice, make it billow and settle just right. I go around, tucking in edges. I run the flat of my hand over the foot of the bed when I'm done. Perfect.

It's just when I'm putting the pillows into their cases that I realize Mitch is watching me from the bedroom doorway.

"What?" I challenge him, hands on my hips.

He blinks and says my name. Then he says, "Don't leave me."

"I ain't," I tell him, "I already told ya."

He says maybe if he does good at Maluk's, this will turn into regular work. We could move the twenty miles north to Little Woody district. Have our own life.

"Like I told ya before," I say, "I ain't movin' that far away from my fam'ly." I go back to what I was doing. At some point, he's saying goodbye. "Alright," I say. "Goodbye then. Now mind that arm this time, don't go gettin' yurself hurt again."

I turn back and check my handiwork. Beautiful. Just needs one more thing. I open the cedar trunk and get out that pretty patchwork comforter, the one Mother give me and Mitch for a wedding present. I lay it over, very pleased with how the reds have not faded.

Yet Mitch is still standing in the doorway, yacking at me. Can't he see I'm busy?

"Yes, yes, goodbye, goodbye!" I say, waving him away. "Git goin' already!"

Next time I look, he's finally gone. I finish tidying up the talcum powder spilled on my old cherry wood dresser. Then I go stand on the step, shielding my eyes from the setting sun. Maluk's buggy is way down the hill. And never no sign of rain.

At dusk, I sit alone there in the dull heat, watching the road, listening for the first fall of Jonesy's hooves. Aching for what is to come.

Now what was it Mitch was nattering about in the bedroom doorway?

I turn his words over in my mind and click my tongue. *Huh! Why's he gotta try and ruin things for me?*

"Rosie, my darlin'," I think that's what he said. "When yur all finished makin' that bed, you *are* gonna hafta lay in it."

Chapter 3

Mother's Constitutional

(1936)

Six bad years into the Depression, with paying work so hard to find, she had found good work with a wealthy farmer down by Drowning River. Ed Welsh was his name. He had hired Eileen to take care of his children and ailing wife. Supposed to be anyways, but turns out, that's not all he wanted took care of.

I said to her at the time, I said, "Baby sister, you gotta be careful now. Men can get ya into things there ain't no good way outta." But she was young, and how can you tell a young girl about the world we live in today?

She had started at Welsh's after Christmas and when she come home to visit in February, she couldn't wait to tell me all about Mr. Welsh trying to get at her. Me and Mitch was not getting along again, so I was sleeping down the road at Mother's. Eileen and me was whispering and giggling in the back room for half the night, keeping the whole house awake.

"For cryin' out loud, Rosie!" Mother yelled through the wall. "You with six childern of yur own and still carryin' on like a ninny!" She sighed heavy, then softened a little. "Girls!"

But Eileen always got me like that. She had this way of being with a person, encouraging like. You'd be telling her some regular thing you done, she'd be nodding, smiling gentle into your eyes. Like what you were saying was just the biggest thing in the world. She would reach out and stroke back your hair, listening in that quiet way of hers. Every minute you were with her, you just felt important somehow. Adored, I guess you'd say. Even me, old married woman that I was at twenty-five.

Not that she even knew exactly what Welsh wanted—she'd never had a beau. But she'd be doing some sort of work, peeling potatoes or washing windows, then turn and there he'd be, telling her, all low and breathy, what a pretty girl she was. She would roll her eyes and laugh, telling me about it, but I could see the thrill it gave her. These things feel like so much fun at first, yet the stakes are dead serious.

I took her aside the next day before she left to go back to Welsh's and told her that no good could come from it. You keep that man at bay, I told her. But she figured she was old enough to handle whatever was came. That's what she told me, the pure white light of winter in her face. "Don't you worry, Sissy. Yur little sister is a big girl now."

The next month, when she come home for her sixteenth birthday, she was quiet and distractible, not her jokey self, and I figured something had happened. Me and Mitch had that old, cold shack at the end of Mother's property, and I got Eileen to come down and help me clean out the animal stalls.

That's when she brightened up and started telling me about her and Eddy. "My Eddy," she was calling him now, as if he was a kid like her. She said he really loved her—true love—and that she loved him back.

Poor Eddy was so desperate unhappy, she said, his cranky wife always moping and coughing in her upstairs room.

"Oh Eileen!" I said. "Tell me you ain't... given in to the man."

"Well!" she accused. "You was younger'n me when ya took up with Mitch..." she tossed her head, "and *had to* get married!"

"Eileen!" I said. "That is not the same. Mitch was a single man, and I was the one that started things with him. Ed Welsh is yur boss and he has a wife." *How can I say this to make her understand?* "Ed Welsh is taking advantage of you, hun, doncha see? Because yur young and innocent to the ways of the world."

Well, that just got her going quiet, arms crossed and looking vexed. She said she thought I'd be the one person who would understand, the one person to see her side and be happy for her. Pretty soon, she went trudging up to Mother's house, left me there shovelling shit and shaking my head. *Eileen, Eileen, what hornet's nest have you got into?*

It was when she come home for Easter that they had the terrible fire out at Welsh's. Supposed to be a chimney fire, Ed Welsh claimed. Said that by the time he saw the flames from the barn, it was too late to get them out.

That woman and four little girls all burned alive. Only him and the boy saved.

We was just grateful Eileen wasn't there at the time. But Eileen was like a cat in a oven, crawling the walls for want of getting back to Ed Welsh.

Mitch's cousin Velma whispered she heard in town that Welsh had lost a wife and child before this marriage, the bodies buried somewheres in the hills. Died of fever he had claimed, but not attested to by no one else but him.

I wanted to go to Mother then but she had so much worrying her already. We'd lose the farm if taxes was not paid and they was due again in fall. Mother was planning to pay them from sale of crops, and yet we had no money to buy the seed for planting. It was Eileen's pay she was giving Mother that was supposed to cover all that.

Within the week, that cad Ed Welsh come driving his fancy buggy into Mother's yard. Thick built and hard muscled, he had on a red silk shirt and his dirty yellow hair slicked back. Mother come out and give him condolences. He had his boy staying with him in Swan River at the house of his deceased aunt. He still needed Eileen, he said.

My sister could hardly contain herself, dancing and begging to go. So Mother agreed of course, and Eileen ran to get her things. I bit my tongue. Soon as taxes was covered, I'd tell Mother everything and we'd go get Eileen out of there.

In May, when my sister come home that last time, it had already started. She slept at my house up the road, so I was the only one who knew about her puking every morning. She admitted she hadn't had her periods in two months. I said to her right away, I said, "Eileen, stay here with us. Don't go back there. I'm scared somethin's gonna happen to ya." I told her to come with me to Mother. I said, "Eily-Isle, she's got that Mother's Constitutional, the special tea for bringin' on the periods."

But Eileen said no. She said Ed Welsh knew a man, a medical man, with real scientific medicine. Not old mumbo jumbo country cures like Mother had. And anyways, she was scared to look Mother in the eye, being pregnant and not married.

"But Eily," I said, "she can *help* you." She wouldn't hear tell of it. I thought, *Eileen, someday you'll learn. Just like me, some day you will learn that when you got a real problem, Mother is the place to go.*

I seen her from my garden patch that Sunday morning, sitting on the step, waiting for Welsh to come take her back. She had on her new yellow dress with the gay, flouncy hem. Store-bought. Her hair, down loose and pinned back at the temple, shone gold in the morning light.

How long till you're the cranky wife, hun, and the man grows tired of you? That's what I was thinking. Even then, I thought the danger was somewheres off in the distance and we still had time.

Chickadees was chirping in the hawthorns when she climbed into the buggy, life and hope and promise dancing in every move and curve of her.

"Love you, Eily," I called out as they drove away. "I'll see ya at the fair in July."

She waved back, clicking and singing to the horses as they went. "Love you, Sissy. See ya at the fair." But she never made it back for that.

* * *

All during planting, it nags and worries at me. How is my sister Eileen making out? What is this *real scientific medicine* Ed Welsh's medical man knows? I wish she'd just come home. I keep thinking I'll talk to Mother. But then I think what fireworks there'll be and how Eileen will never again trust me with her confidences.

My mom has been making the Mother's Constitutional tea for years. That tall plant with the yellow button flowers she picks over by the train tracks, boiled in water and left steeping at the back of the stove. She always told us children never to touch that tea, it's only for her. She'd be choking down a pint every couple hours, sweating and retching in the nights, and by the second or third day, she'd be having her blood and feeling better.

Mother knows all about helping women. She's been going out to the women as a midwife for a few years now and Doc True much appreciates it. He's getting up there in years and is just as happy to have a woman like Mother do the waiting and tying off with the country ladies. He'll just check on the mother and babe next time he happens to be out their way. And if he gets any pay at all, Doc is always sure to pass Mother a dollar or two out of it.

One evening at the end of May, a nice little breeze is blowing from the west and I sit on a blanket in the grass against the weathered wall of the house, nursing my baby Cathy, as Mother finishes off the dishes. I'm thinking about that tea she makes, Eileen's situation and all, and she comes and sits on the porch steps beside me.

Mother is past the childbearing age by now, her hair gone wiry grey. She always coils it into a bun, wrapped 'round with a kerchief that she ties in a knot on top. She's taken to wearing a old shirt and man's pants, my mom. Hell, she's been doing so much of the man's work for years that she finally got tired of trying to do it in skirts and put on the pants her own self.

A woman wearing man's pants! My, how the tongues did wag in town. "Let 'em talk," Mother would say, holding her head up. "I got no say in their biz'nuss. They can damn well stay outta mine!"

"Mother," I ask her now, "ya know when ya drink the tea to force the blood? Some people in town is sayin' that for a woman to knowingly bring on the blood is a sin. Cuz yur killin' the seed. Do ya ever think it might be alive, what yur passin'?"

"Naw," Mother says. "I don't think nothin' like it. No use thinkin' what ya can't afford to think. It's jist yur periods comin' late, that's all. Ya drink the tea and bring on the blood. Mebbee a few pains more'n usual. But there ain't nothin' livin' in what ya pass. You can see for yurself when it comes, it's jist blood like reg'lar. Nothin' alive."

My James and Carly is playing with a little cat by the step. "These ones here though," Mother says, nodding towards them, "*these ones* is alive. That's what we know for sure. These ones here *is* alive. And if there's too many born, then the ones we got is in peril. God knows there's barely food for the ones we got. But yur little sister Carleen that died the year after we come out to the homestead," she says, leaning in and meeting my eye. "Was she alive?"

I nod, looking down at my baby Cathy, stroking her little sleepy head.

"She was alive, our Carleen. But we had so little food and no money for a doctor. We was workin' like crazy not to lose the homestead. Which we lost anyways, course. But Carleen Margie, she went and died on us. Remember?"

I fade off into memories of my little sister. When she was a baby, I lugged her everywhere in a gunny-sack bag. She'd never fall asleep, except on my shoulder.

"And with the tea," Mother is saying, "the mother never dies. *That's* the thing with the Mother's Constitutional. Whatever might have some day grown into somethin', well, that's gone. But the mother never dies, she'll be there to raise the ones she's got. And when the right time comes for a child to live, well, she could have one then."

Mother lays her hand on my knee and gives it a pat. "But when a woman makes the tea and drinks it," she tells me, "she cannot say that God sent her a child, or God took it back. She cannot hang it on her husband nor the laws of the land nor doctor's orders. That is the real crux of the matter. When ya drink the tea, there's no one else ya can blame nor credit, jist yurself."

She gets up and starts yelling at the kids that it's time to get home. "Whatever happens, ya got to say that ya choosed it and ya done it yur own self." She bends and gives me a little peck on the side of my head. "And it's not every woman," she says, "who's up for sayin' that."

* * *

It was the second day of June when Mitch's cousin Velma come up the dirt road in Erickson's buggy with strange news. Eileen was seen getting off the morning train from Winnipeg, looking pale and terrible sick.

I go running up the north field where Mother and Old Albert is working, her hauling the plow and him throwing seed. "Well, why the hell would Eileen have been in the city?" Mother frowns. Me and her jump in with Velma and hitch a ride to Swan. But when we finally find Welsh's auntie's house, it's all locked up.

Mother's pounding on the front door but there ain't no answer, so I run around the side. There's these tall windows high up, where my chin can barely reach the sill, but I keep moving from one to the next, trying to see in. Finally, at this one window, I see a big empty room with polished wood floors, nothing else in it but a big stuffed flowery chesterfield. And upon it, my sister Eileen.

She lays dead still, eyes on the ceiling and knees pulled up, a patchwork blanket half-kicked off on the floor. Ashen pale, lips blue, gritting her teeth.

And that old coot, Ed Welsh, is planted right at the front door, arms crossed, with Mother yelling and pounding on the outside. I get my palm up and bang the window. Welsh jumps and scowls back at me, purses his lips, and finally steps up to open the door.

Eileen hears me too. She turns her head slow and reaches out her hand towards me, lips moving like she's trying to tell me something. *I'm comin', baby sister*, I think, and go running back around to the front.

Ed Welsh is looking daggers at us, telling Mother that Eileen just has a fever. He's giving her medicine, he says, no need to get all hysterical.

"Well, we'll come have a look at her," Mother says, stepping onto the door sill.

But that man steps right forward, blocking her and almost knocking her down. "No!" he says. "Not right now! Come back tomorrow."

"What the hell?" Mother says. "Well, why?"

"Come back tomorrow!" he repeats, then slams the door in Mother's face and bolts it.

Mother's jaw drops. "What the hell is goin' on here?"

She turns back and hammers the door a bunch of times, swearing bad. But it never budges. I run around the side again. Some flowery curtains have swung over the window where my sister is. I can't see a thing.

"Eileen!" I yell, giving the window a bang. "Eileen!" Nothing.

I run back. "He's closed the curtains now," I'm pretty winded, "but I seen her before. She's on the chesterfield in there, looks real sick. She held out her hand to me, seemed like she was tryin' to say somethin'. Mother, what're we gonna do?"

"Well I don't know what the hell to do!" she says, one hand up and kneading her forehead. "It's not our house. Private propity. And with his money, he'd have the Mounties on us if we tried to break in. We could get the Mounties on him ourself, but I don't know. This whole Winnipeg thing, that's a worry. Why would Eileen have took the train to Winnipeg?"

I kick at the step. "Maybe... she's in trouble?"

"Yes, that's what I was thinkin'. So if she... if she was expectin' like, and... if they've had a doctor at her, to abort it, like, then the Mounties *will* get into it. But it wouldn't be Welsh's ass on the line, it's Eileen they'd be after... if that's the sichee-ation here."

We walk out to the gravel road and stand around. ". . . although why she'd go to some quack in the city when I got my own med'cine to help her," Mother says, "I do not know."

I murmur agreement and look away.

"And then, what if it is jist a reg'lar fever like Welsh claims?" She purses her lips. "Us makin' a big fuss over a case o' the chicken pox or some such? That would piss off Welsh and get Eileen fired for sure. Then where would she find another job? Only three months left till taxes is due again."

We pace back and forth to the house a couple times, Mother pounding hard on the door, but it don't never open. Finally, she shoos me on up the road.

"Might as well go home, I guess, since this prick ain't lettin' us in. We'll stop off, leave a message for Doc True to look in on Eileen whenever he makes it back from his country rounds. Welsh would not dare try to keep Doc out."

She spits into the gravel and hikes hard up the road, me jogging along, trying to keep up. "Come hell or high water, after chores in the morning, I *am* comin' back here," she says. "And I *will* go through that God damn door."

But at first light, when I step off my porch, I see Doc's boy riding up the hill on that sorrel mare. The kid gets down slow, head hanging, and goes over to Mother in the yard. When he speaks to her, she staggers like she been hit by a fist.

I run down the road, bare feet and all, and Old Albert comes out of the house. Mother is pure crazed, howling and moaning. "No, no, no! My girl, my girl!" Albert has fell down on his arse on the step, bawling like a kid.

"What happened?" I screech at the boy, grabbing his two shoulders. "Is it my sister Eileen? Is she dead?"

Eyes big as saucers and lip quivering, he just nods his head.

* * *

It's suppertime on the second day that my big brother Ken Workman comes through the door. I had a telegram sent to him up at Flin Flon. I knew he had worries of his own, what with the miners' strike going into the second month and no money coming in to even feed his family. But I didn't know what else to do—what with the situation.

Old Albert had gone to town the previous day to collect Eileen's body. Going to bring her home on Erickson's buckboard and lay her out on the kitchen table like regular. But they had the body up at Hall's Funeral Home and said we couldn't see her. Said Doc True had called for a inquest, he would do a autopsy, and she would have to be buried closed-casket from there.

The neighbours has all come to the farm. Nobody knows what to do or say. It's crowded and noisy in the house, a bunch of ladies crammed into the kitchen here, trying to help me feed everybody.

Mother sits at the table, eyes wild and mouth agog, like someone slapped her face and she ain't had time to blink. There's a ringing in my ears too, everything seeming so strange, like this whole life ain't even real.

But I look towards the doorway and my big brother Kenny is filling it up, head ducked down to clear the six-foot frame. More solid than ever, hair black and thick with curls, but skin with that unnatural paleness that miners get. He has on a fresh-starched white shirt with his khaki work trousers and good black Oxford shoes.

"Momma!" I croon, taking her hand. "Momma, look. It's Kenny. Kenny's come home."

Her eyes come up slow. But instead of coming back to herself like I was hoping, she starts to moan, some kind of animal sound coming from way down in her, face caving in horrible. She's shaking her head, keening "No, no, no, no…"

But Kenny takes the long stride to the table and gets hold of her. She fights his tenderness and he wrestles her down gentle. They thud onto the floor there with all the feet and he drags her half onto his lap like a child. She keeps wailing, snot and spit getting all over Kenny's good going-to-town shirt. But he don't care, he strokes her head and talks to her quiet till her fight turns to tears and she begins to sob, held into him there.

Folks cast their eyes about, not knowing where to look, and proceed on outside.

I sit on the wood chair by the window, tears coming down.

Late at night, when Mother is put to bed and the neighbours have gone, I go and sit with Kenny on a stump by the fire and tell him everything. About Ed Welsh making advances and taking advantage of Eileen. About Welsh's so-called accidental fire. About Eileen, deathly sick, getting off the Winnipeg train. And Welsh refusing to let her own mother try to help when she was dying.

My younger brother, Junior, comes loping his big self out from the house. I swear, that boy is already topping six foot four. Well, Kenny fills him in and also tells Old Albert what we're thinking. I say Culain and the Kirk boys will for sure want in on this. Kenny seen me and

Culain sitting together in the tree line earlier. Well, it's common knowledge by now that him and me is close. So Kenny don't kick on it neither. Way late into the night, him and Junior go hiking up the silent road to Kirks' place.

On the third day, Mother sits on the bench at the dark table. The iron stove is cold. Blankets cover the windows—don't want no spirits drawn to us that ought to be moving on. I send my sister Beatrice, the next younger than the twins, up the road to help with my kids. I'm just trying to get the last of the plates washed up when Culain Kirk drives their big black team into the roundabout, hitched up to a hayrack. Two of his short, stocky brothers, Crofter and Christian, sit cross-legged in the straw. Kenny and Junior jump on and when Old Albert comes from the barn, wheezing, they take him by the shirt shoulders and drag him up there too.

Culain has already clicked to the team and they're just heading out the dirt drive when I come running and hop on board.

"She ain't comin'!" Junior pipes up. "Kenny!" he complains. "Rosie ain't comin'! This ain't for women! This is for the men!"

"Huh! Well if this is only for men," I fire back at him, "what the hell is you doin' here? Jist cuz yur fourteen years old, Junior Labeau, don't make ya boss to me."

"Kenny!" Junior whines.

Ken has gone to stand with Culain at the front wood rack and he glances back. I raise my chin and bug my eyes at him. Kenny shakes his head. "Well, Junior," he says, "if ya think ya can tell a Workman woman what to do, have at 'er!"

Junior glares at me, I glare back, and he slits his eyes and looks away.

"Besides," Kenny tells him, "yur sister ain't no girlie-woman, you know that." I give a nod to Ken and settle myself. Culain flicks the reins and the team breaks into a trot. "But, Rose," Kenny shouts through the moving air, "when it comes down to it, yur gonna hang back, right?"

"I know," I yell back. "I jist wanna be there."

We go clipping down Pretty Valley Road, the horses galloping good, green willow branches and saplings whipping by. Tearing through the countryside behind a two-horse team, Culain Kirk stands solid and at ease, as if looking out on the world from his own front porch. He holds the heavy reins light in his thick paws.

In a bit, I start working my way up front, crouching to keep my balance as the wagon rocks along. I stand holding the rail alongside my tall, strong brother and Culain Kirk, who's barely taller than me. My sister comes into my mind, how sick she looked, the pleading in her eyes. I bury my face in Culain's shirt and let the silent tears come. He shifts the reins to his other hand and puts his arm around my shoulders. Pretty soon, I can feel we've reached the valley floor and are turning at the crossroads onto the old Northwest Highway. A couple miles outside of Swan River, Culain slows the horses to a fast walk and I go back to sit in the straw.

My brother Ken has done a fair job stripping bark off the poplar club he's brought. The Kirk men have poplar clubs too, laying in the straw beside them. Junior has the baseball bat. I hike up my skirt at the side and fetch that sharp little Swiss knife I have stashed in my stocking top. Not for killing a man, that knife, but for being remembered.

Culain reins the team off the highway heading west and comes up Ditch Road to the Welsh house. It's skinny and high, two gaunt windows like dead eyes on each side of the door. Kenny and the Kirk men are getting ready. Junior has jumped off the rack and is jogging along beside, bat held at the ready.

It's just when Culain pulls the team into the yard and calls, "Whoa," that the front door slings open, crashing on the outside wall, and out steps John Elliott, our local Swan River constable. He's a tall man, even without the blond Stetson hat he always wears. With him is Doc True, who ain't no threat. But then coming up from the fire pit in the yard is three or four other fellows, all Kenny's size or better. There's McKay Junior from the General Store, him I know for sure, and a couple of the Colton boys, farmers from Little Woody district. They all spread theirselves out in front of the house with the constable.

Shit! What do we do now?

Well, Kenny jumps down, sets his jaw, and strides into the yard, so me and the Kirk boys hop down too and go with him. About twenty feet from the house, we come to a halt and form our own line facing their line. There's Kenny in the middle, Culain at his elbow, and the other Kirk brothers to the right. Junior's beside Kenny on our side, the bat thrumming loud and fast into his palm. Then Old Albert, but he looks so frail and pathetic that I just have to step right up too, and come forward with the men.

Kenny glances my way and frowns, but I set my jaw. My brothers is not going to fight this thing without me.

"Good afternoon, gentlemen," John Elliott calls in a amiable but strong voice.

"Afternoon it is," Kenny answers, "but better for some than others."

"Not so good for our sister!" Junior screeches. Startled, me and Kenny both look his way. Junior's cheeks is high red, his eyes glassy. Being young and so big, his britches hiked up and hair snipped short for less sweating, he suddenly looks strange to me. As if they had gave him too small a head for the size of his body.

"Take 'er easy, son," Kenny tells him in a low tone. Junior's breath is raspy and quick, the bat drumming hard in his hand. I don't think he even notices he's wincing with each hit. Kenny looks over the constable and his men. I don't see no firearms myself. "Junior," Kenny says again a little louder. "It's alright, Junior. Slow down, son."

"Ken Workman," the constable calls over. "We are truly sorry for yur sister—for... what happened. We are here today to try and right that wrong."

Kenny says nothing, nostrils flaring.

"We do not want trouble, Ken," John Elliott says, his voice a little stronger. "Do ya hear me?"

"Then git outta our way!" Junior yells. "Git out and let us at 'im!"

"Ken," the constable continues, eyes steady. "We are not here to help Ed Welsh. We are here on yur side, to help you. So you don't wind up doin' somethin' yur whole fam'ly will pay for."

"Bullshit!" Junior spits. "Kenny!" he pleads. "Kenny! He's fulla shit!"

Junior takes a step forwards but Kenny clutches his shirt sleeve and holds him by it. "Hold on, Junior! Hold! Lemme hear the man." Junior's teeth are clenched and he's grabbing breath in gulps.

"Now, Ken, yur mother has already lost one child this week," Elliott goes on. "Think, man! What's gonna happen if you do to Ed Welsh what ya got in mind? You know who his daddy is, the kinda connections he has. The Mounties' down at Dauphin would not be able to let it pass, Ken. You would have yur justice for a day. But then what? All of yuz in big trouble! Yur fam'ly hurt even more."

Kenny glances over my way. It does make sense. I give a quick nod.

"You men," the constable calls generally, hands out and high like a pastor blessing the congregation. "We're not here to protect Ed Welsh! We're here to help you."

"Bullshit!" Junior cries, wrenching his arm away, trying to run at Elliott.

Kenny jumps to grab him back, but Junior rips away again, forcing Kenny to take him hard and hold him by force. Well, that's when Junior starts swinging so Kenny has to slap him once, open-handed, across the head, and grab him hard by the shoulders. Junior flails, cursing, and tries to swing again, so then Kenny has to wrestle him down.

"Hold, Junior!" he's hollering. "Will ya hold, damn it!"

Constable Elliott's crew wobbles forward, nervous. "Whoa, whoa," Elliott coos, arms out and gentle, as if calming a terrified horse. So they all hold in place while Kenny takes down our brother.

Junior thrashes and roars where he's pinned to the ground. "Lemme up, Kenny, ya yella bastard!" He bucks a couple times, but can't budge our big brother. Soon as he quiets, Kenny does let up, and the boy rolls out from under and scrambles to his feet.

Junior's earlobe is split and bleeding, and he backs away, raging. "Lyin' bastards and cheats! Ed Welsh killed my sister! And yuz are lettin' him git away with it!"

"Junior," I say gently, taking a step towards him. "Junior, it's alright."

"No!" he screams at me, but it comes out half a sob. I stop in my tracks. The last thing I'd ever want is to bring my brother to tears in front of the men.

"And you!" Junior howls, stabbing his finger towards Kenny. "You deserted us all years ago. Ya went north for the good life and never cared for none of us! Ya deserted yur own mother! And now yur desertin' Eileen too."

Kenny's throat tightens, his jaws flinch, and he says nothing.

"God damn you, Kenny!" Junior screams, then turns and half-runs up the road, arm to his forehead, shoulders heaving with the sobs he's trying to choke back.

"Junior..." I call weakly behind him. But he's already at the corner.

"Let him go," comes a firm and calming voice at my elbow. I guess while my brothers was scrapping it out, Constable John Elliott has came and stood solid there with us. "He'll be alright," he says. "Jist needs to blow off steam. It's hell yur fam'ly is goin' through these past days. Each one has their different way of gettin' through."

Kenny studies the collection of men waiting in silence, Kirks and Coltons and McKays all mixed in together.

"You men can go now," Elliott tells his people. "This here is alright. This is all took care of now." His extra muscle starts milling about, clubs are dropped, like he said, and they head in their different directions. I stow my Swiss knife back in my big skirt pocket. "Come over to the firepit by the trees, Ken," he says, taking my brother by the elbow, steering him. Kenny don't resist. "Rosie, Albert, come over now and we'll talk."

Me and Old Albert fall in line. Culain catches my eye, nodding towards the hayrack, where him and his brothers will see to the horses. When we get to the firepit, I see that Doc is with us too. Apart from that faded bow tie and the battered old black medical bag he's never without, you would think Doc was a regular fellow. He never puts on airs.

He steps forward now, shakes Old Albert's hand, and helps him sit. He shakes Kenny's hand too, giving it a fatherly pat. I'm just about to sit when he comes over, puts his arms around me and speaks quiet condolences in my ear. I guess that kind of gets to me, and we stand there for a time, me bawling like a kid in Old Doc's arms, the men quiet, looking away. After a bit, I fetch the hankie from my sleeve, give my nose a good blow, and sit. Doc settles hisself on the stump beside me.

Constable Elliott clears his throat and begins to speak. First of all, he explains, that cad Ed Welsh is not even in the house anymore. Seems Elliott and Doc had heard of Kenny's coming and figured on this occurrence. When Kirks' team pulled up, they had advised Mr. Ed Welsh to go quietly out the back door as they went out the front. This he had done immediately and without complaint.

"Coward that he is," Elliott observes, lip curled like at a bad smell.

Doc clears his throat. "I don't know how much ya already know…"

Kenny says we know about Welsh getting around Eileen, for starters. We know about the pregnancy and Welsh sending Eileen to Winnipeg. Figure she met up with someone and then come back… come back dying from what was done to her there.

"Yes," Doc says, "that's basically it." He says the autopsy confirmed Eileen had been pregnant. And that she had been torn, way up inside, in her womb. I flinch hearing this, but I tell Doc just to keep going, because I do want to know. So he just lays it out plain as he can. He says Eileen died from sepsis, blood poisoning, what they call Puerperal Fever. Thing is, Doc explains, this was no home remedy, not some woman in a alley. "It was someone with the right equipment," he says. "Had to be a… had to be a doctor that done it." His eyes drop, head shaking.

So then the constable speaks up again, saying that's all we got to go on. Eileen paid cash for her train ticket and there was no way to tell where she went or who she seen between arriving in the city on the Wednesday evening express, and boarding again to come home Thursday night.

"As to Ed Welsh," Elliott says, "we all know it was him that set it up. But evidence? There ain't none. And with his daddy being a big shot on the Railway Commission, personal friends with the premier of the province and all, Welsh has lawyers coming out his trapdoor. Mounties couldn't even lay charges on him for the deaths at Drowning River, never mind this."

I click my tongue. "More dead girls."

Then Doc starts talking about the Certificate of Death, saying he figures there's no need to be too particular with what he writes there. For cause of death, he would just be putting pneumonia or some such thing. He says Mr. Hall is in agreement on that. He looks to Kenny, then to me and Albert.

"Pneumonia?" Kenny says, head cocked.

"For the official record, like. Published record."

"Oh!" my brother says, the meaning sinking in. "Oh, I see!"

"Anything else would only embarrass the family and foul Eileen's memory," Doc says. "That's our thinkin' anyways... if it's acceptable all 'round?"

"Yes, that's... that's more than fair," Kenny says. "Thanks, Doc."

We sit nodding in the circle, wind sighing soft in the poplar trees.

I think about my Eily-Isle. Years ago, she was but a little gaffer, and I was maybe twelve years old. We was under a tree together on a balmy summer day, her laying over my shoulder, me rocking her, humming. My little sister. The soft weight of her, the feel of her tiny fingers drawing butterflies on my back and flitting them there.

"So, that's it?" I ask. "Junior was right? Welsh will jist go on with his life, walkin' the streets of Swan River, head held high? Like nothin' happened? Like my sister's life was... nothin'?"

"Uh," John Elliott hesitates. "Not in this town, he won't. He was already snubbed at the Baptist Assembly after the fire. And since I had a quiet sitdown this mornin' with Mr. McKay at the General Store, Welsh's business will not be welcome there. Nor anywheres else in the town of Swan River. But..." he opens out his palms, helpless, "but somewheres else, I suppose."

Doc says he heard that Ed Welsh's daddy had already sold the land and machinery from the burn-out at Drowning River. "In these troubled times," Doc says with disgust, "they say he made a profit."

It's too much to take. I stand and so does Kenny. We thank them for their help anyways. Old Albert takes two tries at getting up from his stump, so Constable Elliott goes over, takes ahold of him, and helps him walk back to the horses, Albert stumbling and wheezing as they go. Me and Kenny start out to walk with Doc, but as he bends to pick up his medical bag, the binding comes loose again. Them handles been bound together with binder twine for years now, since the clasp went beyond repair. While Doc kneels to rebind his gear, Kenny catches my eye.

"Rosie," he says for my ears only, "we ain't done with this."

* * *

On the sixth day of June, in the year of our Lord nineteen hundred and thirty-six, we laid down my sister Eileen beneath a young pine tree on the graceful neck of the lovely Swan River. She was sixteen years, two months, and twenty-one days.

My brother Kenny slept at Mother's that night. In the morning, he said he'd be taking a little trip to Winnipeg. The papers was reporting a growing lack of civility betwixt the miners and the owners up in Flin Flon, and Ken was nervous to be away if it came to trouble and he wasn't there on the side of the workers. But he had to do this Winnipeg business first, he said. So he hitched a ride to Swan with Culain Kirk, who had took up a collection of sorts from the neighbours to cover Kenny's fare.

Two days later, I'm in Mother's yard scrubbing clothes on the washboard, my little kids playing in the grass, when I see him come striding back up the dusty road. Mother and Albert had dragged theirselves out to the fields, hoping for God knows what. I go bring Kenny a sealer jar of water for his parched throat and we sit on the step together, waiting till the two of them can work their way up to the yard.

He tells me what happened in the city. He had asked around at the Winnipeg Station and soon located Edwin Welsh, the father, in his office at the Grain Exchange. When he said he was Eileen Labeau's brother, the man got right up and shook his hand. Very cordial. Closed the door. Offered him a glass of ten-year-old Bushmills. Kenny says that would have been about the finest glass of whiskey he ever had, but he turned it down.

Then I guess he just came right out with it. He said it was Ed Welsh's fault his sister was dead and the family was on hard times like everybody. Well, almost everybody, he said, looking around him at all the pomp and burnish. The family couldn't make it without Eileen's pay, he said, and he knew the Welshes had made money on the property at Drowning River.

Well, Edwin Welsh just reached into the drawer of his oak desk there, took out a strong box, started counting up a wad of bills, then put them in a envelope. Then he came around and sat on the edge of the desk in front of Kenny, looking down.

"He chuckled," Kenny says, "and told me a little story. About a time when he was young and his father had to make a payout for him. For his little indiscretion, he said. Indiscretion. There was a girl, a servant, and he said it cost his father a lot more than this to send away the girl and her bastard. That's what he said, them actual words. The girl and her bastard, he said."

"Huh!" I gawk, hand to my jaw. "What kinda people?"

"He handed the envelope down to me and I took it," Kenny says. "And he thanked me. Yes, he said *Thank you*, as if me and him had jist made some sorta fair exchange. I jist sat there for a minute, my mind buzzin', but he had walked around the desk again, sat down, and went back to his numbers. As if I wasn't even there. So I got up and left, envelope and all."

I look over at my brother. I can see the shame of it in his eyes, in the set of his jaw and his shoulders. "Oh Kenny," I rub his hand. "How... how could ya do it?"

He takes a breath, his eyes soft on Mother where she's working her way towards us. "Hadda be done, is all," he says. "Hadda be done, so I done it."

Well, Mother has arrived in the yard and my brother stands and puts his arms around her for a minute. Then he reaches into his breast pocket and hands her the envelope. Inside is three hundred dollars, all in ten-dollar bills. Three hundred dollars! This whole farm cost about half that.

Mother can't believe her eyes. "What is that?"

"That," Kenny tells her, "is Eileen's life insurance."

"Life insurance?" Mother grumbles, the bills splayed out like a deck of cards. "What life insurance? We ain't the kinda people could ever afford somethin' like that."

Kenny studies his dusty boots.

"Oh!" she says when it dawns on her. Then her voice raises. "Money ain't gonna bring my daughter back!"

"No it ain't," he tries to tell her. "But it'll help yuz, Mother, and it'll hurt the Welshes... or, well, prob'ly won't hurt them, but..."

She shoves the bills back in the envelope, lets it fall in the dirt, and flops down on the bench under the willow, arms crossed. "I don't want their God damn blood money!" Now she's raging. "I jist want Ed Welsh dead! I want him hurt and fouled like Eileen was! I want him dyin', tainted and terrified like my... beautiful girl." She turns away, shoulders beginning to heave.

My brother fetches back the envelope, then kneels with his good pants in the black dirt and takes her hand. "Mother..." he soothes. "Mother, with the money, yuz can buy a team—there's a pair of white oxen for sale out at Shadbolt's. Then yuz won't have to pull the plough yurself no more. You can pay off taxes for this year and next year too, so yuz won't lose this farm." He keeps coaxing, cuddling her into him, and she lets him. "Mother, you can buy a stone for Eileen's grave, a real nice stone with her name put on it. You can buy a family plot at the cemetery in town, with room for others." He glances towards Old Albert on the step, coughing and hacking away. "There's more of us gonna need a place in the not-too-far-ahead, prob'ly."

Kenny stands, eyes on the road, big gentle hand cupping Momma's head, and she leans into him, burying her face in the side of his blue homespun shirt. "I shoulda gone through him," she bawls softly. "I shoulda gone through the God damn door."

* * *

Sometimes Mother says to me, "Rosie, if only we had knew. We coulda helped Eileen. Coulda saved 'er, mebbee."

I don't say nothing about it. Too guilty. But I know I should have told Mother everything. I was trying to do right by Eileen, that's all I got in my defense. I didn't want to make trouble for her. But the trouble that found my sister was worse than anything my mother could have ever done.

Sometimes in the mornings, when I light the stove and put the porridge on, I make up little dramas in my head. Better stories that might have happened. I can just see me and Eily-Isle sitting at the table with the checked tablecloth that we keep for special company. Her yellow hair is down loose and pinned back at the temple. It's early in June and Momma has a big pot of the Mother's Constitutional on the back burner. Eileen has one of them fancy China cups, a robin's egg blue, and she drinks, dipping the cup now and then into the pot. I go wait with her at the outhouse and when it's done, she sleeps.

Later on, I see her planting a little garden of her own. I wave to her from my garden patch and she waves back, pretty hair bobbing in the breeze and that big wide-mouthed smile that always makes me want to sing.

But then at night, the dream comes back, playing over and over like a silent film at the Star City Cinema. Eileen in the big empty room. That posh purple chesterfield, giant irises blazing loud and gaudy all around her. Face pale, lips blue, reaching out her hand to me. No one else is there, just her and me. She seems so far off and I seem very low, looking up from the ground as I am. Unnatural, like I'm just too small.

Nothing else happens, that's where it always ends. Just my sister Eileen, gouged out in the tender years, beckoning to me. Trying to say something.

Chapter 4

The Relief

(1937)

I take the path down through the ditch and up into the big field. It used to be a hay field, smelling all pretty with clover, alfalfa, and Timothy grasses. Now it's just a empty mess of dust ruts, bramble weeds, and dried-out dogwood that didn't make it. Good place for spiders anyways, and I'm careful not to step in none of them gnarls where they like to nest. I cut over through a stand of scrub oak and then follow the natural ridge along by Kirks' dugout, which of course is so dry by now it just looks like a mud trough. Their sad old cow must have been trying for a drink, as she's stuck down there, bawling away, up to her knees in muck. They're probably going to have to drag her out of there, looks too weak to unstuck herself. I'll have to tell Culain.

Don't it wear on a person though, just working and scraping, day after day? The papers is calling our times the Great Depression, crops failing and lives crashing, year on terrible year. They say folks is dying from want in the cities, specially children and old people. Like all the other farmers, we got nothing out of them seed crops these past three years, not one red cent.

But Mother says we're not going on the relief. We don't judge them that needs the handout, but we ain't that bad off yet.

Mother says we got to stick together, throw all we got into the gardens, and see if the bush won't get us through. This time of year, late August, there's all kinds of berries and nuts, ripe or soon to be, and squirrels and rabbits that the boys can hunt or snare. When we come out for the homestead, government thought they was smart putting us way up here in the hills in the middle of the bush. But now, with drought conditions general, being up in the hills close to the head of the Roaring River turns out better than being down there on the bare, thirsty plain. We got the bush to fall back on, and Nature seems to fare better when it ain't been fooled with by men.

And our gardens is doing better than many. We stash the puny carrots and turnips in the root cellar with the spuds and cook up and can any vegetables that will preserve. Then some of our neighbours got a cow or a goat and they send milk, if they got any to spare, for our children too. Everybody shares if they can.

Still, the Government demands cash money for the property taxes or they'll put us out on our ear. We would have already lost it all if it wasn't for Eileen's life insurance.

Eileen...

Anyways, I got my sister Beatrice watching my children right now, as Mitch is hired-helping down at Maluk's again. It ain't much money, but the main thing is it keeps him out from under my skin. I do tire of his whimpering and whining at bedtime, how I should do my wifely duty and all. Sometimes, I even give in and climb up there on him, give him a little. Just for relief from the begging, like.

As I come off the trail back behind the bunk house and go around to let myself in, I can see Culain across the yard and I wave. This little shack ain't much. Two bunks on the one wall, a bed on the other, and a skinny space in between. Under the window here, a little table with a washing-up bowl and kerosene lantern, and a deck of cards of course. Culain has left a jug of water for me, I see, so I have a quick sponge off and climb into the bed wearing just my slip. Won't be long to wait.

What people do in bed when the lights are out, all the thrashing and carrying on, used to mean nothing to me. Just something I could use with a man to get what I wanted. A barter, fair trade. Like what I done with Mitch to get me pregnant and get out of home. And it made me feel somehow special. Like I was not just some helpless kid, but a going concern. I could trade my kisses, and other things, to have a say. To be able to—how would I put it—influence? I guess, influence a man. Get him going the way I want.

Still, the act itself, that was just a little sacrifice I would make, something to be got through. What I would allow or give up for the sake of the trade.

But since I took up with Culain Kirk, well this is a whole new kind of situation. Now I understand things I heard women say before, about wanting it, actual wanting it. Just like a man would. Before Culain, I never knew that was even possible, a woman getting her own fun out of sex. Some women say they do it because they must, that it's a woman's duty to please her husband. I don't answer them back, just know that there's some of us craves it. For ourselves.

Course, this kind of hankering can lead a person too far. Look at that Mrs. Ford in town, used to be the shoemaker's wife. She got caught fooling around with somebody else's husband. Talk was all over town for months, how her and the man had to run for their lives down Victoria Drive, half-dressed and in the snow, her husband with a shotgun coming up behind. Lucky nobody got killed.

Mother says that was a case of the *seven year itch*. She said it's usually the men gets that one but it can happen to anyone. You get married and the years go by and you get bored with what you got at home, start looking around for fun somewheres else. You get a itch, see, a yearning for something different. And you know how itches is, she said. They want to be scratched.

Well, I found that interesting, what with me and Mitch being married near seven years when I took up with Culain.

Anyways, it has been weeks and I was near climbing the walls when Culain come by Mother's yesterday, asking why don't I come up, spend some time?

There's a thump on the outside wall, him dropping some gear, I guess. The door swings open with a bang, and here he is, smiling from ear to ear and ready for me. "Rosie Kelvey!" he beams. "Have I got somethin' good for you!" He's out of his trousers, wrestling his undershirt off, and flinging back the covers before I can finish squealing.

Then he makes me squeal some more. Though I do try to muffle it in his shoulder, not wanting to embarrass any of his family within earshot.

After, I lay on his arm like usual, our legs all tangled up and wrapped around each other, just telling him this and that, enjoying the feel of how we are together. I'd give up lots for this, just the way we are right now with the evening coming on. Friends, alone and content together, satisfied, and satisfying to one another.

Culain untwines us a bit, flips onto his stomach, and props hisself on his elbows. The skin over his thick-muscled arms and back, like rich cream, takes my fancy, and I lay my hand on him, soothing and stroking. So soft and manly. Then I see he's looking at me, kind of serious.

"What?" I tell him.

"Nothin'," he says. "Jist that, I do believe yur the most beautiful woman I ever seen. I's thinkin' about these words I heard once in a cowboy movie. *Raven-haired beauty*. That's what they said about this one woman, a Mexican lady. And them's the words I was thinkin' for you, Rosie Kelvey."

"Oh go on!" I tell him. But I can't stop grinning.

"No, Rose, it's true," he says. "Ain't nobody like ya, not a woman on Earth. With that natural curly hair o' yurs, so thick and black. Them dark looks. Why, yur eyes is truly black, too deep to call brown."

I feel the heat coming up my throat. "Stop teasin'!"

"And you got *curves* girl! Here—" He slides his hand down my outside, making me jump and giggle. "And here—" His hand strokes my tummy. "And here—" He fondles my one titty—which starts to get me going again. "And firm, firm, firm. You, Mrs. Kelvey," he takes my hand, linking his fingers through mine, "are somethin' special."

We get to kissing and carrying on, but then I remember their old cow I seen stuck in the dugout and I tell him about it.

"Oh shit!" he says, laying back. "She'll get sick standin' in that ooze too long." We can hear some of his brothers not far off, talking and arguing while they're chopping firewood, which don't make much for romance, neither. So he says he will maybe go round up Crofter and Christian, see can they get the old girl dragged out of there. The children cannot do without her milk, and that's a fact.

I get up, have a quick wash, and slip on my panties. Culain is dressed but still sitting on the bed. "Rosie," he says, that earnest look coming over his face now, "did ya think about what I said before? How we could make a break for it, you and me? Maybe go north if I could get work. We could make a life together up there, you and me, 'stead of livin' with our differnt fam'lies, always havin' to sneak for a minute alone."

"Yeah, I thought about it," I tell him, pulling on my dress. "But I mean, what about my kids and all? My mom's here, my sisters and brothers. It would be so far away." I rake my fingers back into my hair a few times till it gets feeling a little more tidy. He tells me again about how we'd send for my children, how if he got a good job, we could visit Mother regular, and all that. "Yeah, I know," I say. "I don't know. Anyways, I'm losin' the light here my dear, I gotta go." I give him a peck on the cheek and stand behind the door while he goes out, yawning and fiddling with the deck of cards for a minute. Next time I peek out, the coast is clear and I go down the east path so as to miss them at the dugout.

I wish he'd just forget this whole making-a-break-for-it thing. I love Culain, Culain makes me happy. Sometimes he downright thrills me. And there is a drought of happiness in this life to match the drought all-round. But as to moving away somewheres else, why would I? Though the rest of my life is hard and mean and not letting up, when it comes to men, I got it made. I got a husband that loves my children and can't boss me around, and a fancy man that rings my bells and gives me something in this grey life to look forward to. I can't see how upending it all just to look like man and wife some other wheres could improve on that.

* * *

Old Albert is dying. Got some sort of growth in his throat that's killing him. Started with the constant hacking and coughing. Then he got the bad sore throat, grating and hurting when he ate. When he started choking on his food, gagging and shaking and looking like a scrawny old scarecrow, Mother had to get Old Doc to have a look.

Some sort of cancer, Doc said, probably throat cancer. He said if a person had the money, they could take the train to Winnipeg and get the tumour cut out, but it wouldn't really make no difference. Cancer is cancer.

"My death sentence," Albert moaned. "Never no happiness in this life and now I'm done for."

I been wishing that old man gone for years. Still, it ain't good for Mother to have to deal with, nor the children neither. More hard times and bullshit for us all to have to get through.

On Sundays, the Pentecostals have a free luncheon after their three hours of Sunday School, so Petunia and some of my kids go jump onto the wagon they send around. We call it the Hallelujah Buckboard. Well, I guess the kids must have mentioned the old man taking sick because first thing Monday morning, Mother's out in the garden when I go down to get started on canning them carrots, and here's old Preacher Bondage coming through the porch. Albert's just got out of bed, coughing and hacking at the table there, but Old Bondage doesn't care. He gets right down to saving Albert's soul.

Tall and crookedy, shaved but with the constant dark jaw like it weren't close enough, Old Bondage holds that enormous leather Bible high overhead like a servant with a platter of beef and goes to preaching at him. "Repent!" he commands, the huge finger of one hand stabbing up to heaven and snaking down through the air to his thick oily chin. "Repent, oh sinner! Repent yur evil ways! For I bring you salvation in the name of Jesus! Redemption from the everlasting fire!"

Albert clears his throat. "I ain't Pentecostal," he croaks from the chair. "My people don't go for all that fire and brimstone." He says in the Universalist Church where he went as a boy, they was taught different. "God is like a great river and we're but drops of rain," he teaches, as if the two men are equals, having a reasonable conversation. "All are redeemed and go back to God," he rasps, "with or without repentance."

"Sinner!" the preacher howls, black eyebrows thick and vexed, face crimson. "For I say unto you, ye must be saved! Or face unending torment!" A torrent of words comes spewing loud. Wickedness, damnation, eternal pain, and woe. "Repent! Repent, oh sinner! Come to the altar and be saved!"

I turn towards the counter there, trying to tidy up. Everything a person owns looks so dirty and wrong when you know you're being judged.

Old Bondage is good and riled now, laying in with the Revelations, the Four Horsemen of the Apocalypse, and the Beast of the Sea. There's loud thumping and crashing. What is that? I sneak a peek and see he's whacking that huge Bible on the table again and again, jarring Albert something awful. The old man's eyes, casting about for help, cling onto mine, giving a imploring look.

But uh-uh. I turn back to the counter. I ain't getting in front of that preacher, no-way, no-how.

Well thank God, here comes Mother through the door. "What the hell!" she glares at Old Bondage. "Who asked you into my God damn house?"

Bondage blinks. "Watch yur profane tongue, woman!" he commands. Mother's eyebrows raise. Bondage proclaims, all huffy-like, that he has come bearing the means of Albert's salvation.

Mother steps in, reaches up, and grabs him by the shirt. "Out!" she says, shoving him backwards through the doorway.

Bondage flails and kicks where he's half-fell over into the woodbox, and finally gets hisself standing. Fuming and righteous there in the dark porch, he rants at Mother that salvation is the key to heaven, it's only through repentance that Albert can attain salvation and avoid the everlasting hellfire.

Mother squints from one man to the other. Albert's shaking his head, eyes beseeching. "Well he don't want it!" she tells Old Bondage. "So git!"

When the preacher is gone, Mother makes a pot of Red Rose and pours Old Albert a cup. My God, the man don't look good. He tries some bread with his tea but ends up choking, so we have to smack him hard on the back a bunch till it clears.

Well, we're way into canning season now. We got to preserve everything that will preserve before another winter sets in. Today, it was the green beans and a bunch of dill pickles me and Mother done. Got her house all hot and steamy, and by the time we get the supper over with, I'm just bone-weary.

And yet the kids is begging, "Let's play a game o' ball tonight! Let's have fun!"

"Alright then!" Mother says. "Batter up and let's see what yuz can do!" Pretty soon they're throwing down old coats and tack for bases in the big field. Junior and the boys finish up chores in a hurry while my James has ran up the road and come back with a bunch of Kirk kids, and we have a nice little game of ball.

We play scrub baseball, no teams, each one just circles around from batter to field to pitcher and back. Everybody plays. We roll the ball on the ground for any of the little kids, age about four or five. Mother plays too, holding out her apron like a big scoop to catch the fly balls. And though she's a grandmother now, she's still got a better arm for hucking them in from the field than most of the big boys.

"I'm gonna whoop yuz buggers!" I tell them. But then, just when I'm on deck, there's a clattering and crashing in the house, so I have to miss my turn and run to see what's going on. It's Old Albert, with water spilled all over the kitchen floor. He complains that he was thirsty, there wasn't hardly water in the pail, and when he tipped it sideways to pour the dregs into a cup, he got weak and dropped it. Petunia goes for another pail of water and I have to get down on my knees and sop up the mess.

He sits shivering on the chair. Even in this heat, the man is cold all the time. His throat feels like raisins on tar paper, he says, any solid food will make him choke and sputter. Yet he's hungry as hell.

"Well eat then!" I tell him. "I ain't stoppin' ya!" He says he's too scared to try. Even eggs or mashed potatoes won't go down no more.

"Terrible," I say, clicking my tongue. Petunia gets the dipper and gives him a drink and I go outside to dump the dirty water.

I get back out there and sit down, cuddling my little Cathy while I wait my turn. My Margie and Hope Kirk get on base, then Junior hits a big homerun, everybody yelling and cheering, all three of them already home and the fielders still trying to dig the ball out of the far weeds. I hand Cathy over to Margie and get ready for my turn at bat, but then Petunia starts yelling, "Gramps is hurt! Gramps is hurt!" I can see him on his face in the yard, thrashing around like a idiot. So I have to miss another turn and go see what the hell is going on.

"For Christ sake!" I tell him, as we strain to put him upright.

"You okay, Gramps?" Petunia asks kindly.

"I wanted to be at the ball game," he whimpers.

I click my tongue and sigh loudly. "Come on then!" We take hold of his arms and help him walk. He's really lighter than a man his height ought to be. "Petunia, bring that chair and put it up against the house for him." Then I go back to the game.

Mother comes in from the field and sits with me under the poplar tree. I tell her about Albert and all his dropping and falling. "Mm!" she says, shaking her head and loading up the bowl of her big old corn cob pipe.

She strikes a match on the tree trunk and lights her pipe, just as any man would. She puffs shallow and fast till it gets smoking up good, then takes in a nice strong pull and blows out a long, leisurely trail of smoke, filling the air with the oaky smell of Burly tobacco. She holds the pipe bowl gentle near her breast, looking off peaceful to the distant trees.

We don't really talk much about our man-situations, me and Mother. We'll say a few words when there's no other ears nearby. She known about me and Culain all along and never kicked on it.

I think Mother understands what it is to be a living woman with the wrong man in your bed. I don't know if she ever loved Albert. In my own heart of hearts, I think maybe she just ever loved my poppa, James.

I know she put her faith in Albert, though, when we first come west, trying to start over and raise a family with him. But that faded fast, what with us losing the homestead and him driving Kenny out. I know she never forgave him for that. Nor did I. And for years now, the man has had no end of excuses why he can't do this work and can't do that work. Lazy old sod. If he would ever have worked like a man, maybe me and Mother wouldn't have to. And always blaming someone else when he fouls things up. Well, Mother ain't the kind that suffers fools gladly.

Streaks of pretty pink have painted theirselves above the distant fields and trees. Me and Mother sit together and watch the children, hitting and running and shrieking in the evening air, till we begin to lose the light. Then we start to collect ourselves up and say our goodnights before the swarms of black flies and mosquitoes descend and hurry us all indoors.

* * *

"But why, Mother?" I complain. "Why would it hafta be me?"

I've came down to borrow some porridge for morning, and Albert's just had a choking spell so Mother's had to whack him on the back a bunch of times. It's when she walks me out into the yard that she tells me her thinking about the situation. That we'll have to move the old man down to my place now, until the end.

"But, Mother, you know how he wears on me," I tell her.

She says it just makes sense this way. He can't be left alone for too long, yet she got to be working outside if we're going to have anything to feed these children come winter. And her big girls and Junior got to work with her. She says I got to be closer around the house with my little ones anyways. She'll send the supper for both families every night and I can cook it.

I hem and haw and try to come up with reasons not to do it, but Mother has already said it, so I have to purse my lips and give in. "When's he comin'?" I ask. She says now's as good a time as any. I blink my eyes and go get Albert Junior to bring the hayrack around.

"I do *not want to go down there*, Josephine," Albert moans as we walk him outside.

"I know," she tells him. "Nobody wants it, but it can't be helped."

He sputters and complains as the hayrack rocks and jiggles down the road, but the girls—my Petunia and Mother's Beatrice—jump on and sit with him, trying to make him feel better. "It's gonna be alright, Gramps," Pet tells him, stroking back a greasy wisp of his grey hair.

"It'll be better actually. Cuz now you'll be at my house and I can sit with ya lots."

Well, then we got to get him off the wagon and into my kitchen. "Why do I have to *be here?*" he whines, which brings on the coughing and choking again. What a show to get him settled.

"I'll send Junior to Ruddock's Drug Store tomorrow," Mother says, going out to the wagon for the potatoes she brung along for supper. She's made Old Ruddock a deal for quinine to dope Albert out, for when it gets real bad.

Albert's sitting on the edge of the rickety chair by the window, looking pure miserable. He caws at his throat a couple times, trying to clear it, but that don't do nothing. He sighs and gazes up at me, all pleading like.

"Huh," I ask myself out loud, "why does he hafta do his dyin' in *my* house?"

"I ain't deaf, ya know," he tells me, eyes falling to the floor.

"I do not care!" I tell him, pointing my chin up, and get out a pot to help Mother get them potatoes peeled.

His sickness goes fast. Inside a month, he's lost so much weight his trousers would fall right off if he were to stand up, which he can't do for long. He mostly stays in bed, just drinking milk now, and eating pudding, as nothing else will go down. But that gives him the trots and he can barely make it outside on his own.

"Help me, for God sake!" he's pleading one day when I come in from the garden. "Help!"

But it's too late, he's already messed hisself.

"God!" I moan, half choking and gagging while I'm trying to clean up. It ain't enough I'm washing shitty diapers for my two youngest?

Now I gotta wash poopy pants for a grown man? That shit smell ain't never going to come out of that old cotton mattress, I'll tell you that.

"Sorry!" he whimpers. "You wout'n come! You wout'n come and I cout'n hold it!"

Why don't he jist die and be done with it? Give us all some relief.

I send James up for Mother and she helps me wash everything down, the old man laying on the cold wood floor, ribs and bony arse exposed.

Mother says this is ridiculous, this ain't working. He can't really lay down no more without choking anyways, even though we always buttress him at night with that big gunny bag full of straw. She says we should prop him up in that old mate's chair by the kitchen window. We can tie him in at the waist with a tore-up sheet so he don't fall. And then at least if he makes a mess, it'll just wipe off with a cloth.

"It won't be much longer anyways," she says.

So we get him set up in the chair, though he complains that it's too cold by the window, shivering away.

"Tough titty!" I tell him.

Petunia says we could move the wash stand over by the window and put his chair by the stove. Mother says okay, so then we have to move the whole riggamarole over there.

I get them dirty things washed and on the line before I have to come in and make the supper. Old Skin and Bones has drifted off in his chair but wakes long enough to complain about the smell of the food. Petunia brings a cup of warm water from the cistern and he sips, then closes his eyes and nods off again, still shaking and shivering.

After dishes, Mother goes home to get the last of her peas picked and the children go back around the house to play hide 'n seek. I put Cathy on my hip and go walk out to the road. Grey dirt up and grey dirt down, that's all there is, and lines of thirsty, dusty trees on either side in both directions. I sit on the edge of the ditch for a hour but there ain't no human soul goes by. I sigh and walk back.

The old man's head is lolling forward on his chest, those ties looking mean and dug in at the waist, like he's a man's been folded in half. I stop for a minute, studying him. All these years, I been wishing him gone, thinking what a relief it would be. But this here seeing it, having to watch the suffering, that don't feel right neither.

Why should I hafta feel bad for him? Ain't this life hard enough already?

I put Cathy down in the back room then swipe the deck of cards from the drawer and go out to the step. I turn that old tub over for a table and play solitaire, game after game, till the dusk falls and the children tire theirselves out and we all go in for bed.

The neighbours has been coming up to take their leave of Old Albert. Mrs. Mares was here on Monday, and Charles and Elvie Kirk yesterday. After supper, I got my big girls playing quiet with the babies in the back room, and water heating on the stove for dishes, and what do I see but Kirks' rig coming up the dirt drive again. I'm hoping I know who that might be. I run in to the basin, wash my face, put a couple pins in my hair, and dab some powder under my blouse.

The rig pulls up and out jumps a bunch of Kirk brothers. There's Crofter and Christian and yes, my man Culain! I go stand on the stoop, greeting them as they come by. Crofter tussles my hair and Christian gives me a little squeeze, calling me Dear.

Culain stands, looking up from the bottom stair. "Uh huh," he tells me, "there she is, the apple of my eye!"

"Speakin' of apples," I tell him, stepping down. "Why don't we go for a little walk in the trees and see if we can't pick some forbidden fruit." I give him a big old hug and a kiss. My God, he's solid built and it's been weeks.

"After," he tells me. "Not right now." I hold him at arm's length and give a good pout but he just takes my hand and walks me up the steps. "I wanna have a visit with yur dad while I still can."

I feign being persnickety. "Hmph!" I tell him. "And he ain't my dad."

But I go in and give them all some of that rhubarb loaf I made, to have with their tea. The Kirk brothers fill up my little kitchen, Culain on the bench at the table, his brothers sitting on chairs pulled up nearby to Albert. Culain does most of the visiting, telling about the lynx that run havoc on his trapline last year till it got caught in its own game. He made six dollars on the pelt.

Albert sits nodding and shivering, glad for the company I think, wearing his terrible grimacing smile. But then he goes into one of his coughing spells, hacking away, and something pale and frothy comes spewing out of him. Petunia grabs a rag and starts cleaning his mess, but the men go skittish, not knowing how to be. Crofter and Christian both down their cups in a hurry and start taking their leave. They grasp onto the old man's hand to shake it, him sputtering and going red, trying to hold back the next storm of heaves till they can get out the door.

Culain sits quiet at the table. Petunia gets some warm water from the cistern and, when the old man has settled somewhat, takes his shirt off and washes him down. Then she brings a clean shirt and puts it on him, retying the ties as gently as she can while still making them hold.

"Cold," he croaks.

Petunia goes over and grabs a couple slabs of wood for the fire but I say it's warm in here already and we need that wood for morning. She stops, the wood in mid-air, and purses her lips at me. I'm tiring of that girl's scowls and complaints and just about to take it up with her, but then Culain says don't worry about the wood, he'll chop up a box full before he goes.

So I say, "Oh, well, thanks," and let it slide. Pet stokes up the fire.

Culain has taken up the chair nearest Albert, not saying much, and the old man seems to calm and rest a little, kind of slumped over there. I go sit on the outside of Culain. The house feels pretty cozy now, the fire snapping in a friendly way, and Pet has sat down on that old stool, holding Albert's pathetic hand, looking up gentle into his death-grey face, her dark ringlets dangling.

Culain starts talking low, telling the story of his own granddad, how he left home at the age of thirteen and took work on a dairy farm down by Hamilton, Ontario. How he come out for the homestead with his wife and six children, how he worked the soil till the soil dried up and then he had to go to the bush, hauling timber, at his age. Albert seems to be listening. Then Culain tells about the logging accident his granddad had, the size of the tree that fell and how it bounced twice, how terribly hurt the old fellow was, every bone in his back and legs snapped like kindling. How Culain had sat with him at the last, the ungodly ship of pain he was swept away on.

I say that must have been a terrible way to go and Culain says, "Yep." Then he says, "But there ain't many good ones, though, that I know of." There's just the quiet crackle of the fire now as I sit holding onto Culain's arm, watching Daddy Albert on the other side of him, seeming like parchment paper, so frail he might blow away any minute.

I don't know why he had to be the way he was. Just always been weak and different than us. Always giving advice nobody asked for, yet not knowing his own arse from a hole in the ground. His fits of rage in the early days, till Mother put a end to them. A very consternating person, really. I can barely remember a time when hating him wasn't part of me.

He seems to rouse now, eyes bright. "I seen the angel agin! The dark woman, full of love."

"The dark woman?" Culain asks.

"He's addled," I tell him. "Thinks he sees this woman, dreams her probly. Unless there's angels for real, which there ain't. It's jist him, goin' crazy while he's dyin'."

The old man tells in his high-cawing whisper about this dark angel. How her face is full of love and forgiveness. How she told him God *is like a great river*, just like they taught when he was a boy in the Mohawk territories, and we're all drops of rain and we all go back to the river. That's what Heaven is, he says, we all go back to God at the end. And Culain and me will go back to God. And Albert will too.

Hating is so much easier than feeling plain desperate and sorry for the man.

"Ya jist dreamed it," I tell him. "There ain't no dark angel and God ain't no river. He's jist a big man up in the sky. And kinda mean, far as I can tell."

"Rosie," Culain says low, shushing me with his hand. "Why not let him believe?"

I feel perturbed for some reason. I purse my lips at Culain and he cocks his head at me. "I'm... goin' outside," I tell him and I go.

I'm thinking he'll follow me right out to the step but he don't and I sit alone for long minutes. It ain't fair for me to have to watch this old man die, all pained and suffering. Why can't I just have a happy life?

Finally, Culain does come out, giving my shoulder a gentle squeeze as he steps down past me. "Ain't ya gonna sit with yur dad?" he asks.

"No," I tell him, "I had enough time with him long since."

He goes over and starts splitting wood. "Like I said, there ain't a lot of good ways to die," he tells me, raising the axe deftly, the cut landing perfect with a resounding crack. "But there *is* some ways more terrible than others." He collects up the cut wood and starts a neat stack by the step. "And I think this is a bad hand yur dad's been dealt." The axe drops again, neatly splitting a big hunk of wood. "Poor bastard," he says.

"Ain't my dad," I tell him, slapping at a fly on my arm. "And he don't get no pity from me."

"What d'ya mean?"

"Why should I pity him?" I say. "He been nothin' but a weight 'round our neck ever since we known him. All the years he sat on his arse, complainin' of his aches and pains, makin' me and Mother do all the work. It was his fault we lost the homestead."

Culain pauses to fix me with a look. "Rose," he tells me, "he was a old man! He was in his fifties already when yuz come here. Old men cannot work the way young men can."

"He was the one drove Kenny outta home!"

"Yur brother Kenny?" Culain frowns. "Well, Kenny don't seem to bear him no ill will on it. And that was... a lotta years ago."

"Don't matter!" I tell him, raising my voice. "He done it when he done it and now my brother's gone!"

His eyes stay on me. I look away, head shaking. I don't want to spoil our time together by arguing. And yet, I do want to argue. He goes back to chopping and I go back to watching him chop. The axe raises, the axe falls with a crack, the boards fly, he bends, picks them up, stacks them, stands at the stump, and the axe raises again.

He did drive Kenny out. And Kenny was the only part of my Poppa James I had left.

Culain sinks the axe in the stump, then begins to grab up the cut wood by armfuls and truck it into the woodbox in the porch.

"Besides," I tell him. "I think it's like Old Bondage says. He ain't repented for his sins. So he ain't fergivin'. He got punishment comin'."

Culain has finished with the wood now. He comes and stands in front of me, taking my two hands in his.

"Now is that for one and all, Miss Rosie?" he asks.

"What?"

"Is that for *all sins and failins*?" he asks, a cheeky grin growing on his face. "Is it sins like yurs and mine that needs repentin' too?" he teases, kicking playful at my foot. "Or only his kinda sins?"

I grin in spite of myself, giggling. *Honestly, this man!* "Stop it," I tell him, wriggling free.

"Rosie, Rosie. You turnin' mean in yur old age."

I laugh. "Twenty-seven, same as you."

"Well, I ain't no big Christian, claimin' the be-all and end-all a knowin' right from wrong. But I do think that when it comes to leavin' this world, everbody deserves a little grace at the end. Whatever yur dad done or didn't do, it's his last chance. And it's yur last chance, too. Maybe ya should jist stop bein' mad and forgive him."

"Oh well..." I tell him. I'm tired of thinking about that old man. Bad enough I got to see him every time I walk through my own kitchen. Right now, there's better things I'd rather be doing.

I reach out, touch the inseam of Culain's trousers, and run my hand up there to where it is warm, warm, warm. "Mmm," I purr.

He lays his hand over mine, moving me off and stepping back. "I gotta git goin', Rose," he tells me.

"What? But I thought—I thought tonight we was gonna..."

"Uhh," he says. "I still got chores waitin' at the house but... come up on Saturday, in the afternoon. Or if I ain't around, come on Sunday."

"Huh!" I tell him, all sarcastic. "Well, then, I'll jist wait and wait and wait till *you* feel like it!"

He's grinning to beat all get-out. "I always feel like seein' you, Rosie, my love, you know that. Jist I got work to do is all." And off he goes.

"Hmph!" I say, shaking my head. And I sit right there, not moving nor caring. But then one mosquito bites me and so does his brother and I guess their cousins have arrived for the feast. So in I go.

* * *

It's Trooper Roaring Kirk who brings us word about John Elliott, Swan River's town constable. Died very sudden-like. They figured it was his heart. He was found in the alley on the back steps of the jail, propped up against a beam like he was just having a nice nap, the big, blond Stetson still shading his eyes.

We all want to go in for the wake as Constable Elliott is much respected, and was particular decent to our family in our recent troubles. But then, what about Old Albert? He's so close hisself that he shouldn't really be left alone. Mother says I can take the hayrack, and whatever older kids I want, plus my little Cathy, and go in. She'll stay here with the old man and the rest of them. She knows I get fearful of them oxen, Baby and Sunshine, they're so damn big, but she says Junior can go and drive them for me. We can camp out overnight at the fair grounds nearby to the Elliott house and be there for the funeral Thursday. But be sure to give her condolences to the family, she says, and explain the situation. So that's what we do.

It's terrible slow going down the mountain with the oxen, but by dusk, we're camped out at the fair grounds and got the team grazing on the grass. There's other families, too, have driven teams in and camped out there. There's even motor cars parked on the roadside, and must be sixty people, I'm sure, between Elliott's yard and the house at any given time. It's exciting, but sad at the same time.

We all go in and pay our respects, have a bite to eat, and then go sit by the fire in the yard, see who all's around. Our kids take off to the big field across the way, playing tag and hide 'n seek and whatever else they can think of. But my goodness, the stories people have to tell about Constable John Elliott! Funny stories and touching stories about all the folks he helped, and also about some fellows he wasn't too helpful to at all, on account of they needed to be behind bars. A very fair man was our constable, but not one to cross, and not a man you'd want to see coming your way if you was up to no good.

The time flies by, night is falling, and my little one is nodding in my arms there, so I give her to Pet and Beatrice to take back to camp.

Not a few minutes later, I see the Kirk brothers and Culain coming into Elliotts' yard, saying they're camped out next to our tent at the fair grounds. Soon as Culain comes out of the house, I say we should go walk the half-mile to the river, having my definite plans for him. But he's acting odd, not meeting my eyes but taking my arm, not saying nothing, and leading me down the road aways.

"What's eatin' you?" I ask. Is he that upset about John Elliott?

Well, that's when he tells me he ain't going back up the mountain tomorrow with the rest of us. He's thumbing his way north instead. Says he's had a letter from his friend Carl up at Sherridon, saying they're getting ready to open up the mine again and there's a job for him if he'll come. Culain says Jake Mares works there and would probably say a good word for him too, what did I think?

"I'm sure Jake Mares would say a good word for ya," I tell him. "And I hope you and him and yur friend Carl at Sherridon will have a damn happy life together too!"

I yank my arm away and walk by myself. So then he's begging me not to be that way, saying how he'll send for me once he's solid. How he'll get a place for us and the children, and we can be happy together, living as man and wife. Nobody will say boo about it, because the people won't know us. He's jogging along there, trying to talk to me, but I got my head up, arms swinging, and I'm just going.

"So!" I tell him. "What am I s'posta do till then? Sit around like a bump on a log, waitin' till you decide to send for me? *If* you decide to send for me?"

We're at the river by this time and I lean up against the trunk of a willow, looking out at the dark water. He stands by, twisting his hands all desperate, pleading that he *will* send for me though, he *will*.

"Well, what if I don't wanna go?" I tell him. "I already told ya! I got a life here, Mother and my fam'ly! Why would I wanna go to some other wheres and start over?"

"For me! That's why!" he pleads. "To be with me!"

"But I can be with you here!"

"Yeah!" he glares. "And you can be with yur God damn husband here, too!"

"Huh!" I tell him. "I ain't *with* him, really. As you very well know."

"Do I?" he demands. "Do I know that? Or do I jist know that ya come see me ever now and then when ya got a hankerin' for some dirty fun?"

I cross my arms. "Oh! Ree-diculous!"

So then he starts saying about how this ain't fair to him. And it ain't fair to Mitch, neither. How it grates on him what we're doing, knowing he's the fly in the ointment of another man's marriage. He says we can't go on our whole life paying for my mistake of marrying Mitch when

I was young. He says there comes a time when a man would like to be on the up and up, not sneaking around like a kid being bad.

"Rosie," he says, trying to cuddle me up. "It's our chance, doncha see? It's a chance for you and me to be happy together."

I keep my arms crossed, side-step him and move in front of the tree, staring out at the black river. "But I *am happy*," I try to tell him. "Doncha see, Culain? I'm *happy now*."

He tries again to put his arms around me. "Aaah!" he gripes. "Well, I ain't."

I pull away again, spin around, and give him a real piece of my mind. About how selfish he is, only thinking of hisself. About how he just uses me for his own pleasure and don't care none about how he hurts my life nor Mitch nor my children.

He flinches. Even in the dim light, I can see him studying me. *I got to settle down here.* "Why would ya say them things, Rose?" he frowns. "Why would ya say such hateful things to me? Ya know they ain't true. Ya know I love ya, true love."

I do feel shame for my harsh words, but yet I clench my jaw and point my chin up. He says nothing. I wait a while but still nothing. So I say "Hmph!" all defiant.

Is he really gonna go north and leave me here alone?

I sigh and finally look in his face. Some sort of sad, consternated look there. "Listen, Rose, I..." he finally says, "I'm gonna go back to the wake now. I wanna visit with some folks yet tonight, say my goodbyes."

Mad again. "Go ahead!" I say, just snotty. "I do *not* care!"

He don't rise to it, though, just goes on calm-like. "Come mornin', I'm gonna be thumbin' to Sherridon. And I will write to ya, Rose, and

I want ya to come to me when yur ready. Bring the kids and come and live with me at Sherridon."

I blink, feeling like I might cry. But I hold it back.

He turns and starts to walk away. Then he stops. "Rosie? Come to me at our camp after. Come and spend this final night with me before I go." I bite my lip. "Will ya? Rose? Will ya come?"

I stand like stone, willing back the tears.

"Because I do love ya, Rosie. I only ever loved you."

Still I stand, refusing to meet his eyes, intent on the black current ahead. I don't even budge when I hear the soft sound of him moving away. Finally, when I look, the soft reds and blues of him are headed north up Ninth Avenue. And ain't nothing I can do about it.

All I got now is my anger. I turn on my heels, going west, just to be walking away. I charge ahead, one block, two, three, the breeze whipping my hair back. I don't want him to go. And I don't want to go with him. Why is he making this problem? I want so much to sleep with him tonight, be in his arms, feel the joy he always gives. I want this whole fight to not be happening.

But it is and that's his fault and so I *am mad. Damn it!* I stride up one street and down the other, all around town for what seems like hours. I cross the Swan River Bridge and walk out into the country in the dusk, way out the Ditch Road, walking, walking. Trying to walk my mad off.

When I finally get back to the Elliotts', the house lights is off and the fire in the pit has burned low. There's only older people sitting there, folks I do not know. But there's a couple guys at a truck out on the road so I go out there. One of the guys is John Elliott's son, young Jack. He's not as tall as his daddy, but he's very handsome, got a cool wave in his blond hair. He looks me up and down with them blue eyes.

I tell him my name and give him condolences. He nods and says, "Oh," then I go lean on the truck beside him. He says they got some liquor there and are willing to share. "Will ya help me drown my sorrows, Rosie Kelvey?" he asks.

I say, "Sure, I will."

I don't know what I'm doing nor why I'm doing it. Just know it feels like the bottom come out of my world tonight. So I drink a swig of the whiskey and another swig and one thing leads to another and it's after dawn by the time I make it back to the fair grounds.

I trip and crash my way around the Kirks' campsite, trying to find Culain. His brother Crofter, groggy and snarling, says that's where his bedroll was but he must have already loaded up and headed out to the highway to hitch his way north.

Serves you right, Culain Kirk, I think. *You had to go away with no kiss goodbye.* But it's a empty satisfaction just the same.

My baby Cathy is wet and crying, been crying for hours, Pet says, wanting nothing and nobody but me. I hush her with milk and sit there hunched against the wagon wheel, feeling the chill of the morning. Don't that spot look forlorn where Culain's bedroll is supposed to be? My head ain't right and my guts ain't right and I just feel terrible all round.

One thing I know for a fact. I ain't never doing nothing like that again, drinking and flirting with boys and carrying on. I am just going to settle down now, stop being mad, and wait for Culain to send me a letter. I know me and Culain will fix things up between us. From here on in, I'm on the straight and narrow.

* * *

Back in my usual hell, waiting for my stepdad to finish dying and go to whatever place is waiting for him. I'm up early today and get the porridge over with so the kids and me can walk the three miles to the quarry early and have them berries picked before the sun gets too hot. Beatrice is coming with us, and Mother's youngest one, Vallee, same age as my James. We got them syrup cans and the buckets the oats come in. We slide a belt through the metal handle and do up the belt. The can hangs at the waist, leaving two hands free for picking the berries.

"You wear them long sleeves now," I tell the kids, "no matter how hot it is. Mosquitos and horse flies and God knows what'll be hidin' in the shade, waitin' for blood."

Pet gives the old man water and medicine before we go. He's shivering there and begs to have a little fire started in the iron stove but I say no. It's already eighty degrees in this house. Mother'll come check on him later.

"The dark angel come to me agin," he tells us in his croaky voice. "All are redeemed, she said. All are forgáve and go back to God."

"Yes, yes," I tell him, trying to get the children through the door. "The dark angel, full of love." It's all he talks about now. He gazes up at me, eyes sunk deep in their sockets. I didn't know a person could get that wretched-looking and still be alive.

Not much longer and he'll be gone.

We're back by noon, with two water pails full of blueberries for pies and preserves, plus that carpenter's box filled right to the top with pincherries for jelly. I get some back bacon in the iron pan to fry and potatoes and carrots on to boil. The big girls come in from where I sent them to feed Mother's chickens.

"Eileen," the old man says. I look around. His bony face is alive with joy, smiling up at Beatrice. "Eileen," he coos to her, half-crying. "Eily-Isle, come to Daddy."

Everybody gawks at Beatrice. She's all doe-eyed, looking back, but she goes over and stands wooden while he tries to hug onto her. "Dad," she tells him, "it's me, Beatrice. I ain't Eileen."

He looks up into her face, the smile fading. "Beatrice?"

"Yeah. See, it's me, Beatrice," she tells him.

He studies her, confused. "Beatrice?"

"Mmhm," she says, untangling herself from his grip and going to stand with the kids. "I'm Beatrice. Eileen is dead. Doncha 'member? Dead 'n gone."

"Beatrice!" Petunia gasps. My jaw drops. The children murmur.

"What?" Albert squeaks.

"Well she is!" Beatrice argues loud. "Eileen *is* dead. She been dead a whole year!"

His face falls, tears rolling down, and he's bawling like a kid, though it comes out in croaks and snorts.

"Thanks a lot," I tell Beatrice, "for ruinin' our dinner."

"Well, it wasn't a lie!" she glares. "Eileen *is* dead! And I *ain't* her!"

We're back in the garden by the afternoon. Petunia goes in for water and comes back, saying the old man is shaking something awful. Can't she go sit with him? I nod my head, though God knows I could use some help digging these spuds.

He lasts through the night again, shuddering and trembling between snatches of sleep. At some point, there's a fearsome racket, he's cawing and squawking there in the dark. I get the lantern lit and run out. He's moaning that there's hot knives in his guts. Petunia gets the quinine drops in the water and pours some into him. The baby's crying back in the room, and my other children are scared, peeking around the doorway.

"What's the matter with Grampa?" my little James calls from the doorway.

"Nothin'!" I tell him. "He's jist dyin'. Go back to bed." But me and Petunia is up for another hour before the medicine numbs him and he goes under.

This is my prison. I am the jailer and the jailed.

Mother comes up in the morning and sits with him, holding his icy hand, dipping a cloth in cool water for his head. He fades in and out, and in awhile she has to get back to the garden. "Jesus!" she tells me in the yard. "We know it's comin' for all of us. But does it hafta be so God damn mean?" She says come the weekend, she'll start sleeping here overnight. To be with him at the end, like.

He lasts another day, sweat like gas sheen on his grey face. I turn from the counter and his head is cocked up against the chair frame. Makes him look like that tormented Jesus on the cross the Catholics keep.

At some point, he chokes again, wheezing and thrashing. Petunia goes over and bashes his back till he gets breath. Then she sits on her stool, talking soft, telling him stories she learned at the Pentecostal. About the pearly gates, no more pain, and angels singing.

From where I stand, I suddenly see the line of Eileen's face in my daughter's. Petunia is dark where Eileen was fair, there's a toughness to her where Eileen was honey and light, yet I somehow see the two of them is more same than different. For some reason, tears sting my eyes, my throat goes tight, and I stand there alone, watching as my daughter feeds the old man comfort in a little tin spoonful of hope.

After supper, I spend a hour chopping wood and come in, back aching, covered in grime and sweat, relieved that the house is finally cooling off. But there's Petunia loading up the stove again.

"Leave it," I tell her.

"What?" she says, eyebrows vexed.

"Leave it. It's warm enough in here, save the wood for mornin'."

"But Grampa's cold," she says. "He's cold."

"So what," I say. "He don't chop the wood, let him be cold. I don't care."

"Jeez! Why?" she yells. "He's dyin' and all he wants is a little wood in the fire. Would it kill ya to jist be nice to him one time?"

"I said get outta there!" I yell, going over, taking a swipe at her head. But she ducks me.

"No! I ain't gonna!" she hollers. "I'm makin' a fire for my Grampa. Now git away and leave me alone!"

I step up and smack her a good one across the cheek. "Don't you speak to me like that, Missy!"

"You have no right!" she shrieks, rising up. "You have no right to treat me that way! And you have no right to treat my Grampa the way you do! He's dyin'! And yur nothin' but mean!"

"I'm..." I try to tell her. "I jist—I jist said to leave the fire. Now listen to me. I'm yur mother."

"My mother, huh!" she tells me. "When? When you ain't too busy with yur boyfriend?"

My jaw drops. "Matters that do not concern you!"

"Ha!" she bawls, her face splotchy and wet. "But my Grampa does concern me! He's the one that always loved us! He's the one that took care of us, him and my dad, when you and Gramma was always gone somewheres. Workin'!" She says *working* as if it's a dirty word.

"And why was we somewheres workin'?" I answer back. "We was out there workin' because the men was not!"

"What the hell? They worked how they could!" she screeches. "A old man! And one without a arm! And you have no call—" she's howling, "you have *no call* to treat my Grampa the way you do!"

"I... I..." I'm flabbergasted. She goes stomping outside, bawling away.

The old man is half-slouched in the chair, eyes staring nowheres. I shake my head and go clean up the scraps, do the dishes, and take the slop pails out. When I come in, the stove has been loaded and stoked, the room getting warmer, and Petunia is sitting with him again.

She don't look at me and I don't look at her. I finish up and light the lantern.

The children are in bed when he begins to seize. Petunia helps me get him out of the chair and he has a bad fit on the floor, then another a few minutes later. His guts feel hard and hot to the touch. I tell Pet to just leave him there, he won't be long now. She sits on the floor cross-legged, holding his hand, weeping on and off.

I stand around, don't know what to do with myself. I sit at the table and deal out some solitaire. I play the hand, shuffle up, and deal, play the hand again and again, never winning. Petunia has laid down and fell asleep beside him. I stare at his chest for long minutes before I believe I do see some movement. I shuffle and deal again.

What? I catch myself falling sideways. Must have put my head down on the cards and slept. Them two is still there on the floor, Petunia laid out beside him. It's dark in here but looks like grey light in the sky outside. The hour before the dawn.

I dreamed about my Poppa again, my real daddy before the war. I haven't dreamed of him in a long while. But it was some sort of dream where the sun was shining and we was under a tree looking out at a blue bay. Happy. I was little, getting held in his lap.

Or maybe... Was that my Poppa? Or? God, I think it was actually Daddy Albert. Shit. I hate that. Why would I dream a happy daddy dream about him? Bad enough to have him dying in my house, never mind taking over my dreams.

It's cold now. And they do look pathetic there on the floor. I get a couple big coats from the hook in the pantry to lay over them. Then I throw that wool sweater over my shoulders and go out to the biffy, the grey light just beginning over the poplars.

Rosy Sweet Cheeks. Was that... wasn't it my Poppa James, my real daddy, called me that? I seem to remember, could that be right? Didn't Kenny say it was my poppa's name for me? Did Albert only take it up after?

My head hurts from thinking.

But when I step into the house, there he is, choking. Rigid on his back, eyes bugged out, mouth open and tight, like a caught fish that ain't been clubbed out of its misery. I shake Petunia, yelling at her to run quick for Mother. I grab the brown quinine bottle but it's empty. "And tell 'er bring more quinine!"

"I don't wanna leave my Grampa!" Petunia frets. But there's a sudden high whistle to his breath, ungodly, his head starts to wobble, face crimson and twitching. Petunia blanches. "Oh Grampa!" she wails, and goes running out the door.

"Albert!" I yell, down on my knees. "Dad! Albert!" I take hold of his back and roll him towards me. Rasping air hitches back and forth somewheres and he strains, desperate for it. "Jist keep breathin'" I yell at him, not knowing what else to do.

The wind has gone out of my hate, just when I need it most.

His eyes snap open, staring up at me, a grimace of pain or joy. One shaky finger rises ever so slowly, like the flag at Reveille, lightly touching my cheek. A word quavers out of him, half whisper, half rasp. "Angel..."

What is happenin' here?

His eyes roll back, whole body shaking, chest seized. "Dad!" I yell, grabbing onto his shirt. "Dad! Petunia's gone for medicine! Jist hold on!" He grabs a clipped breath, squawking awful, then balks again, nothing in his face now but terror. "Jist breathe!" I'm yelling.

A horrid whistle of air tries to be dragged to the lungs, followed by a thick, final silence. His upper body stiffens, eyes gleaming with fear, arms thrashing and fighting. I should let go but I don't. I hold on, head ringing from the blows.

"Dad! Albert!" I cling to him, trying to shake him or quiet him or make him live. "Dad! Dad!"

It don't matter. He dies like that.

When he's still and staring up with dead eyes, I struggle to my feet and go lean on the counter, back turned away so I don't have to see. Tears roll down my face, some intolerable pain breaking in my chest. *Why?*

The children have heard the commotion, I can hear them crying softly back in the room. I get my hankie from my sleeve and try to fix my nose and eyes. When I know my voice won't break, I call out to James, telling him get his trousers on. "Go meet Gramma," I say. "Tell 'er it's too late. Grampa is dead."

He peeks around the doorway, big-eyed, then shoves his back along the far wall, spooked and jumpy, till he can get past it, and bolts for the porch.

"My dad is dead," I say to nobody. "Only dad I ever knew, anyways."

I reach to the little window and sweep back the curtain. The rising sun glows red beyond the poplars. What's that saying? *Red sky at night, sailors delight. Red sky at dawning, sailors take warning.*

I suppose that means another hard day is coming.

I see the form of my son plodding his way across the yard and out into the field. He don't look too keen on the job he's headed for. Then I see the shadows of my mother and my daughter moving off Mother's step, coming this way in a hurry. They don't know yet they ain't even going to make it.

Chapter 5

The Terrible Twinning

(1938)

On the Wednesday, Mother's twins and my Margie come tearing up the dirt road yelling that Beatrice got into a truck with two old guys and they drove off with her.

"Lord, Lord, what now," I says, grabbing my baby Charlotte. We run on up to Mother's, the big girls hauling my little ones, Carly and Cathy.

Mother ain't in the house so we leave the kids there with my brother Vallee and start yelling in the yard. Then we see her coming up from the field behind the oxen, Baby and Sunshine. I get all of us over behind the wood corral while Mother drives the team in.

"Mother," I yell, "Beatrice has took off…"

"Eh?" She looks mad, shakes her head and waves us towards the house. I send the girls up with the kids and go around to where she's throwing down feed. She's wearing her old brown farm boots, her hair bunned and wrapped around mulatto-style with a cotton scarf that must have once been purple. In her faded-out woman's top and mannish dungarees, her stocky little frame shows through, and when she forks the hay from the stack to the ground, her arm muscles bulge and pop just like a man's.

Mother jams the fork into the stack and climbs through the fence, her face red with sun and work. She grabs the empty water pails, starts heading for the well, and I hurry along behind, telling her what the girls said. It was Old Bob Hay and Billy Boy, a queer pair of characters shacked up on the edge of Swan River, known for bad goings-on. Well, they pulled up in their half-ton, yakked with Beatrice for a minute, she got in, and they took off with her.

I figure Mother'll start cussing and go storming into town to get her. But she don't. Just stands stock still there by the well, kind of with her back to me. Not moving.

"Mother? What are we gonna do?"

"So this is the day," she says. Or I think that's what she says, her head cocked to one side and not moving.

"What?" I get a bad feeling, my mom standing still, saying strange things. "I know where their place is," I insist, "over on the Ditch Road... Mother?"

She takes a breath, drops the well bucket down, grabs the rope, and hoists it up. Then she pours the glistening water into the pails, tosses back the bucket, picks up the pails, one in each hand, and carries them, sloshing a little, back to the oxen while I follow behind. I try to help by taking a pail, but she shrugs me off as usual. "Git" she says, sidestepping, "or you'll throw my balance."

"Mother?" I try again. "What do ya wanna do about Beatrice?"

"Wanna have my pipe, soon as I finish this," she says in a strange, flat voice.

She pours the water into the trough and sits the pails on the slick wood platform. Sunshine's the first one there, and when Baby crowds in close, I can't help but take a step back. They're so huge and always make me nervous. Mother's head barely tops their shoulders. But she reaches in and strokes Baby's enormous neck, where her thick white hide ripples and flicks. She croons to them like they're small children.

"Mother." I shake my head. I can feel the worry like a wedge in my gut. "Those guys... Beatrice is jist a young girl."

She starts walking on up and I follow her. "Well, Rosie, what the hell can I do? Can't make these girls come back. They only run agin."

I lower my eyes, remembering myself at fourteen, running away time after time till they finally had to let me marry Mitch. Now I'm a couple years shy of thirty with seven children. Wish I'd done different, but they couldn't tell me nothing at the time.

Mother stops at the wash basin outside the house, washes up, towels off, and sits down on the rough-hued bench under the willow with a little breeze blowing. I don't know what else to do so I sit with her. Vallee, now age nine, has got Charlotte down for a nap in the basket and the little girls playing grounders in the field. Mother fetches her red can of Velvet tobacco from under the bench and her corn cob pipe that she stores in the cleft of the trunk, then loads it up. She grabs a match from her pants pocket and strikes it with a flourish on the rough bark of the tree. It flashes to flame. She gets her pipe smoking up good and then takes a long, satisfying pull and lets it out, eyes way off in the distance somewheres.

"Look what happened with you," Mother says, low and soft, the sweet perfume of her rummy smoke wafting round us in the cooling air. "Run off to the Kirks' and I brung ya back. Ya run off agin and I brung ya back. Next day, where was ya? Gone agin." She sighs deep. "And lookit what happened with Eileen. Out at Welsh's and got into somethin' she needed help outta. But now she's keepin' secrets, and wout'n tell. Ya know how that turned out."

My throat gets chokey and I shake my head. "But Mother."

"Turned out with my girl in a box. Doc put down pneumonia, but we know it was... that other thing. Died of bein' a girl, bein' poor, and keepin' secrets." She smacks a mosquito on her fleshy arm and flicks the tiny carcass away. "Girls want out, that's jist how they are," she says. "Come to this age and they want it bad. Wanta git away from the dirt and the work and the kids. Git away from havin' nothin', goin' nowheres, bein' nobody. They ache for it." She snaps off a little twig from the tree base, pokes around in the bole of her pipe to loosen the tobacco a might, then takes another draw and breathes it out. "So here comes some man danglin' a cure and off they go. I know I done it. And you done it."

"Well I was wrong. I know that now."

"My girl, I know ya know it *now*. But ya dit'n *know it then*." She smokes some more and the kids run hard to the back field, trying to catch a fly ball. "There comes a time when a young girl will fight ya. Seems to be how all our girls is, from me on down. And mebbee that's how it's got to be. Otherwise they'll be weak things, suckin' at their Momma's tit all their life." She slaps my leg and gets me laughing. "You turned out good!"

But then she gets serious again, kind of choked up, which shivers my back because Mother ain't the choking-up kind of woman. "Rose, I'm shakin' in my boots here," she tells me, "because out there is no game. And Beatrice always was so like my Eileen. Looks jist like her, everbody says. But Beatrice ain't smart like Eileen was. Got the fire but not the spark of our Eileen. Beatrice is one to speak without thinkin', act without knowin' what comes next. And she is headin' down a dangerous road." She takes another pull, cocks her head back, making a 'O' with her mouth, and blows the smoke skyward in a narrow stream. "And I jist—I cannot—I can *not* see another one a my girls in a box."

"Oh Momma..." I hug her up and rub her shoulder.

"I been thinkin' about this for awhiles now," she says, patting my arm. "Long nights I thought about it. Thought about these girls and what to do differnt. Can't keep makin' the same mistake. Go tearin' down there and drag 'er home. Only to run agin."

She taps out her pipe in the grass, swirls a finger round the bowl, and rubs off the gunk on the outside leg of her dungarees.

"What are we gonna do then, Mother?" I ask as we start heading for the house.

"Gonna make supper," she says, bending over the potato bin in the porch, throwing enough in the bucket to feed all of us. "Make supper and wait. We'll give 'er a couple days and if she don't come home by Friday, then I'll have to go to town."

"So you *will* go get her?"

"Not me," she says, "Gonna tell the town constable, Young Jack Elliott, yur friend... or whatever ya call him. Get Old Billy and his pal arrested."

I scoff. "Jack? What's he gonna do?"

"There's laws nowadays against what those guys is doin', I know that for a fact. There's a law called *Contributin' to Minors*. That's what they used on Injun McGee when he tried to run off with Sarah Murphy. They charged him with that—*Contributin'*."

"But Mother," I laugh, "Jack ain't... well, I mean, I ain't nothin' special to him. Not in town anyways, in front of the high muckity-mucks. And them Mounties upstairs of him, they jist look down their nose at the likes of us."

"Jack is not the Mounties though," she says, putting on the potato water to boil. "He's the local constable, hired by the town, but still has to uphold the law. And there *is* a law. Men can't go messin' around with young girls anymore—not even here in the north. So I'm gonna go see Jack Elliott, tell him where Beatrice is and who's got 'er. He'll hafta go get 'er outta there. And arrest them dirty buggers."

I fill the washing-off bowl with water from the cistern and dig out a potato. Mother takes the paring knife and a big spud from the bucket, skillfully whisking away the thinnest of layers, then flips the spud into the bowl with a splash and grabs another. "Then what will Beatrice do?" she says. "No place to harbour in town. She'll hafta come home. That'll give us some time to figure out what the hell to do with 'er."

I get my knife going too and pretty soon we got the pot full and heading for a boil.

This is dicey, because I kind of like young Jack Elliott. Ever since me and him done some serious smooching at his Daddy's wake, he been kind of sweet on me. And with Culain away for months at a time up at Sherridon, I can use a little man-attention now and then. Sometimes on a Sunday, me and Mother has took the children to a baseball game in town, and there would be Jack Elliott. He'd be giving me his google eyes and trying to get around me. Bringing me a ice-cream treat or a little glass of soda pop from the booth, all polite and sweet. It's fun and gives me something to look forward to.

But as to getting him into my family's business, 'specially embarrassing business like Beatrice's shenanigans? This I do not like. I agree with Mother that something's got to be done and I do want to get Bea away from them guys. I just hope Jack don't screw it up. Because if he runs afoul of Mother, well that would just ruin everything.

* * *

It's the still dark of Friday morning and Beatrice has not come. I wake from another one of them dreams. Eileen alive again after all. In the dream, it's a beautiful afternoon and we go walking together through a field of silver sage, swaying and singing in the summer breeze. Eileen's hair is pulled back at the temple, the blush like wild rose in her cheek, and when I call her name, she smiles so bright it shames the sun.

I heave myself up and go shake Petunia. She swings her legs over the edge of the bed, sighing, and I put my baby Charlotte in her arms. Then I go shake Mitch where he's on the cot. "Git up!" I tell him. "Help Petunia with the childern whiles I go to town with Mother." Maluk has sent him home, two weeks ago now, what with his coughing and sputtering and the pain always in his chest. I hope the rest will get him right again and back to work.

I get the stove lit and the porridge on before heading down to Mother's. She's got on a old dress for town. By the time the sun has topped the poplars, we've got the cow milked, the animals fed and watered, and we're clipping off down the road.

We sweep down those miles of dirt road going north past four sections all the way to Cleary's corner, then we follow the fence line west another three miles through grass and bramble and grain fields. Sun's beating down good by now. I'm sweating and mighty glad to see that little coyote trail leading down through thick willows to the Roaring River. It's shady and cool down here, the river singing and sighing. Mother steps onto a little gravel bank, tucks her skirt hem up into her belt, squats, and starts scooping up water in her palms to drink. I do the same. The water is cold and clear, the little songbirds twittering in the bushes, and the smell of the blooming honeysuckle all around.

There's a stand of saskatoon bushes just back behind and we go to picking the tasty purple berries by the handfulls, gobbling them down.

When we've had our fill, we go wash our hands of the sticky juice. I wash my face while I'm down there, scooping the water onto my arms and even slicking it into my hair. Lots of time to dry off before town. Then me and Mother sit for a bit on the big rock there, just quiet together, watching the river as it courses and churns and rolls its way around the bend, the pigeons in their little bands, winnowing out and around and back again.

It's time to start moving again so we jaunt up through the willows into a big clover meadow, following the trail north for a while until we top a ridge and see the railroad tracks. We step up onto the rails of the CN line and walk the rail west for miles, then up around the broad, slow curve just south of Swan River, waiting in the high grass by Eisner's Slough as the morning train goes steaming by. There are yards and houses on our east and people call out and wave to us as we go by. Kirks and Mareses and such, all moved to town with the last crop failure.

We swing into the town of Swan River proper on the east branch of the "Y" line and head towards Main Street. I'm starting to get nervous now that we're finally here. I want to get my sister away from them guys but I dread having to go into the jail office. I mean, I keep thinking, what if they won't let me out? I just hope it don't take too long getting Beatrice back as this is town day for the farmers, and if we ain't too long, we'll be sure to get a ride home on the buckboard with some neighbour or other.

There's all kinds of horses and rigs and even automobiles on Main Street when we cross. We're heading for Colonization Avenue where the municipal office, the post office, and the town constable's office and the Mounties are all together in the one block.

Going past the Ladies' Auxiliary Hall, we see a huge banner for Farm Women United and a bunch of placards nailed to the fence. That's different.

"What's these?" Mother asks, and I read them to her as we go along. There's a big event going on for the ladies this afternoon, I tell her, a lecture with some big speaker from the city, a Mrs. MacPherson Murphy. There will be crumpets and tea service, no less. I have to sound out the next part. "Sump-tu-ous," I tell her, "*A sumptuous supper will be laid out for the gentlemen later.*" It's by invitation only.

"Hmph!" Mother jeers. "Guess we was left out of the invitin'. By accident, like."

My stomach is rumbling. "Mmm! Crumpets!" I say. "Jist think. Crumpets!"

"Too rich for our blood," Mother says. "Mark my words. We ain't their kind."

We've finally arrived and we stand at the end of the sidewalk, facing the big new municipal jail, built of solid red brick. Mother sets her jaw and moves forward, stomping up the three sturdy steps, and shoves open the heavy oak door.

Inside is all wood, a little waiting area on our side with a bench, and then the big plank counter, about four foot tall with a wood gate at the end that I suppose they must unfasten when they let folks in or out. There's a dirty little window on that side, hardly gives any light, but as our eyes get accustomed, we can see better. There's a small iron stove, not lit I'm sure, a table and a couple chairs, wood supply boxes and such, and coats hanging on hooks in sort of a closet area. On the wall facing us is the gun cupboard, hanging open, with a bunch of rifles and a big .303 British.

Behind the counter is not Jack but that young Ted MacPherson, the truant officer supposed to be, but I think he's just kind of a glorified dog catcher. He been gawking at some sort of magazine, mouth agape, and jumped to shove it under the counter when we come in. Mother goes over direct in front of him and stands solid, waiting. Ted's jaw opens and closes like a fish out of water, then he blinks and rallies. "Why Old Jo Labeau!" he smirks, all cheeky. "To what do we owe the pleasure of yur fine company?"

Mother looks the guy straight in the eye for long seconds, not missing his drift, and says not a word. He begins to blush and look away.

"Need a man," she comes back at him, "if ya got any here." Ted goes all sour-mouthed, eyes squinty and blond eyebrows pointed. "Lemme talk to Jack Elliott," she commands. He glares, red-faced, but finally shuffles over to the backroom door and calls out to his boss. Then he stands, hands on hips, sulking.

In a couple seconds, Jack steps in. He sees me, glances at Mother, nods and starts to come over. But Ted takes ahold of his shirt sleeve, squeaking something about wanting to go over to the Ladies' Auxiliary to see his Auntie Murphy.

"Might as well," Jack tells him, and he hightails it through the back. "God knows, he ain't doin' nothin' here," Jack tells us confidentially, stepping up to the counter. Then he nods, showing proper respect to Mother. "Josephine."

"Jack," Mother returns in kind.

He glances my way, all innocent and polite. "Uh, hullo... Mrs. Kelvey, is it?" he says.

"Oh, hullo, Jack," I say, lowering my eyes, "I mean, Constable. Or whatever... Jack Elliott."

Mother turns her gaze on me, frowning and shaking her head. *I would like very much to fall through a hole in this floor right now.* She turns back to Jack.

He pays attention, taking the tone of business. "Now, what can I do *ya for,* Josie?"

"My girl Beatrice is over on the Ditch Road with queer Bob Hay and that hooligan Billy Boy, that's what," Mother says. "I want her outta there."

Jack is silent for a minute, nods and takes a good breath, then steps into it. "Well now, Josie," he says, like explaining to a child. "I think I mighta heard somethin' about that. Thing is, as I understand it, she went there of her own accord."

"Own accord or not, Jack, it ain't right," she tells him. "Ain't a man in this town would stand for it if it was Rupe Davis's daughter. Or McKay's daughter."

"Well now, Josie, but it ain't McKay's daughter though, is it?"

"Jist cuz she come from a fam'ly a nobodies like mine, Jack, don't make it right. And ya know it ain't."

"Hell of a situation for ya, Josie, I see that."

He's fiddling with a wood sliver there on his side of the counter. He pinches it between the thick, smoke-yellowed nails of his thumb and index finger and yanks it out.

Mother stands waiting, not making it easy on him.

"Well, what exactly is it ya want from me in all this, Josephine?"

"You the police, ain't ya?" She's getting consternated already.

"Local constable, strictly local."

"You are Jack Elliott?" she says, bugging her eyes up into his face, as if she ain't sure. "Jack Elliott? Son of John Elliott, thirty years the law in the Swan River Valley? Is that right? Or have I got the wrong fella here?"

"Yeeees," he pushes his lips up into a smile, "that is who I am. And that was who my daddy was. But this ain't my daddy's day. And I ain't him."

"Well, no you ain't! And that's a fact!" I guess the pleasantries are over. "But yet, tryin' to do his job, ain't ya?"

"Tryin' to do *my* job, yes."

"Well, ain't there some kinda law? I heard there was a law aginst men takin' young girls for evil purpose. Called *Contributin' to Minors*. Now, is there, or ain't there, such a thing?"

"Well yes, but..."

"When old Beezley bootlegged to them Robinson boys, whose daddy owns the feed store, they got him on that one. *Contributin' to Minors*. Put him outta biz'nuss. When Injun McGee tried to run off and marry Sarah, the postmaster's daughter, the priest annulled it and Injun went to jail. *Contributin' to Minors*. He's still down at Dauphin, ain't he? They say he got ten years."

"Well, Josie. Them there is differnt cases. Law frowns on nare-do-wells interferin' with decent folks." My jaw drops. Jack glances my way, hurrying to correct hisself. "No offense to yur girl," he says, "No offense to yur whole fam'ly."

I give a quiet, "Hmph!"

"And Josie, ya know yurself, yur girl Beatrice was caught in the field behind the Legion, doin'.... bein'... shall we say, bein' a bad girl."

"Well as I recall, Jack, she was not bein' a bad girl all by herself. I believe there was a certain son of the mayor in the tall grass with her." Jack hems and haws some more, which is beginning to aggravate me. "Look! I ain't claimin' Beatrice to be no saint," Mother tells him. "God knows she bin a handful. But these guys that got her now, they ain't no kids. And you know damn well what they's doin' to her. She's only thirteen years old."

"Awful young for actin' that way," Jack says, raising a brow to make his point.

"Huh!" Mother raises her eyebrows right back, and juts out her chin for good measure. "Well ya know, Jack, I ain't above gettin' her outta there myself."

"Now, now, Josie," he tells her, "that we don't want neither. I told ya last time, there'll be no more of you fightin' the citizens of this town. Yur lucky the mayor went easy on ya when ya messed up his suit and hurt his arm."

"Went easy on people findin' out he got roughed up by a woman, more like."

"You hear me, Josie! No more fightin' the good folks of Swan River."

"That's what I'm sayin' now, Jack. I ain't took matters in my own hands. I bin waitin' patient two whole days. Talk'll be all over town about my girl, who she's with, what they's usin' her for. Ya said it yurself—ya knew it before I come here."

"Well uh... Josie, it is, uh... the sort of thing that will make tongues wag. A young girl, choosin', well, a bad path to go down."

"She ain't *choosed* it, is what I'm sayin' to ya, Jack! She's thirteen years old, a kid for Christ sake! She ain't old enough to know what the hell she's in for!"

Mother is yelling now, stepping back from the counter, gritting her teeth. Her eyes have gone mean, arms tense and fists clenched. I move over out of her way. Jack's eyes are big and his mouth keeps opening, but ain't no words coming out. "Girl is jist gone wild and runnin'!" Mother is screeching. "And them guys is givin' her a place to run to! A few years on, she'd know they ain't doin' her no favours, lettin' her ruin her life for their pleasure."

"Well, let's not get..." Jack says, holding his hands up like he's under arrest hisself. "Let's jist calm down here."

"I ain't calmin' down!" Mother yells through gritted teeth, lips gone snarly. "I don't want no God damn calmin' down! I want the God damn law to do what it God damn says it will!"

Jack looks truly flummoxed. "I... well, I..." he stutters. He glances my way, kind of a pleading look, but I just look to Mother and then down at my shoes. If he thinks I'm getting between him and Mother, he is dead wrong. "Well, Josie, now..." he starts again. He nods his head, then shakes it a little, then nods it again. Then sighs. "Well I suppose... yur right." I look up. Jack smiles weakly at me. "Them guys?" he tells Mother. He looks my way again, so I nod back. "Well, I guess..." He shrugs. "I guess they are actually *Contributin' to Minors*, now that ya put it that way."

"Damn right they are!" Mother says. Her chin is still jutted but she actually is calming a bit. "Now do the God damn job of the law, Jack Elliott," she tells him. "Git that girl outta there."

"Yes," Jack says. "I guess I could... take a little gander over to the Ditch Road. Go pick 'er up."

"Oh! Oh, good!" I say, giving my biggest smile.

"Well..." Mother says, relaxing herself down. "Well, all right then."

"Uh-huh," Jack smiles, head nodding. Then he goes serious again. "Course," he says, shaking his head, "it's a little dicey. For me, like. Ya prob'ly know but, that Bob Hay fella is the nephew of the Presbyterian minister. They got a lotta... lotta pull, I suppose you'd say, in that fam'ly."

"Shouldn't be doin' what he's doin' then," Mother says.

"Yeah. And then Billy Boy. What with his father holding a seat on town council, makes him, if you look at it that way, well, my boss."

"Yup," Mother agrees. "A bit dicey."

Jack sighs heavy, not moving from the counter.

"Well, good then," Mother says. "You drive out there, bring Beatrice here. And we'll be back in a bit to fetch 'er." She smiles at Jack approvingly and steps up to the counter, sticking out her thick little hand.

Jack gawks at the hand, confused for a minute, then "Oh!" he says, the light dawning, and shakes her hand. We all laugh.

"Thanks, Jack." Mother says, laying her other hand warmly over top of his, blue eyes fairly twinkling. "We knew we could count on ya."

* * *

Well now we got time to kill in Swan River on a going-to-town day, but not a cent to do it with. The Swan River, the one the town's named for, weaves between the yards and empty lots just north of here. Mother has brought some boiled potatoes and pork rinds in a sack and she wants to head down the hill, sit under the willows there and have a little fire, see can she maybe catch a squirrel or something to roast up. That spot there is right across from Eileen's grave

I got other ideas. I tell Mother I'd like to go look in the back door of the Women's Auxiliary, maybe see if I could get a taste of one of them crumpets. Mitch's cousin Myrtle often times will get work serving these high-faluting deals and I wonder, could she get me one of them crumpets? I say I'll catch up with Mother right here in a couple hours.

"Lady`s Auxiliary?" she sniffs. "La ti da! Ain`t you a big deal?"

"I know," I tell her. "But crumpets!"

So she heads off and I walk towards Main Street. But it ain't really crumpets I got a hankering for. When I see she's way down the block, I turn in between the shoe maker's and the butcher, go up the alley and come around to the back of Jack's jail. He's just coming out onto the step, putting his hat on, and I say, "Hey you."

"Hey yurself," he tells me back. I step up and he checks the alley, then gives me a squeeze. He's going to hitch up his big horse to the country rig so's he can bring Beatrice back, he tells me, and teases that I should come to the barn and help him. With his big horse, he says. We're giggling away there.

But then there's a racket up above and Jack gives me a little friendly push. I step down to the ground, looking all innocent. And tromping down the wood stairs from the Mounties' office comes Sergeant Bill Dumtree, all six foot six of him.

I seen this guy before, when I was with Culain. Always showing up with the game wardens, trying to catch you poaching. So called. Meaning you was trying to shoot some game to feed your starving family. Game wardens know this and make clear they're just doing their job. But Dumtree, he always got to be a prick about it, shoving people around, doling out insults and threats.

I'm not sure how to act now, kind of embarrassed, but he don't even look at me. Starts telling Jack he's got to go out and run some halfbreeds off the road allowance north of town, wants Jack to go with him.

"Off the road allowance?" Jack says. "Well, they're only there cuz they got nowheres else to go. What are they hurtin' by livin' out there in the ditches?"

Dumtree says they're hurting plenty, shouldn't be this close to town. He says he has his higher-up in town today, Major Murphy, whose wife is making the big speech to the ladies, and he wants everything shipshape for that. "Don't need no halfbreeds gettin' drunk and criminal, makin' us all look bad."

He steps down and goes over to his Mountie truck, motioning for Jack to follow.

Jack hesitates, twisting his hat in his hand. I roll my eyes and he gives me a little shake of the head. Then he goes over to Dumtree, starts explaining he's a little busy, giving the excuse about having to ride out and pick up Beatrice from the Bob Hay place. "Her sister," Jack says, nodding to me.

Dumtree gives me a stare. I know Jack just said that to get out of going with the guy, but I do not care for it. Dumtree grins at Jack and snickers. "Shit!" he says, giving him a elbow as if I ain't even there. "You can get you a little piece of sumpin' dirty later!"

Arsehole. I bite my tongue.

Jack guffaws obligingly, avoiding my eyes, and tries to make a start for the stable. But Dumtree slides his big arm over Jack's shoulder, drags him back playfully, and steers him around to the passenger door. "Tell ya what, Jack. Here's what we'll do." He says they'll go scare off them redskins together, then they'll swing by to where the Major is at, pick him up, and the three of them can drive out the Ditch Road and pick up Beatrice.

Jack purses his lips at me and can't do nothing but get in the truck. As Dumtree is heading back around to his side, I bug my eyes at Jack but he only shrugs and off they go.

"Oh for cryin' out loud!" I say to myself as the racket of the truck gets fainter. I hope they just hurry up. It's already been a long day and I want my sister back in time to catch a ride home.

Now what am I going to do?

I'm famished. Yet the thought of Mother's cold potatoes and pork rinds don't do nothing for me. I start thinking about crumpets in earnest. Crumpets and cream puffs and a big pot of steaming tea... My mouth is watering and I head off for the Ladies' Hall. *Myrtle, Myrtle, please be working!*

I slip into the back of the hall by the kitchen and it's lovely cool in there. It's dim lit and I stand flush of the wall, letting my eyes adjust. There's a lady behind a podium making a speech and rows of chairs all set in front of her, a bunch of women in the seats. The only ones I recognize is that elderly Mrs. Leary and her daughter from out our way.

Then sure enough, I see Myrtle coming out of the kitchen, all gussied up in a white serving outfit, one of them Dutch maid caps sitting all prim and proper in her hair. There's another girl working too, dressed the same way, and the two of them is going back and forth to a long table along the west wall, laying out fancy biscuits and little cakes and a silver tea service and China.

When she sees me, Myrtle gestures to stay put, finishes off what she's doing, and in a few minutes comes over. I whisper to her about what's happening with Beatrice and when I tell her I ain't ate no dinner, she goes to the table, shuffles some things around that don't need shuffling, and picks up a couple cookies and a biscuit to slip me. Then she takes me by the elbow and steers me over to a chair at the far end of the empty back row.

"Am I allowed?" I whisper.

She wrinkles her nose and sets me down.

So I sit alone at the back, enjoying the cool and the dark and the tea biscuits. Some sort of nutty batter with shreds of something my mouth ain't never tasted before. My Lord, I think it might be real coconut. Just beautiful.

The lady at the podium is very thin and serious looking, wearing some lacey getup with a big flouncy-feathered hat. I bet that hat cost more than taxes on our farm for a year. This must be the special speaker the signs was raving about, Mrs. MacPherson Murphy. I notice that layabout Teddy MacPherson leaning up against the side wall, thumbs in his belt loops, looking proud as punch. Guess this is the Auntie Murphy he spoke of back at the jail.

Mrs. MacPherson Murphy sure knows how to talk. She's numbering out all the advances been made for the ladies these past years. Having the vote, being able to own land, getting to run for public office, now even being allowed into Law and Medicine up at the university. Don't say? Well, I had no idea. I knew we was allowed to vote but seemed to me the men was pretty much still running things.

Well now Mrs. Murphy starts on about some other women, women she calls "the Unfit," and how tragic it is that they have the same benefits as their betters. "Every washer woman, serving wench, and harlot is now endowed with the self-same privileges so necessary, so prized by those dear hearts here present," she complains.

I cock my head. Seems like a strange thing to say. What's the matter with making a living by washing people's clothes or helping out with meals? Seems like that wouldn't put a person in the same class as a harlot anyways. But the ladies in the audience seem in agreement, nodding their heads. I look over where Myrtle and the other serving girl is standing silent by the table, just gentle and waiting, looking straight ahead. Are they hearing this the same way I am?

"Some women are not equal," Mrs. Murphy continues. "The yellow peril of the Orient," she says, "the Red Indian, and the unwashed Barbarian of Europe." Such people make up what she calls, "a ghastly plague of the unworthy and irredeemable that threatens our Canadian way of life."

Holy Moly. If that's how she feels about all them folks, I'm sure she wouldn't be crazy about the likes of me. Poor as dirt and Poppa's mulatto blood in my veins.

She sings the praises of this doctor fellow named Darwin and his theory that he made, called Survival of the Fittest. It don't just apply to dumb animals, she says, but to human beings too. "Society has no business permitting degenerates to reproduce their kind. While encouraging breeding by the right type of citizen, we simply cannot permit the perpetuation of the wrong type."

I can see some of the women's faces from the side here, starting to recognize quite a few. Why, there's one of the teachers from Bennett School and that new doctor's wife. And in the front row, Mrs. Smith-Jeffers, wife of our member of parliament for Nelson Riding. I keep expecting one of them to rise up and object to what's being said. Instead, they seem to encourage the woman, all nodding and murmuring, agreeing together.

They even clap when she mentions that Hitler fellow over in Germany and how he's helping the cause. Hitler? I thought I heard tell he was a bad man. Yet Mrs. Murphy seems to like him. "The dearest gains of our highest ideal could yet be jeopardized by the unchecked propagation of the inferior stock of the human race. We must not fail!" She gets downright Pentecostal now, half-crying out her speech. "The stakes are too great! We must not fail!"

The ladies shout and clamour, cheering her on, but I don't.

I know I don't understand all them big words the woman is using but I get her gist. I never heard of half them fellows and their big ideas she's all google-eyed about. Doctor This, Doctor That, Professor

Something Else. And far be it from me to claim being smarter than such a wealthy and educated person.

But you know, what this lady is saying just don't seem right to me. That some folks is superior and others is faulty. That people born to hard times and troubles is not hardly people at all, but more like animals. No, I just cannot listen to this. I think I'm going to get up from this nice comfy seat and go somewheres else. Them coconut biscuits is done anyways.

When I rise, Myrtle looks over but I nod towards the door, so she smiles and gives me a little wave. I tiptoe my way out while Mrs. Murphy starts going on about some sort of a "eugenical" program, which she says will stop the dangerous over-breeding of these "unfit" people through what she calls "compassionate programs for sterilization." Sterilization? Ain't that like castrating a bull?

As I reach the door, she starts slugging her way down a long list of the kinds of people these programs is meant for; the indigent, the pauper, the retard, the syphilitic, the schizophrenic, the depressive, the epileptic, the juvenile delinquent.

Released into the parking lot, I take up Mrs. Murphy's stringy voice and help her out with her list. "The big-nosed, the fat-arsed," I whine, "the knock-kneed, the pigeon-toed, them that can't get it up in the night." Jesus, if that was my first Ladies' lecture, please let it be my last.

There's a nice breeze blowing now, still must be a hour before we go collect Beatrice from Jack's jail, and I could sure use a nap. I take myself over under the willows at the edge of the gravel lot, take off my sweater, wrap it around one of my shoes for a pillow, and lay down in the tall grasses for a nice little snooze.

What do these kind of people believe anyways, behind their closed doors? That folks who is poor like Mother, or retarded like the twins, or bad-behaving like Beatrice, is not worth living?

I've been dozing for a while there when the Mounties' truck pulls into the lot and swings to a stop in the gravel not ten feet from me. I roll onto my elbow. Sergeant Dumtree gets out on my side and there's Jack Elliott on the other. The doors slam and they go in the side office entrance of the building. Huh, what are they doing here? In just about a minute, out they come again with some older-looking, mustachioed fellow, and the three of them come lean on the truck, talking and smoking. I duck my head down.

"The Major here knows just how to handle this sorta thing," Dumtree is telling Jack. "Him and his lady wife. Ain't that right, Major Murphy?" He tells all about Beatrice, how she's only thirteen and shacked up with grown men twice her age.

"Ah yes," the Major guy grunts, "the promiscuous juvenile female." He starts talking about some joint run by the Sisters of Loving Kindness in Winnipeg where they got arrangements to send such girls for rehabilitation. He says he can get Beatrice in immediately.

Rehabilitation? What the hell is that? Beatrice ain't going to Winnipeg, she's coming home with us. I'd like to find out what the hell is going on, but I feel somehow scared of those Mountie guys. Plus wouldn't I look foolish, coming up out of the grass like some queer old hobo?

Jack don't seem in agreement at least. He says it's the men that's in the wrong, in his estimation, taking advantage of a wayward kid. He mentions the *Contributing* law, saying he'd like to get Beatrice back to her mother and let the family work it out.

"No," the Major says, a real take-charge kind of guy. "That is not the preferred course of action." He says this sort of thing needs a firm hand and he starts asking Sarge about train times. Sarge says sure, there's a schedule for Winnipeg late tonight.

"Society's needs must prevail," the Major announces to Jack, like a stern father addressing a foolish kid, and they all start piling into the truck. Sarge is driving, so Jack winds up sitting between the two Mounties like a girl, the stick shift jamming back and forth between his knees. As they pull away, the Major's words waft back to me. "This aberrant female presents a perfect case for sterilization."

Sterilization? Are they saying they're going to do that to my sister? I jump up and go hiking down to the river, yelling for Mother. Breathing hard, I tell her about the Major and his mean-thinking Missus and now they're going after Beatrice, planning to take her away and give her that operation, like castrating a woman.

"Nobody's takin' my damn girl nowheres," Mother glares, and we go hoofing hard back to the jail but it's all locked. Back door's locked up too, so we come around the front again to wait for them to bring Beatrice. I'm just telling Mother about the strange things that woman was saying, Mother scoffing away, when we hear a muffled commotion up above and a yell that sounds like my sister.

"Shit!" Mother yells. "They already got 'er in there!"

She bashes on the oak door, yelling for Jack to damn well let us in, and pretty soon he does, looking sheepish. He goes to the gate at the end of the counter and touches something that clicks, lets hisself back through and closes it up again.

"Well!" Mother demands. "Where's Beatrice?"

He hems and haws about the Mounties and the laws and how there weren't nothing he could do. He won't meet my eye at all, keeps telling Mother that he tried, he tried, but the Mounties took her and she's upstairs and there you have it.

Mother is flabbergasted. "You tried?" she yells at him. "You tried? Well what the hell, is you the police or ain't ya? You the son of John

Elliott? And you tried but the Fuzz upstairs wout'n let ya? Are ya a kid waitin' for a say-so from the big boys?"

She's fighting mad now, sweeping his tally book onto the floor, and goes stomping over to the wood gate, all four foot eleven of her, rattling and shoving at it, trying to go through. "Give me back my God damn daughter!" she's bellowing.

Well, now the Mounties come thundering downstairs and in from the back, Dumtree, that gigantic oaf, and the Major, almost as big. I grab onto Mother and try to hold her but she yanks away from me. That Major guy is yammering about Beatrice, saying she has been incarcerated under the Juvenile Delinquents Act and is to be sent for rehabilitation to the Winnipeg Home for Delinquent Girls until the age of majority. Twenty-one years.

"Oh my Gawd!" I gasp, hand to my mouth.

Mother stops, her jaw, her fists, her arms, everything in her tense and ready to blow. Then she speaks. "Age of majority," she says through her teeth, each word deliberate and exact, "up... yur... God... damn... bloody... arsehole!"

Then there's a row.

Mother has clicked the latch on the wood gate and slammed it into the Major, causing him to sprawl back and crash into Sarge, them both lurching backwards like a pair of idiots, near falling on their arses. Mother is through the gate and plowing ahead, on her way to Beatrice. But the Major grabs hold of her. Dumtree rallies and the two of them got her shoved against the wall.

"Mother!" I'm yelling, coming through the gate to help her, but Jack Elliott pushes out the other way, walking me backwards, got me pinned against the wall by the bench.

"Rosie, no!" he's muttering. "Rosie, stay out of it! You'll get hurt." At the same time, trying to look back over his shoulder, he keeps calling, "Now, now, boys!" like a ninny. "Go easy there, boys, go easy!"

"Lemme go, Jack!" I'm screeching, seeing how them pricks got my mom pinned against the wall. I struggle and shove against him but he's too close to punch so I reach up and claw my nails into his face. He's trying to shield hisself while he's still got his weight against me and I'm pinned.

"Momma!" I'm yelling. They've took my mom down and they're both on her, holding her to the floor, but she lashes out and clips that Major guy a good one right in the face.

He flips back holding his nose, blood oozing between his fingers, going, "Oh God, Oh God" in the same nasally voice his stupid wife has.

"Momma!" I'm screeching and crying, as the Sarge is punching my momma right in the face, how a man would punch another man. *Momma!* Her head bounces into the floor, and while she's kind of passed out for a minute, the Sarge half-stands, flexes his knee and comes down hard on her with all his weight. Sarge gets up and she's just laying there moaning, but yet he hauls off and kicks her in the hip for good measure.

"Momma!"

Jack's still leaning on me, but half turned around, calling out, "Jesus, fellas, that's a woman there!" like he don't believe his eyes. "Jesus," he tells them, "yur beatin' up a old woman."

"Lemme go, Jack Elliott, ya God damn bastard!" I rant. But I'm also sobbing into his shirt and clinging onto him. Mother is trying to come around, flailing half into the closet there, growling like a wounded bear while the big men stand over her, laughing.

Eventually, she stops struggling and just lays there dazed, gazing up at them. Jack has let me go and I slouch down onto the bench, bawling away.

The Major stands smirking down at Mother, face writhing with some foul emotion. "They're going to split her open and *do* her good," he croons.

Mother gawks at him. "What?" through puffed-up lips.

"Your harlot daughter," he grins, eyes weird and bright. "They're going to stain her and split her and gouge out her filthy womb."

Mother closes her eyes and clenches her jaw and I'm just sitting there crying like a kid. *If only Kenny was here. Or Culain. Or somebody. If I had a dad. If only I had a dad, he'd kill these fuckers.*

Jack has gone through the gate and shouldered his way towards Mother, the big Mounties smirking and elbowing each other. Jack kneels down and is talking to Mother quiet, then he helps her stand and she lurches towards me, face swollen, welts and bruises coming up on her forehead, and bloodied all-round. When she's through the gate, I take ahold of her, she's limping bad but together we stagger out the door.

"Rose," Jack says low, eyes darting around. "I'll... I'll come find ya after."

"No you won't!" I screech at him. "Git away from me!" And I get my mother down the three steps.

But that damn Sarge has come and followed us outside. He stands on the step all crazy and excitable, laughing behind us. "Ya lost, Old Jo Labeau! Ya lost agin and ya always will! Yur the bottom a the heap and ya ain't never gettin' up. What's the point in fightin'?"

Mother stops and turns us around. I can just make out Jack's face in the little dirty window, looking pathetic and upset. Mother lets go of my arm and stands alone, gazing up at Sarge.

"Momma?" I say. She's very still, just standing there, like the calm before a storm. "Momma, let's go!"

But she swings her right hand up, almost like she's waving at him, the fingers and open thumb forming half a frame for his image. Her jaw is set, eyes cloaked, like she's looking towards Sarge more than at him, and she speaks in a low, clear voice.

"I damn you, Bill Dumtree," she says. "If ya ever agin come near me or mine. I damn you and yur evil heart. I curse you. I curse you. I curse you."

Well, Sarge laughed that off. "I been cursed by the Witch of Roaring River," he would announce at the Vimy Hotel. He would put Mother's name into that dirty joke about the man having sex with a bear instead of a squaw, and the story bought him drinks for weeks. But if Sergeant Bill Dumtree wasn't fool enough to fear a old woman's curses, he was smart enough to steer clear whenever he saw us in town. And he never did come near our door.

Not till years later, when Mother had left this world and he went to her little house with a bunch of the volunteer firefighters. When poor folks die owing taxes, the firefighters like to torch their homes, to get in some practice, like, with their hoses and axes and such. But poor old Sarge had to knock off early, turned out, with crazy pressure like a weight on his chest, the cramp becoming pain till hell wouldn't have it, and that very night, Sergeant Bill Dumtree was heading off hisself to the great squaring-up on the Other Shore.

Mother picks herself up unsteadily from the boardwalk by the town well. We've washed off as much of the blood as we can from the brawl with the Mounties. Her left ear is stinging her something awful where it's split and we've pulled a fluff of grey, blood-matted hair over it. Her nose ain't broke, so that's good, but her leg is a torment where Dumtree drove his knee into her.

It's too late for home now, there ain't no rides tonight. So we're going to head out south of town, we know lots of them folks along the railroad tracks and someone's bound to offer us a bed for the night. My kids'll be fine with Petunia and Mitch. Mother leans on me, breathing and shaking her head. "What's gonna happen to Beatrice now?"

"I do not know," I tell her. There's a clutch in my throat and a clench in my guts and things at the edge of my brain that I don't want to think about.

"Another girl took from me," Mother says. "It's a twinnin' of sorts, a terrible twinnin'. Eileen took to death, Beatrice to God-knows-what."

She tests out a couple of steps for the hip and it's bearable if she lets herself swing the other way and limp on this side. So that's our plan and we head off.

Outside the Ladies' Auxiliary Hall, young Teddy MacPherson is back at practicing the stance of a man of leisure. With the solid wall at his back, he has slid his one foot up with the knee jutting out. Displaying his manly presence, I suppose.

What a pair me and Mother must look, crossing Main Street by the Vimy Hotel, me with my one blouse sleeve tore half-off, Mother all swelled up and hair cockeyed, limping along like a couple of hobo hags.

"Tough day in town, ladies?" Teddy sneers as we approach. "Got all boozed up and slapped around, did yuz?"

Mother ignores him, just trying to put one foot in front of the other.

"Hey, Old Jo Labeau!" he yells, stepping out all impudent as we pass. "Ain't ya gonna come listen to yur friends inside? They're 'bout to save the world for the ladies."

Mother sniffs and slits her eyes at him. "Ain't no God damn friends a mine," she says, and spits a thick wad of blood-nasty towards his feet, making him screech and jump back fast like a pansy boy. I giggle and keep going.

He shrieks, rubbing the elbow he whacked on the wall. Then comes rushing after us, trying to make a show of being a dangerous man.

But when Mother checks her pace as though she may return, he thinks better of it and takes a step back, stands there pouting and cursing us softly with his little-boy curse words as we continue along our way.

Chapter 6

A Seven Year Ache

(1939, Spring)

The Winnipeg train will be in by noon bringing Mother and Beatrice, but why should I sit on them hard old benches in the grey shadow of the grain elevators, looking at nothing but six tracks of rail? I got myself waiting over here on a patchwork quilt in a sunshiny spot of new grass. Ain't going to do nothing but enjoy the break from the work and the worries and the noise.

I have left all my children and Mother's with my second girl, Margie, and Mother's twins Pan and Tan. Should have been Petunia but she pushed hard to come into town and I'm beyond tired of arguing with that girl. She's took off now, saying she wants to do this and do that, but I told her, "Jist tell the truth and shame the devil! Ya know damn well yur gonna go over to the lumber yard, see that Beaulieu boy!" She flubbed and faltered but didn't argue the point. For a change. If she ain't back when we're ready to go, she can walk back up the mountain. I mean it.

Well, now I see young Conan Kirk, the next one younger than Trooper Roaring Kirk but older than Grace. Him and his sister Hope has got jobs on that big Henry family farm out by Durban and he's in town doing errands. He says they're looking for another hired girl and Hope told him, if he could track me down, get me to give it a try. She will speak up for me.

That would be real cash money.

So I tell him I'm waiting on Mother to come back from the city, and if she says yes, I'll come out there directly. He says not to take too long though, as there's lots of folks would give their eye teeth for a job right now, and I say I won't. He goes hiking off for Main Street and I watch him go, thinking how he does favour Culain in the set of his shoulders and the lope of his walk, brisk-like, meaning business. But he don't have the muscle and the solidness of his big brother.

I miss Culain something awful. He's a teamster now, up at Sheridon, caring for the heavy horse teams, and driving the iron ore all the way down to The Pas, where it's shipped out for B.C. Every once a season or so, he'll jump on the train and come home for a visit. He's making good money, which is much needed. All my children has wore holes in their shoes and I know they'll be getting new ones on Culain's next visit.

Still, every time he comes, it's the same. Starts out happy and exciting, him and me finding somewheres to go, get our passions out for a day or two. And I feed him good. Then starts the arguing. Him begging me to go, me begging him to stay, that turns into fireworks, me stomping off, him coming next day to smooth it over, and both of us having to put it all aside and make up before he has to get on that next train north.

I do not like it. I am not happy.

Many is the night I lay and ache for him. Or ache for something, some bit of sunshine in all the long, grey days. But there ain't none, just Culain, whenever he comes. So we just got to go on working, me and Mother, just keep on slugging.

Well, here's the train, and once the commotion clears a bit, I see Mother, all four foot eleven of her, coming my way, no Beatrice. Her face is red from the heft of her suitcase. She slings it down and flops onto the quilt there with me. She's got on the lady dress with lily patterns she sewed for the trip but that just makes her look more odd, built so manly as she is and with the short-cropped grey hair, always oily no matter what she tries. She ain't saying nothing and that can't be good.

Half a year now we been trying to contact that Sisters of Loving Kindness joint where they got Beatrice but not getting no news back. So Mother had went to the Orangeman's again and Mr. McDiarmid had got the address for her and give her some cash for the trip, and she put that together with the bills Kenny had sent. There's a relative of the Kelveys who works at Eaton's in Winnipeg. He wrote back to us and said that yes, they would put Mother up, so off she went. We was hoping that joint would agree to let Beatrice come home, as both Doc True and McDiarmid had give Mother letters of testimonial in support of it.

"How was it, Mother?" I ask, pouring sugared tea from the canister into a thick glass cup and handing it to her. Still tepid anyways. "How is Bea doin'? What did they say?"

Mother grunts, taking a slurp of her tea. She looks off away, eyebrows knit, and I sit waiting. "All Catholic nuns runnin' it," she says. "They're the sisters, I guess, of lovin' char'ty, like, but the one I seen in the big, fancy office, Mother Superior, I guess she's the boss."

Mother sits so very still and says no more, which I find hard to take. "And?" I ask. "Well, what did she say? About the letters? About lettin' Beatrice come home?"

"Said a lots," Mother says. "All about wayward girls, sinfulness, sins of the flesh, sins of the fathers, all that. Very preachy. I dit'n follow all of it. I showed her my letters and told her Beatrice has a fam'ly that wants her back, that I'm sure she learnt her lesson now."

She balks again and I try to wait. Finally, I ask, "They dit'n... they dit'n let us?"

"She droned on and on, a lotta big words. I dunno," Mother says. "She showed me some kinda damn papers, the law or somepin like that. I cout'n read what the hell they said. But I knew what it meant, meant I cout'n get my daughter back. So I said, 'Well I wanta see 'er anyways, see my girl.' So they put me in a room to wait and she come in."

I follow Mother's eyes to the pigeons winnowing back and forth from the tops of the elevators, flying out and around in their little crews, then back home again. I wait.

"She's even skinnier'n before. Eyes all sunk in, but bright and crazy. Yackin' away 'bout the place, the mean bitches of nuns, how they beat the girls everday. And some guy in charge of 'em, a social worker, whatever that is, how he's her only friend and treats her nice. And rantin' loud 'bout the other girls they got there, that they's all bitches too and she's gonna beat 'em up."

"Oh, sissy..."

Mother shakes her head. "I told 'er, 'Beatrice, ya gotta settle down now. You'll get yourself in trouble.' But then she started shriekin' at me. 'Trouble! Trouble!' she yelled, laughin' loud, 'Worse trouble than this?!'

And then she done the damnedest thing. She stood and pulled up her dress. Pulled it all the way up to her titties right there in the room, showin' her bloomers and everthin'. Flauntin' the scar they give her. Big ugly scar, all healed crooked and red, slashed across her tummy there where the..." Mother shakes her head, eyes downcast, ". . . baby would've bin... if she could've ever had a child. Which she can't no more."

"Oh no! Sissy... oh no!"

"Bastards!" Mother says. "They done it. They done the operation to her. Now how will she... How will she ever make a good life for herself if she can't ever... be a reg'lar woman?"

I cannot fathom it. I just sit there gawking, trying to understand. "What did you... say about it?" I ask Mother. "Say to her, like?"

"Nothin'," she says. "Never got the chance. She was jist screechin' and yellin' at me, mad as hell. Sayin' they told her it was me sicked the cops on her. Screechin' this was my doin'! Her own mother. That I took everthin' from her! 'This is yur fault!' she kept screechin' at me. 'This is yur fault!'"

"What? But, Momma, ya fought for her! You was, we would never..."

But Mother is up off the quilt, packing up the tea things. She ain't much for tears and feelings and girlie talk, Mother, so I get up too. We pack our things, fold the quilt, and start heading over to the livery where Junior has the ox team.

This is monstrous. This is all so wrong and hard to believe and hard to bear. Them people have got my sister and how do we get her back? I keep thinking of things I want to ask Mother, maybe come up with something, but I can tell by the set of her jaw as we steam down the street that talking about this is over.

So then I just tell her what Conan Kirk said about the job out at Henry's.

"Well, that would be money, real cash money," she says. We talk about it for a bit and she says, "We all can pitch in with yur little ones. Charlotte's pritty much crawlin' anyways and can be fed without the tit if need be. You go."

Within the hour, I'm hitching a ride out to Durban. But all the way, my mind churns, full of questions there ain't no good answers for. Why would them people hurt my sister like that? To fix a human girl the way you'd fix cattle? Just for being a kid and doing wrong? How will my sister ever be right in life now that she's had stole from her the one thing that grows a woman up and gives her hope? Motherhood.

The Henry house is like a castle, three stories high and a railed-in veranda all around. There's bunk houses down the yard and a huge garden, the soil well plowed and black, even a few green rows peeking through.

But now, ain't that Mrs. Henry a sour-looking woman, all frowning and sharp-questioning me? Hands on hips, glaring down from the front steps. "You a hard worker? Or jist one a these that does enough to get by? Where you work before? Nowheres, I suppose!" So I tell her I worked the threshing crews before the hard times, I ain't afraid of work, and I got Hope Kirk would speak up for me. She takes another hard look, then clicks her tongue and says, "Git to work then!" I go find the girls and tell them I'm in. And we go right to fixing the big supper for the family and their eight children, plus Mister Henry's two brothers, and their wives and small children.

I'm dog tired by the end of the day. Hope shows me my tiny room next to hers at the back of the third floor, and then we go outside where there's a bunch of us labour sitting around a fire over by the trees. I see Norma Mares is here, same age as me, used to be our neighbour out by Roaring River but now moved to town like so many families that lost everything. There's two of the Mitchell boys too, plus Conan Kirk, of course. Pretty soon, the young fellas finish off their stories and jibes they was giving each other and head for their shack, me just yawning away.

But then Norma starts telling me how things is on these jobs, as she's done this before. She says to watch out for the husbands, they'll grab you if they can. At every job with rich farmers, you got the two things to contend with. The wife, who's your boss and has every intention of working you into the ground. And the husband, who figures if he's paying you, you're at his service too, so to say. He'll just scowl or ignore you when his wife's around with her eagle eye, Norma says, but come a hour where you're somewheres on your own, he could just give a try to getting his hands on what you got. Or even in your room, sometimes they try to get in your room at night. So you have to do whatever you can to protect yourself, Norma says. Always. And we got to help out each other. Because when it comes to any strife between the likes of us and the likes of them, we all know who's going to come up with the short end of the stick.

When we get back to the rooms and say good night, I take my little bed and shove the foot of it right up against the door, then put my dresser sideways between my head and the wall. Ain't nobody's sneaky husband surprising me in the night.

Well, the good thing about working yourself silly is, time goes crazy fast. For some reason, the Missus has picked me as her special helper for all the inside cleaning and this is a huge house. Downstairs floors washed every day, upstairs floors weekly, plus all the walls twice a month. My back aches just thinking about it. Plus, I still got to help with the meals like all the other girls.

Two weeks goes by like a filly in a thunder storm. I can hardly wait to see my first pay. Supposed to be a dollar a day for a twelve-hour day but we're working sun up to sun down so I got my hopes for maybe a few cents more.

One evening, us labour sitting on stumps by the fire, Hope asks in her slow, quiet way, "Did ya have any letters from my brother Culain lately?" All the neighbours know what Culain is to me, but there is kind of a unspoken agreement that we don't come right out with it.

"I got a letter from him Thursday, he put in a couple dollars for my kids, what he could spare," I tell her.

Some people think Hope Kirk is simple, because she always talks so slow and low. But she ain't. Actually, she's kind of smart, loves to read books whenever she can, she got *Little Women* in her lap right now. And Hope is about the kindest person I ever met. Like for instance, I got so many kids and Mitch with but the one arm. I'm always busy working to try to feed them, but, well, they're not always clean and took care of. Some folks look down their noses at children like mine. Yet, when Hope comes over, she always treats the kids so nice, bringing them little food treats and sitting with them to comb the tangles out of their hair. Or picking up a rag and washing their little faces. I like Hope Kirk a lot.

She nods at me now, meeting my eyes. "He's a good man, my brother. Always helpin' folks, don't matter who they is."

It's a cool night, smells like rain coming. I'm shivering a little in the breeze. I start thinking about Culain Kirk, wishing he was here right now with his arm around me, keeping me warm. And going up to my lonesome bed with me after.

But then, Norma Mares starts joking me, about how I must be something special, what with having two men on my hook and all.

Hope's jaw drops, she gawks from me to Norma, eyes bugged out.

But Norma keeps on, a big grin building dimples in her chubby cheeks. "Must have more needs 'n reg'lar wimmin, like," she says. "And more to offer." I can't help but giggle, denying it all of course. "Rosie, you must have somethin', well, jist bigger or better'n the rest of us. Can't be satisfied by no one man, like." We're tee-heeing and snorking together, even Hope Kirk, laughing in her gentle way, hand covering her mouth.

Later, in my skinny bed with the foot against the door and the dresser at my head, I get to thinking about the needs of the flesh. The reason why I got to barricade myself in here at night. They say that men is just weak to such needs, that they can't control their urges. But I don't know. I'd say that I like the thrashing and the moaning pretty good myself. Lots of women do, I bet. Yet we ain't out there sniffing and grabbing at those that ain't ours to have. I don't know why it's like that, but that just seems the way of it.

But then, I go back on myself. I couldn't argue that women is some sort of saints or nuns. Well, except those that is. Nuns and saints, I mean. But apart from them, I think maybe lots of married women come around to... to being sexy, I guess you'd say. Like, wanting it. I think at first, the young ones just start out tolerating it, letting the husband have his way, which women are taught is supposed to be our duty. But when a woman gets satisfied out of having sex, gets the pleasure at the end I mean, well, I think that gets her, like, wanting it. Women I talk to anyways, women's been married awhile like my Auntie Ede and cousin Velma and my mom, well, we ain't shy about liking it and what we like and that. So maybe we're more like men than not like them in that sense.

Different times, when I been in town or going somewheres or when folks drop by our yard and there's men there, I find myself looking. Not that I ain't happy with Culain Kirk, that ain't the point. Just that I get to wondering, What would it be like with him? That wiry young husband of Bess Reed down the road, or that Swedish farmer at the highway with his thick-muscled sons, all blond and eager? Or them handsome Metis men living along the road allowances, with their high cheek bones and coal-black hair, their easy laughter, and every one of them playing the fiddle or guitar? What would that be like?

But then some women never do like it. Maybe they got men that don't ring their bells, or maybe the men gets sour of the women that don't like it, or whatever. Maybe that's why they get that hankering for a new one, what mother called the *seven year itch*.

What I got can't rightly be called a itch, though. A itch, well, you scratch it and it's over. This here that I got is like a dull pain that goes on and on, a ache, a suffering and a longing there ain't no cure for. Seems to me I always had a ache, over one cause or other. Ached for my Poppa long ago, ached for fun and change and getting out of home, ached for Culain. Guess I'd have to call that one a *seven year ache*.

Culain's been away for a long whiles now and oftentimes, I'm just crazy to have him with me, giving me joy like he does. He only comes down from Sherridon for a few days every couple months. He was here in March for half a week. But then, as usual, we spent most the time arguing about moving. He keeps pushing me about pulling up stakes and bringing my kids north to live with him. Has to bring it up every damn time. Why? He knows what I've said about it and I ain't never said nothing else. I ain't going.

This last time, we'd been through it again and sort of made up and I was just getting lovey, but then here it comes again. He hates living away from me like this, and when am I going to come north with him? I told him, I said, "Culain Kirk, you are turnin' into a dearth of fun! If you don't stop this bitchin' and moanin', you are gonna drive me into the arms of another!" I kind of giggled, couldn't help myself. Just kidding, of course.

He looked at me, a long look, kind of a quizzical expression on his face. I wiped the grin off my chops. "The things ya say, Rosie Kelvey," he told me, shaking his head. "The things ya say, there ain't no way of takin' back."

* * *

I feel myself tossing and shifting in the darkness. Maybe I'm sleeping way up in a tree, the bough being jostled in the wind? No, I'm in the little room at Henry's farm in the dark of night and my bed is jiggling because *somebody is trying to open my door*. Jesus! I lay perfectly still, my heartbeat pounding in my ears, trying to breathe shallow and not make a sound. The movement stops and I lay still as a bunny.

"Open the door," comes a man's hoarse whisper. "Darlin', open the door. Lemme come in and make ya happy." The jiggling starts again.

Is my dresser going to hold?

"Go away!" I whisper back. Silence. "This ain't yur room!" I whisper louder. "You got the wrong room, mister! Go away!"

The movement stops but there's still some hard breathing and shuffling going on. I lay perfectly still, my eyes bugged out in the darkness, concentrating on breathing without a sound. Through the wall, I can hear the little clock on Hope's dresser going tick, tick, tick. After forever, I realize I ain't heard no more from out there in the hall. And forever after that, the blue of morning starts to shade the blackness. But my night of sleep is done.

When I finally hear Hope moving around in the morning light, I jump up, put my skirt and blouse on, take a breath, and open my door. Nothing. I step over to Hope's door and tap on it, tell her what happened. She says to just yell if they ever get in, she'll come help me if she has to, she could always go home to her mom's if she gets fired. She says she always shoves that old shipping trunk in front of her door and I tell her I got my door wedged with the bed and the dresser. Thank God.

"Oh, watch out!" she says, steering me back from the wall by my elbow. There's something slimy and clear on it right by my door, about waist height.

"Oh, no!" I say. "That's not... Oh God!"

Hope blinks, head shaking, and says in her slow, quiet way, "That's just not what people should do." Then her finger jabs suddenly, accusing-like, at the mark. "Yuck!" she says really loud. I snort and start to giggle, it's just funny to see Hope so lively and excitable. And she starts to giggle too, shoulders hunched up, eyes squeezed almost shut, and her and me just hold onto each other, giggling and snorting and getting some fun out of being disgusted with it all. Because what else can you do?

After morning chores, I come back with a pail of water, a cloth, and a bar of lye soap and wash the wall down once, then twice, and then once more for good measure. I ain't living with some man's slime marking my room.

On the Friday, we get our pay, but it ain't what I hoped. Missus says it's generous, what they give us, as they hardly charge us anything for the rooms we sleep in and the food they provide. Thirty miles from town here, it ain't like we could go down the street to a café. She also says that with her folks coming Tuesday for the week of Dominion Day and with the field work ongoing, there's too much needs doing to have us all traipsing into town with our pay. She says us workers can just have a little party here tonight, have a break, and then get to work again tomorrow. So I have to send my money to Mother with Conan when he borrows a horse and takes him and Hope's pay down for their mom.

We do have fun that night anyways. They got a guy out for the week, guess he's helping to break in a couple horses. Name of Vie LaRocque. A Metis from up Birch River way. My God, he's handsome and dark. Quiet like all Native people, but smiling right into my eyes, giving me them dreamy looks on the sly whenever I glance his way. The boys got a little bottle of whiskey they're passing around. Hope don't take none, but me and Norma take a slug each time it comes our way. We're all laughing and teasing each other, telling stories about funny things that happened, silly people that fail at simple work, and head-shaking events where it sometimes might seem like there could be ghosts in the world for real.

One of the Mitchell boys has a guitar and starts singing cowboy songs. So Hope and Conan start dancing a two-step, then Norma grabs the other Mitchell boy and joins in. I'm sitting there, looking across at Vie LaRocque, all cutesy with my eyebrows raised. But he just grins, his eyes bright and black looking right at me, and he don't get up.

A couple more songs go by, I'm just toe-tapping away. So then I get all brave and go over to him, put my hand out, and say, "Would ya like to dance?"

"Dancin' don't do it for me, honey legs," he says, looking right into me and taking my hand. His hand is very big and very warm. "But if ya'd like to take a stroll over into them trees with me," he purrs, "we might try out a move or two."

Shocking. And exciting.

My breath catches and there's a flush coming up my throat. "Oh... Oh, well, um..." I say foolishly.

He slow smiles at me, not looking away, and I just stand there stammering. "Well, I... Well, um..." His hand, so large and strong, has somehow turned mine over and his fingers are stroking my palm. Inviting, like a very private sample of something else he has to offer.

I feel weak to him, thirsty and weak like my knees might buckle. I yank my hand away but yet I'm still standing there, gawking, and he's still grinning up at me.

"I... I..." I can't make my brain work so I just shake my head, huff out my breath, turn on my heel, and go stomping back to my log.

Holy Moly, just to come right out and say it!

I frown my eyebrows and make a show of watching the dancers. But my breath is caught and my ears are hot. All through "Cowgirl's Lament," I can just feel Vie LaRocque's dark eyes on me. When they start the next song, a jig, I sneak a glance. Sure enough, he's still looking. His eyes are soft and, I don't know, kind, or something. But yet, he looks like he thinks I'm funny.

I jump up and go join in with Norma and Willie Mitchell. The boys play a couple more jigs and I'm just dancing away, laughing, having fun. *See that, Vie LaRocque? I'm not interested in you!* When they start the lovely waltz "Always," I grab young Conan Kirk and dance with him, making Hope sit one out. There's a couple two-steps and when I finally get tired and go sit with Hope on the log, I see that Vie LaRocque has took off somewheres. *Oh good, I'm glad he's gone!*

The fire is burning low and the whiskey bottle is empty. Beau Mitchell is playing the lovely and slow, "Hobo's Lullaby," and Norma and Willie has sat down too, the mood gone quiet and lonesome. And when he plays "Nobody's Darlin' But Mine," so sad and beautiful, I shiver in the chill, dark air.

"I'm pretty tired," I tell Norma, "gonna go up now." Truth is, I'm a little drunk and I feel very much like going to look for my Metis friend. But I won't. Hope says she's going up too and will walk with me, so we go in.

* * *

Missus' folks arrive and we get even busier, trying to keep up on the regular work plus all the extra food and comings and goings. The old folks, Thornefinch is their name, have brought their son Ronald with them. Well, what a loudmouth that guy is. Tall and skinny, jittery and high strung, always jumping around. Supposed to be real smart, they say, went to Normal School down in Winnipeg, and going to be a teacher.

More of a smart aleck, I'd say. We can hear him all the way from the kitchen. He's one of these guys thinks he knows everything and got to be right all the time. Always talking loud about how the world should be, if he was the boss of it. The Indians is one of his favourite topics, how they're a bunch of savages that needs civilizing. Which is why he's going to dedicate hisself to saving the Indian children from their drunken families. Apparently, he's got a job lined up at the Indian Residential School over in Prince Albert.

And big on politics, too, is Ronald Thornefinch. Well, he sure does hate the unions. Always on about the workers being spiteful and lazy, communists to a man, and how they need a strong hand in government to be kept down. On behalf of my brother and the other union fellows, I do not appreciate our Ronald's fine opinions. But it's their house and we need the jobs and we're too busy working our fourteen-hour days to be able to speak up much about the lazy workers.

We get the holiday over with, their holiday, I mean. If I had the time to sit for a minute, I'd be missing Mother and the kids, I'm sure. But because of my work here, at least I know they'll be having a nice meal at home. So I'm thankful for that.

The following weekend, the Thornefinches are finally heading for the train. I guess their son's job up in P.A. don't start till after summer, so he'll be staying on till then. Oh good, more mean ideas held forth at the table for all to hear. Anyways, we ain't getting much sleep as two nights in a row, there's a commotion downstairs. The oldest daughter, Cecilia, must be about twelve years old, apparently keeps having the night terrors.

It's the Sunday night, when I'm so bone weary again, just falling into sleep so I can work again tomorrow, that I guess I must have been sloppy wedging my bed against the door. I'm woke in the dark hours, hands pawing at me. It's pitch black, a man is on top of me, got me pinned. He must have threw the bottom sheets aside and he's thrashing at me down there, trying to get the thing out of his trousers. Oh God, the top blankets have my arms pinned! I struggle and wriggle, get my right arm out and try to shove at his chest, squeezing to keep my legs together, but he overpowers me and cranks my arm down. He's breathing hoarse, his slobbering mouth trying to kiss me, and I fight and squirm, the rot of his breath half-gagging me. He gets his bony knee worked in between my two legs. *Oh God, he's pryin' them apart!*

Terrified, I rip my right hand free and go wild, grab onto where his ear must be, tearing and raking. He screams and I claw at his face, just vicious, ripping whatever I can get at. He screams again, his knee pops out from between mine, he flips away from me, and crashes onto the floor. I roll off the other side of the bed, slide in underneath the edge against the wall, and keep absolutely still.

I can hear his moans and soft curses coming from over there by the wall. I don't move a muscle, nostrils flared to breathe without sound. There's quiet for a long minute, then I hear the muffled sounds of him getting stood up and moving away. "Fuckin' whore," he whispers loud from over by the door, and it sounds like he's went out.

Silence. Just my heart beating in my ears. I think he's left, but I wait to the count of three hundred before I move. "Dirty sonofabitch," I tell the silence. Then I get up in the dark, lift the end of my bed, and wedge it in tight, tight, tight.

Next day, I tell Hope and Norma what happened. I say Mother's bills is far from caught up, I'm sure, and I need this job. They agree to just keep it between us.

"I learnt my lesson," I tell them. "I will never again be careless about wedging my bed in right, that's certain." And I tell Hope to never forget that heavy trunk in her room, and she agrees that she will for sure will be careful to bar her door at night.

"You gotta watch for 'em in daytimes too," Norma reminds us. "Inside, outside, or in the lady's chamber. No matter how reg'lar the time, jist don't never let down yur guard."

All day, I work hard and keep my head down, just watching them men from a distance. I want to see but not be seen. It's in the afternoon when I'm taking out slop water after doing floors that I see Mr. Henry's brother, the younger one that's already going bald, coming up from the field and going into the barn. He's got a white cloth bandage on his left ear and a good, mad-looking scratch right across his cheek.

"Dirty bastard," I say low to myself. Why? He's a got a pretty wife and two sweet little boys there. Why would he do it? And then, who bandaged him up? Like, how would he just come in all scratched up in the wee hours of the morning, and his wife would just bandage him up, and there wouldn't be no fight about where he was and what the hell happened?

* * *

A week later, it comes to a head. One of the men gets hurt in the barn and us kitchen girls have to clean and bandage his hand. That gets us behind a bit. It's already eleven, Norma and Hope is busy making the noon dinner, but the eggs still haven't been collected so Missus sends me out to the henhouse with a basket. These leghorn hens sure are excellent layers. Most of them have a nice big egg in the nest.

I've got about twenty eggs collected when I hear a whining or whimpering sound, seems like it's coming from back behind the chicken house. I go out the door and around back, and here's Ronald with that young girl Cecilia, got her pinned against the wall, with one hand under her skirt and the other one rubbing his thing where he's got it out of his pants there.

"What the hell?" I say.

He jumps and struggles to get hisself right and his thing put away. "Not doin' nothin'!" he yells, fidgeting with his buttons. "None of your business!"

The girl seems frozen but turns her head slowly towards me, a terrible look of anguish on her face, tears streaking her cheeks. "Come here, girl," I say to her kindly, holding out my hand. "Cecilia. It's okay. Come. I'll get ya to yur mother."

She comes over slowly, shoulders hunched, head down, still scared and trying to tidy her skirt. "Please don't tell Mother," she says. "She gets very angry when I tell her."

That's when Ronald comes charging past me, bashing into the basket, which flips right out of my hand. There goes the eggs, smashed on the ground. I get down on my knees and save the three or four that's only cracked, then I take the girl in the back door. Me and Hope is just trying to figure out what to do for her when Missus yells down for me to come up. She's there in the big dining room, tall and busy, setting out plates for the dinner.

"Rose," she says, facing away. "I am told you broke the whole basket of eggs."

I am flummoxed. Who could have told her already but him? And if he told her already about the eggs, what did he tell her about what he was doing at the henhouse?

"We can't have people here breaking our things. Having no care for our belongings and our business. Take your pay." I see the five one-dollar bills she has laid at the end of the table. "Beau Mitchell is hitchin' the team to drive to town for supplies. Take yur pay and go."

I stare at her back for a minute. Then I step up and grab the bills. I do not care, I'm going to say it. "He was diddlin' Cecilia," I say. "Yur brother, he's a kiddy diddler."

"Dirty mouth!" she says with disgust. From the side, her face looks blanched and hawkish. "Dirty liar! Get out!"

"These men is doin' bad things here," I say. What have I got to lose? "They come after us girls in the night. They're diddlin' yur childern."

She turns towards me, sharp eyes glaring down, brows vexed. I step back. "That cannot be true," she says, seeming strangely still and calm. "You *must* be a... liar?"

The word at the end comes out like a question, high and confused and alone. And I suddenly see Missus, where she's standing, on this rich farm with these powerful men. In this big, dark house, with the dark hardwood hutch behind her, the expensive China closet on the wall, the long heavy table she must set. What in the world would a woman do if she did know? None of this is hers, really. It's all only hers through the men.

"Missus," I say kindly. "You. Yur in a hard place now. But you. You got to stand up, stand up for yur girl's sake. Maybe, maybe you could…"

She turns back to the table, her head shaking no. "Just go," she says quietly. "You will have to go. That's all there is to it."

"But… But yur daughter—"

"Go! Go! Go!" she screeches, her voice queer and mannish and shaky all at once.

I take a breath, feeling strangely calm, not even angry. I've got money in my hands and I'll be packed and out of here before Missus has finished putting on the knives, forks, and spoons. Back to my own people.

My God, with all we don't have, I'd rather be me than her.

I gather my things and make my way to the wagon where Beau Mitchell has just finished hitching up the horses. I sit on the wood seat for the ride into town, my little bundle of belongings tucked in by my feet. We don't talk much. It's a hot day but there's quite a breeze blowing, so we'd have to shout and our words would be lost anyways.

That poor girl Cecilia. Who's going to help her? I feel so bad for her but yet, look what happened to Eileen. Look what happened to Beatrice. We can't even save our own.

When the team is way down the road, Beau yells over, "Did ya get fired?"

"Yeah," I yell back. "I broke all the eggs. Well, big-mouth Ronald did, but I was blamed."

Beau nods and shifts the reed he's sucking on into the other corner of his mouth. "Ain't that the way of it," he returns, nodding. "Ain't that always the way of it."

My plan in town is to buy a can of tea and some burley for Mother at McKay's, pick up her mail, and maybe get me a little piece of pie and a cup of tea at the Vimy Hotel Restaurant. Then I'll look around, see if I can hitch a ride from anyone going south to Roaring River country. Even if no one's come to town, I can always walk down to Elvie Kirk's place on the Y-line, sleep over, and leave early to walk the twelve miles home.

There's a letter from Culain and when I'm sitting at the sunny table, my nice hot tea with milk and my nice slice of cherry pie in front of me, I open it. I tuck the small wad of cash into my pocket. "Thank you, my darlin'!" I tell him. I'll go back to McKay's and get that cotton fabric I passed up, make my girls each a little dress for summer.

Culain says he's fine, tells about the team he's driving, Flicka and Beauty is their names, a pair of big blacks. He hopes to be home by the end of August, and ends off reminding me that he's keeping a eye out for a place for us and the children to live. He says he hopes that will be by Christmas.

Culain. Culain. How many times do I have to tell him? Yet, this is how he is. Once he sets his mind to something, he's like a dog with a bone. Got to keep gnawing at it, gnawing at it, then he gnaws on it some more.

I've twisted it back and forth in my mind, back and forth, back and forth. But I just can't see it. Living in that damn rocky place, even colder than here, no farms nor gardens, no friends nor neighbours nor people I know? There's hardly any women up there, from what I hear, it's a town full of miners and roughnecks. They say up north there's six men for every girl. And no jobs a woman could do. Making me totally needful of Culain, having to rely on him, like. Playing the nice little wife at home. Well, that's not me.

I have my mind set on not moving north as much as Culain has his set on getting me there.

Well, first thing when I walk by the livery, I see that nice old Mr. Sinclair, moved in last year just a couple miles uphill of our place, and he's loading up his feed and heading out. He says sure he can give me a ride, so I jump on his rig and off we go, heading south. Out the Saskatchewan highway and up Pretty Valley Road all them miles. I'll be home in time for supper.

But then, as we come around the last curve about a half mile north of our road, I see some folks camped out on the road allowance. Must be Metis people, mix-bloods, as they can't live on the reserves, but then, they don't like the town living neither. These folks here got one of them miners' tents set up and a lean-to with hides drying in the sun, a bunch of stuff strewn about, traps and carcasses and whatever. Looks like they're working on a wood shack too. As we get closer, I see they got a fire pit, a soup kettle hanging on the iron there, a couple old people sitting by the fire and a younger woman, standing, swaying, with a baby about a year on her hip.

And standing behind them, I swear, looks like Vie LaRocque. Well, how could that be? But as the team moves on by, I crane my neck, and sure enough, it is Vie LaRocque. Oh shit! Almost in my back yard.

And who is that woman with the baby? Is he married?

I give a wave, all cheerful and friendly, and he gives back that slow smile and tips his hat. I think about the touch of his hand that time, the heat of it, his cheeky smile and them words he said to me, inviting me to go into the trees with him. My breath is catching just remembering. And all the whole two minutes it takes for Sinclair's old team to mosey on by, Vie LaRocque stands looking right at me, clear-eyed and handsome, not blinking. Brazen.

I make myself turn to the road ahead, but all the way home, feels like a ball of pleasure keeps wrapping around itself deep in my chest, making my heart flip and race and jump and want to dance.

A bunch of the children come running up the dirt road to meet me, and I scoop up my little Cathy, grabbing my baby Charlotte from Mitch's arm as I go, smooching them all, swinging this one, tussling that one's hair. Mother puts on the tea water and I tell her about getting canned, and all the dirty boys that's out there at them rich people's place.

"Ain't that the way of it," she says. "Never mind. We gotta couple months' pay out of 'em anyways."

* * *

Well, now it's coming up to the end of July and we're working hard on them gardens. We got about a acre planted all told, between Mother's and mine. And we got high hopes. There's spuds, corn, carrots, beans, peas, turnips, onions, and pumpkins. And a row of them blue forget-me-not flowers Mother always splurges on, no matter what else she has to do without.

Every day, we're weeding and shoring up rows, watering, and picking off bugs. That's back-breaking work, I'll tell you, getting down on my knees in the dirt, pulling out those little weeds so they can't choke the young plants. Or standing up, swinging that hoe, cutting and swiping at the slivers and dandelions and quack grass, shoring up again, keeping the rows tidy.

What the hell is Vie LaRocque doing living a stone's throw away from here? I mean, we're always glad of neighbours, but that Vie is a strange one. So cheeky and forward, must think he's really something.

But then, come to think of it, he is really something. And would rock a girl good, if he's anything in the real world like how he is in my dreams.

I got them little dresses made for the girls for summer, so now I'm just back to my same old grind. Besides the garden work, I'm making meals, trying to clean up a bit, keeping my kids busy, and putting up with Mitch. That cough of his ain't good. He's been hacking up thick phlegm for a while now.

Mitch tries to be nice in his own ways. I know he likes having me at home. He's very patient with all the children, I must say, and ain't much trouble, just sitting on the bench by the window when he ain't helping with the cooking. The consternating part is his begging me to do my wifely duty the odd time at night. I don't like it, it does nothing for me, but sometimes I do give in, just to be nice, if he's been nice to me in the daytime, by doing some work, like.

What Culain don't know don't have to hurt him.

Between Mitch pawing at me and dreams of Vie LaRocque, I get no sleep at all. I'm in a foul mood this morning, yawning away at the table, snapping at my big girls that the porridge ain't cooked right, can't they even cook porridge. Then Mother yells across that this should be town day for our neighbour Sinclair, did I want to go in with him and pick up some dry goods at McKay's for her?

"I'm comin'!" I yell. Anything but another regular day at this damn boring place.

I go first to the post office, mail that parcel to Beatrice, the little summer dress I made for her when I done them for my girls, some of Mother's date cookies, the licorice allsorts that Bea loves, and a letter I wrote from Mother saying to be a good girl and we'll try to come visit after harvest. Then I go pick up the chicken feed, a can of lard, a bag of sugar, and the hundred pounds of flour Mother needs from McKay's.

But after two trips hauling it all to the livery, turns out that loose back wheel of Sinclair's was because of rot on the axle and a major overhaul is needed before we can go home. McFee's plough and Eichler's buggy is ahead of us though, so Smitty won't get to Sinclair's rig till tomorrow morning. Well, Sinclair says he'll just camp out by his rig tonight, but have I got a place to go? I say I do and go walk down Roaring River Road, south of town, where a bunch of our old neighbours is living.

The Mareses have room for me so I join in with Gladys and the girls putting supper together. Irene is all het up about the dance in town tonight, some of the Metis boys from out Camperville way is playing at the Legion Hall, and she says I got to come too. She says, "Rose, you need to have some fun now and then."

So after we finish our chicken and dumplings, mashed potatoes and young peas, and dill pickles and butter buns—God, it's good to eat real food for a change—us girls get all gussied up. One of the younger girls lends me a grey tweed skirt, which is a bit tight, showing off my curves I think, and a red silk blouse to go with it. We put on lipstick and rouge and powder, and Irene sweeps all my crazy black curls up into a little bun, but with the kinky spirals of hair dangling like a water fall. She stands back to look and smiles big.

"Rosie," she tells me, "you are a knock-out! Anybody didn't know you would never guess you ever had a child. Never mind seven!" Us girls is all giggling and excited and telling each other how pretty we are, and Mrs. Mares yells at us to stop the cackling and get going!

Up at the Legion, the lanterns is lit on stage and some of the Camperville crew's already tuning their fiddles and such. There's that old Michel Beauchamp with his guitar, looks about as old as him, and Mr. Demerais, Grandy Fagnan, and young Joe Chartrand. A few men of different ages, some white, some Indian, are sitting around them on church chairs, with guitars and fiddles, an accordion and a mouth harp, also getting ready to play.

Down here, the blue of the coming evening wafts through the long windows, lighting the rows of wood tables on each side of the dance floor. People young and old mill about or visit at the tables, married ladies and their daughters yacking across the rows as to how the gardens has done, or some new thing in the Eaton's catalogue they can't afford, and who's keeping time with who. A few men are sitting with their families, but most are standing around in clusters at the back of the hall, talking about the crops they put in, or how much *too much* that new John Deere would run you, and how the Grits ain't never going to do nothing good for the farmers.

Children run in and out, little boys taking turns sprinting the length of the hall to the wide-open double doors and then leaping off the top of the outside steps, see who gets the farthest. Little girls in twos and threes promenade around the floor, holding hands, chattering and laughing, some with patent leather shoes clip-clapping and Shirley Temple ringlets bobbing round the napes of their necks.

Single girls sit waiting their chance for a sly-glance at that special boy.

Single men aren't interested in all this, so it seems, only grinning sheepishly when a girl catches their eye, then standing up, sudden and awkward, for no good reason, striding outside, striding back in, back out and back in, finally having to settle on a spot to lean up against the wall, hands shoved into their pants pockets and eyes on the floor, hoping against hope that the music will start and folks will stop looking at them.

Well, the Camperville Boys start it off with some jigs and reels—the "Red River Jig" of course, "Turkey in the Straw," and "Annie's Reel." That gets the juices flowing, everybody up and on their feet. Then they do some cowboy songs and yodeling, "Blue Yodel #9," "The Lovesick Blues," and "The Lonesome Cattle Call." Boy, can that Chartrand kid ever yodel! Well, then they start a bunch more songs everybody knows. "Nobody's Sweetheart," "The Great Speckled Bird," "Georgia on my Mind."

Most all the women and children are dancing, and a few of the young married couples, while a lot of the men tend to dance when they have to and then go disappear outside. There'll be a fire burning out back of the hall where the teams are tied, a couple Fords parked with them, and bottles being passed around. Well, when they start playing the waltzes, all the couples take over the floor, the children groaning and wandering off, girls playing dollies and telling secrets under the tables, boys jumping around out by the steps.

I go sit down too, watching the dancing and the comings and goings, kind of lonesome all of a sudden, missing my own family and my man. And that gets me thinking about my Culain problem again that I don't have no fixing up for. I shake my head, get up, go outside, and walk around back behind the hall. See what's going on out there.

What's going on out there is the fire burning as expected, the guys sharing bottles, the rigs and teams, and over by the edge of the firelight, leaned up against a tree, Vie LaRocque. I skirt the fellows sitting there and walk right up to him, just calm and easy as pie, as if it's what I had planned all along. And he smiles as I come over, shifts his weight and hands me the bottle, as if he'd been expecting me all along.

"Rosie Kelvey," he says.

I take the bottle, swig back a good swig, and wipe my mouth with the back of my hand. The whiskey fire hits me fierce, making me pop open my mouth and bug my eyes for a minute till I get back my breath. Then I blink, shake my head, swallow again, and smile back. "Vie LaRocque," I say.

He chuckles, sliding his arm around my shoulders, and I lean into him, shivering and glad for his warmth in the evening chill. Nobody pays us no mind, they're all laughing and storytelling at the fire. Vie takes another pull at the bottle and hands it to me, and I take another pull and hand it back. My guts is nice and hot, that's truth, though I can see my breath, and my head is getting warm and fuzzy, me and Vie leaning together there like old friends, drinking down that whole bottle of whiskey.

Back behind us is nothing but friendly dark, a sky full of stars, and McCoy's matching team of blacks, whinnering softly, tethered out beside their hay rack with half a load of nice, cozy hay on. Vie steps back, smiling at me with them dark eyes, a tall drink of temptation in boots and dungarees, holding out his hand. "Well, honey legs," he says, "you ready?"

And I am.

The hay is soft and welcome, and the booze has my mouth wet and hungry. Truth be told, I'm wet and hungry everywhere. He comes into me like a tornado. There's nothing but his warm whiskey mouth, his smell of buckskin and hides, him moving strong on me and in me, the rippling, building rhythm of our bodies, and the heaven only this can bring.

Sometime later, I open my eyes and we're cuddled up warm and fine together in the hay, his thick cotton bedroll wrapped around us. I breathe deep the smell of fresh-mown clover and night air. The stars have moved. I wake again and there's just a hint of light, enough so's I can make out his face. Coal black hair, soft and thick, framing his dark features. Untroubled eyes, innocent like a child.

I move gentle and quiet to unwrap myself from him, squatting down for a pee by the wagon wheel, the steam rising, before I hoof it down to Mareses'. The darkness is beginning to open, my head is pretty clear, considering, and I just have time to sneak in the porch and crawl in with the girls on the big feather tick, my cold feet causing moans and complaints in their sleep, before the rooster gets around to waking the house. After eggs and bacon and beans and bread, and helping with chores, I walk up to the livery and Sinclair lets me sleep in his bed roll till his wagon is fixed and we head for home.

What the hell did I do last night? I'm shocked with my own self, might as well say, not even recognizing the me that done them things. That Vie LaRocque, he just caught me off guard, and I was drinking, which I drank way too much, that's a fact. And I just. I just *done things* that I didn't mean. I am not *that kind of woman*.

I know I ain't no Sunday school teacher, what with Mitch and Culain and all. But that don't make me loose or something. It's like, Culain is my man, my mate I guess I'd say, I love him. And Mitch is just, well, just my husband. He lives at my house and loves my children. And it sounds strange, I know, but I always been true to Culain. Well, mostly true. Because I *ain't* that kind of woman. I'm not. I just got this deal going on, with the two men I'm married to in different ways.

And this thing with Vie LaRocque, Holy Moly, this is just crazy. This just cannot happen. I was caught unawares, I let my guard down, and I done wrong. And I ain't never going to do that again. Never. I see Vie LaRocque coming down the street? I will run straight in the other direction.

* * *

Well, Mother is very glad I'm back as my boys have got into a bee hive and covered theirselves in stings that she had to poultice, my baby Charlotte is teething and fussed all night, my other two little girls near school age had tummy aches and was up running to the biffy twice a hour, and then Carly went and had a accident in her sleep so there's sheets need washing. And the arthritis in Mother's fingers is paining her bad today but yet the weeds is taking over the garden.

I jump right in and get to work. I put Mother's Vallee, nine years old, in charge of my kids, and got the twins, now sixteen, doing the shitty diapers and sick clothes. Then we got my big girls Petunia and Margie, along with Mother's Lily, helping Mother with the other clothes, while my Kenneth and James work with me in the garden. It's either hard, back-aching work outside, or inside in the heat, with the kids running back and forth to the well for more water and bringing wood to keep the stove burning hot as hell.

All the while, I got Culain worrying at my mind. I finally decide to tell Mother about how he wants me to move up to Sherridon yet before Christmas. She frowns big and shakes her head. "You got work enough takin' care of all these childern," she says. "But without me and mine to help? And then, which ones of yur kids would go? Pet's got the boyfriend there in town and yur two oldest boys has got places here where they might make some cash soon enough. I s'pose you would jist take the young ones. But then, who's gonna help out mindin' them if you don't have the older ones, like?"

"But, Mother," I tell her. "That ain't even the problem I got. What I'm sayin' is I don't wanna go up there a'tall. It ain't the kids I'm worried about. It's that I don't wanna go a'tall. That's my stickin' point."

She looks at me close. "Well, what about Culain and what he wants?" she says. "Ya think he's gonna hang around f'rever while ya live with another man, like a kid, jist happy that yur lightin' his nights now and then?"

I'm kind of shocked she's saying this, truth be told. I mean, we both know she knows what me and Culain's situation is. But to say it? I feel kind of mad and cornered here. But yet, she keeps on going.

"Culain's a man," she tells me, pouring the big pot of steaming water into the wash tub. "He's more of a man than most of 'em we known." Mitch is sitting in the dirt by the house, trying to light a smoke in the wind with his one good hand and taking four tries before he gets it. "You can't expect a man like Culain Kirk to jist keep waitin' and puttin' up with a nowhere sichee-ashun." She pats my hand. "Rose, you gotta think what yur doin' here. What means more to ya? Keepin' up yur fun and games? Or the one thing in yur life that will see ya through? Yur actual helpmate, like. Culain."

I just feel consternated with it all, knowing Mother is right but yet, not having no plans to go in the way she's pointing. I grab the hoe and head for the garden, leaving her to get the trousers load done without me. I'm whacking away at the weeds between the corn stalks. I see Jimmy over by the well, teasing his sister, and I screech at him to damn well quit it! I'm tired of his bullshit! He gives me a sneer, mumbling that *he wasn't!* So I go stomping over and smack him one, even though he throws his hand up and tries to shield me, but I grab his arm and give it to him on the arse twice as bad.

Then after supper, I say I'm going to catch a ride into town tomorrow if anyone's driving by, need a break from this bullshit. Mitch starts griping me that I'm away more than I'm home, seems like, ever since I come back from Henry's, and how the little kids don't never seem to see me and I don't rock them no more nor even seem to want to hold the baby.

I tell him that ain't true. I go over and snatch my baby Charlotte out of his arm, but then she starts to scream, bending her little body away from me, reaching out to Mitch. The more I try to cuddle her and jiggle her, the more she just screeches and wails for Mitch.

"Damn you, Mitch!" I tell him. "Take 'er then!" and throw her down into Mitch's arm.

"Jesus, Rose!" he yells. But he caught her okay, don't know why he's making such a fuss.

I throw on my dirty work coat and go clomping outside even though it's nearly dusk and the wind is howling harsh tonight. Smells like more rain coming.

I want Culain to come home, yet I don't want him to ever come. Because that will mean a big fight and him going away mad and hurt by me. Either that, or else me having to give up all I got and leave home and go to that cold, rocky place where he's living.

I go lean my back up against Mother's house on the chimney side, craving the warmth that barely seeps through, and wondering why the hell a grown woman would stand alone, shivering and bawling in the cold, when there's not one but two warm houses she could be sitting in, being happy.

It's around noon the next day that I hear wagon wheels squeaking and squawking their way down the road. I run, throw on my last clean dress, yell at Vallee to help Mitch with the kids, and take off.

I can hear Mother yelling from her stoop, "Rose! Rose! What the hell? Rose! We need ya here!" But I pretend I don't hear nothing.

It's not Sinclair though, but old Mr. and Mrs. Henshell on their way to Bowsman to visit their grandchildren. As we head down around the big curve, there in the shanty yard by the fire are the old folks and Vie LaRocque. He stops what he's doing to watch me, smiling smooth and pretty. I can't help but smile a little. He picks up a handsaw, says something to the people, and comes out towards us, swinging along beside the team on the path at the edge of the road. He waves to the Henshells and they call out their hellos. As we pass him by, I crane my neck around. He stops still, plants his feet, and points with his lips in the Indian way towards the bush, showing me where he's going. He grins me on, just cheeky and playful, points again with his finger, then disappears onto a path in the tree line.

I ain't comin'.

But then I am. "Stop!" I yell to the old fellow. "Hold on! Whoa!"

I tell them I just remembered something I forgot and that I got to go back home now. They're kind of concerned and Mr. Henshell asks if I need him to drive me back up to get it, whatever I forgot, as they don't mind waiting for me. But I say, "No, that's okay. Thanks for yur kindness, but I jist gotta… I gotta do somethin'. Thanks agin."

They pull up and I get out and start walking back, as if I'm going home. But then, when they turn back towards the valley, I sprint over into the bush on Vie's side.

I go into the trees and follow where he went. I'm pretty deep in and ain't seen him yet, but I ain't scared. I just lean up against a young poplar and wait. I hear him when he steps up behind me and slides his arms around my waist. I'm aching for it and he ain't shy. I turn my head to the side and let him kiss me. We get to necking up a storm, his hands feeling good on the front of me, getting my blouse open and gripping my titties, washing them all around with his big hands. Somehow, he has my skirt up too, at the back, and is grinding hisself into me, half-lifting me off the ground. I have to grip the tree with my right hand to steady myself while I'm off-kilter, dying for his mouth on mine. I just want him in me now and try to flip around so we can get at it on the ground, but instead, he's got his other hand down my panties from the front and is rubbing that spot, the lady's joy spot. My God, it's working just like that, and I'm bucking and joyful, going on and on with just his hand in front and his thing grinding into me behind through my clothes. Only after it finishes off does he let me turn. While I'm still dazed there, panting and leaning back on the tree, he's got my bottoms off, my legs spread around him, and my arse against the tree. He's come into me still standing and is humping me hard and fast, me getting my joy over and over and both of us getting the pleasure at the end.

Up the road aways, I step off and go wash up in the crick, my nose telling me I need it bad. "Who's that woman at the campsite with the baby?" I asked him. "You got a wife that's gonna try and scalp me now?" He just grinned and said it was his niece, Margaret Mary.

Mother is surprised to see me loping back in the yard, she's pretty mad I went to begin with, but then I hug her up and tell her I'm sorry and explain about how I come back because I realized how much she needed me, and the kids needed me. I'm in a lot better spirits now, happy with my children. I get a lot of the work done and even make biscuits for Mitch's supper.

I wind up going down there three more times in the week. I don't know what I'm doing nor why. I just know my whole life feels tough and dull and uncertain. Except for Vie LaRocque, who gives me something wild and satisfying. Vie LaRocque, that I did not intend but that ain't like nothing I ever known before.

I do feel wrong about Culain, how I'm sneaking around on him. Each time I walk back up the road, I think I better stop this. I better stop because what if Culain found out? But yet, Culain ain't here. And Vie LaRocque is. And I just can't see giving this up. Not right now anyways. Alls I got besides this is kids and dirt and worries and barely making ends meet. And Culain forcing my hand. So every waking minute, all I think of is Vie LaRocque, and nothing else but a needful yearning to go Tom-catting down the road.

This here *seven year ache* is in full swing.

We got sort of a regular deal, I guess you'd say. He sees me walking by on the road, I get around the big curve and cut into the bush. It ain't a long wait and then comes heaven.

Once, when we was finished our fun, me sitting on a moss bed by the Roaring River and him having a smoke, his niece come walking through, Margaret Mary. She talked to him in the Indian language, he answered, and she smiled her strange quiet smile, like a cat in the sun, and said some words back. Then they both laughed loudly and she went on her way.

"What did she say?" I frown.

"Oh nothin'," he chuckles. "Jist that you got me all sweaty. She said, 'Watch out uncle, them white women will work ya to death.'"

I do not like it nor find it funny. But what do I care what she thinks? Margaret Mary LaRocque ain't nothing to me. Still, it is irksome when she quits what she's doing and stands watching while I walk by on the road. Feels like she ain't looking at me, but into me. Just quiet, smiling to herself, knowing everything.

* * *

I had a upsetting dream last night. There was a big room with a bunch of wooden tables and skinny chairs and a girl at one end of the tables all alone. From behind, I thought it was Eileen, and the gladness welled up in me. I reached out my hand to her shoulder, saying "Sissy, oh sissy!" But she turned and it was Beatrice instead, looking mad and scared and crazy all at the same time. She threw the table over, leaped up on the chair, and flipped her dress right up to her chin showing her dirty legs, dirty underwear, and everything else. "You done this! You done this!" she screeched at me. On her tummy was a horrible gash, red puckered with white edges, thick and angry-looking. And as I stared, it had a movement to it, like it was a live thing, growing and writhing and getting bigger.

I lurch up out of bed feeling sick, like actual sick, rush outside, and puke off the back step. I been having this in the mornings all week and I ain't bled this month at all. This thing with Vie LaRocque was a fling and it's over. I ain't going down to the big curve no more.

And Culain should be home in a week, which is lucky, because then if a baby should happen to be coming, it will for sure be his.

Chapter 7

Six Men For Every Girl

(1939, Fall)

The fourth of September, I'll never forget. Me and Mother was out in the garden picking beans, another good crop, and here come Trooper Roaring Kirk, tearing up the road, white T-shirt sweated through and dust puffing in and out the holes in his boots. Prime Minister McKenzie-King declared war on Germany!

"War?" I say, glancing over to Mother and, sure enough, her brow is knit. I know what she's thinking. War. Men dying. Kenny. I step over, put the flat of my hand on her back, and give her my eyes. She purses her lips and we turn back to Trooper.

He's all het up about it. How he'd enlist in a minute, if only he could. I believe he's all of sixteen years old, our young Troop. But he says all the fellows is going and man, is he itching for it! Folks in town been talking about the troubles in Europe all summer. Seemed like there was a fight brewing and now here it is.

"You plannin' to save us all from Old Hitler, Troop?" I tease. "Give yur all for God 'n Country? Take the battle over there?"

"Nah," he grins, eyes blue as spring rain. "Me, what I want is the three square meals a day. Three squares, new pair a boots, and a snappy uniform." He jerks to attention like a soldier, chest puffed out and face all exaggerated serious. Salutes just as if he knows what he's doing, then relaxes down. "And if I should happen to pick off a few Germans while I'm at it..." he fires off a couple rounds with a make-believe rifle like the boy he is, "... well then, that will be a bargain!"

That afternoon, me and Mother tries to figure out who dear to us might have to go. Praying they *don't*, matter of fact. Last war Canada was at, supposed to be the *War to end all wars*, took my Poppa from us. Took thousands of men, all somebody's daddies or husbands or sons. So me and Mother, we ain't too crazy about men going to war. Ain't innocent about what it really means, I suppose I'd say.

Mother says Kenny is coming up to thirty-two at Christmas, that seems a might old to be going to war. Wouldn't they want the younger fellas? Our Poppa was twenty-seven when he died and yet, Kenny's older than that now. I say I don't know. Thing is, Kenny's a big, healthy man, strong from working hard down in the mine. I figure Kenny might be just the type they'd want but I don't say so to Mother. She's already gone quiet and worried-looking.

After Kenny, Culain is first on my worry list. Junior is too young, same age as Trooper, so we don't have to worry about him just yet. And Vallee's still a kid. Mitch, of course, has already done his duty for the country—and missing body parts to prove it. But Culain, what if he was called up?

Mother is plain pale and distractible for days. "They gonna take 'im! Gonna take my boy!" I hear her muttering to herself. "I jist know it. Same way they took 'is daddy!"

End of the month on town day, me and Junior drive in for supplies and mail. Going around the big curve, I keep my eyes looking straight ahead and away from that shanty. I did go down there that one time in the summer, I admit, but I'm trying very hard to be good these days. Specially now that I got a bun in the oven, which Culain is very happy about. Should be due sometime in May.

The war is all the talk in town, men falling over theirselves to get in the army. There's government papers nailed up on the post office wall. Army only wants the best, I guess, and is mainly concerned about sorting out the ones that don't deserve to go. Says the men must be between eighteen and thirty-two, in the prime of health, with no physical or mental defects. Okay, so Kenny's right on the edge of their top age. Maybe that's too close and they'll let him pass?

There's a long list of these "disqualifying defects" wrote down underneath. I notice right away that rheumatic fever is a show-stopper. Culain had that as a child and Doc told him it give a murmur to his heart, so I figure that means Culain's out of the running. Which I know will be irksome to him, but it gives me a big old sigh. Flat feet is another one, and Junior has flat feet, so if the war should happen to last the next two years, he'll be off the hook. How can you march thirty miles a day with flat feet? So that just leaves us the main one to worry about. Kenny.

There's a letter from Culain up at Sherridon and I take it with me to the Winnipeg Café to read while Junior goes to get the feed. When I'm sitting in the booth, my nice hot tea with milk and my nice slice of cherry pie in front of me, I open it. I tuck the small wad of cash into my big skirt pocket, smiling. *Thank you, my darlin'!* My older kids will definitely have boots for their feet this winter.

Then I read the letter. He says he's doing good, the work is hard, but he's got a line on a nice little house not far from Main Street with five rooms all told that will be open in January. A bit pricey, he says, but it will be worth it when he brings me and "our family" home with him. He says he's going to work all through Christmas, saving every cent, then he'll be coming to get me and the children at New Year's, and for me to be packed and ready to go.

Well, shit! Shouldn't have read it till after I had a chance to enjoy my pie. I been trying my damnedest to stave this thing off, about me moving north. Knowing that when Culain sets his mind to something, he's like a dog with meat. Get your hand in there and you'll get bit.

At least he ain't going to war, so there's that. Thank God for rheumatic fever.

On the Tuesday, old Mr. Sinclair stops by on his way from town so we all sit there under the willow and have a cup of tea together. He's what you call a confirmed bachelor, that one, and a mighty good neighbour.

Well, he's a reading man, Old Sinclair, orders in the newspapers from far and away, and reads every page of every one of them. Very educated. He goes to explaining the war now, all the reasons that caused it and which countries is on which side and such. Real interesting stuff. So then, Mother mentions about Kenny, wondering whether he'll get called up. And the old man explains that mining is considered what you call "essential services" just like the police and doctors, so men who work mining don't get conscripted. Because their work towards the war is needed here.

Mother's jaw drops. "So Kenny won't hafta go then!"

"Prob'ly not," Sinclair says. "Not if he's workin' at the mine and don't wanna go."

"Hallelujah!" Mother sings, grabbing my arm and we whirl each other around in the dirt, me yelling too. Tears of joy is rolling down Mother's cheeks.

"Yippy!" my little guys chime in, jumping and dancing and wrestling about. "Yip-yip!" they sing, like a bunch of little coyote pups. I don't think they know what we're celebrating, but anyways.

Oh Lord, what a relief! Because sure as shit, being one of us, if Kenny was to go to war, he'd get killed. That's our life, and no two ways about it.

Well then, the week after, Trooper Kirk comes up again. He's hired-handing for Goodales, a mile down the road past LaRocques, and he's still on about enlisting. "Gonna drive me a tank, that's what. Full metal tank that no bullet can pierce. Just think of it! A have-nothin' Kirk boy from Swan River, Manitoba, drivin' a tank! Yessir, there's the ticket!"

"Ah, Troop," I tell him, "everbody knows you ain't old enough. You gotta wait a few more years." Ain't nobody in this valley getting in the army without Doc True's say-so. And Doc knows as well as anyone that Trooper Roaring Kirk is the boy born on the banks of the Roaring River in the flood of '23 when Elvie couldn't make it to town on the buckboard.

Trooper smooths back his blond hair and twinkles them blue eyes. "Can't wait too long," he says. "Folks is sayin' the war'll be over by Christmas. Gotta get in there, not now but right now! And me, I got a plan how I'm gonna do it."

But we keep teasing. This big plan now, what is it? Is he going to wear a mask to his attestation? Put on stilts and a funny nose? But he just grins. "Never you mind," he tells us, faking all persnickety-like. "I will get in that army, come hell or high water. And not in two years neither."

* * *

By the end of the week, I'm antsy and mean, yelling at the kids when they come whining at me while I'm working in the garden. What the hell am I going to do about Culain? I keep thinking I'm holding him off till he changes his mind but now, here he's renting a house. *You are bringing this thing to a head, Culain Kirk! Which one of us is going to win?*

It actually is getting to me, worrying at my mind day and night, making me feel cornered and trapped. And having to do without is getting to me too, specially with a whole lot of fun just down the road, ready and willing to make me happy.

Around noon, I see Old Sinclair's buggy in the yard and Mother yells over, "Do ya wanna go to town, get that chicken feed for me?"

"Hell ya!" I yell back. Anything but this damn ugly worthless place.

I get in better spirits on the drive in, as the old fellow is very good company, always funny stories to tell. He starts in on a tale about his old mule, Sara, who always stood behind him when he read the papers in the yard, looking for all the world like she was reading too. She also loved a drink of whiskey, that old girl, so on special occasions, he would pour half a bottle in her trough. Then, he swears, she would dance a two-step around the yard, weaving her head back and forth, with the biggest, goofiest smile plastered on her face. Well, I just laugh and laugh and laugh till I have to make the old man pull over by a willow grove so I don't pee myself.

I got another task, a hard one, to do in town. So after I pick up the chicken feed, I go sit on the steps of the United Church across from the post office with a pencil and writing paper and try to compose my letter to Culain. I sit for long minutes with the pencil ready, just getting more and more fretful and unsure what to write. Then I scribble down some words, cross them out, groan, and tear up the paper. But time is passing, Old Sinclair will be ready to go soon enough, and so I just have to get it done.

Finally, I write down:

> *How are you? I am fine. Kids is fine. Things is offul londsum here. Nice you got a house but Mother don't want me goin nowheres. Mabee I could jist come visit.*
>
> *Yur frend Rose*

I know it probably ain't going to fly, but anyways.

When I mail my letter at the counter, there's one for Mother, wrote in Kenny's beautiful hand, which I stash in my skirt pocket. Going around the big curve, I see Vie LaRocque in the yard hammering together some poles, making a drying rack for hanging meat, I guess. He stops to watch as we go by but I look away, though God knows I'd like nothing better than to jump right down and run over there.

"And now for the *good* news," I announce to Mother in the kitchen, digging down in my big pocket for Kenny's letter.

"Aah, my sonny boy up in Flin Flon!" she beams, snatching the letter. She cradles it between her two hands like always, takes a big smell of it like it was a flower, gives it a kiss, and presses it to her heart. Then she hands it back. "Read."

"Dearest Mother and family," I begin... but then I stop, scanning ahead. And then I read the first few lines over carefully and not out loud.

"What?" Mother says, looking alarmed. "Rose?"

"Jist a minute, Mother," I say, my butt finding the bench by the window. "I jist wanta..." One page, hand-written, just a few lines, which I read silently all the way through.

Mother has slumped down into the chair across from me and I slowly bring my eyes up to hers. Her jaw drops like a iron oven door. "No!" she argues. "He's not! He can't be! Why would he?"

"Mother," I say. "It's not… It don't mean… He jist…"

"But he don't *hafta*!" she bawls at me. "Old Sinclair even said, he don't *hafta* go!"

My brother has enlisted. He says he's going to try for the Royal Canadian Engineers as his mining experience, explosives work, should stand him in good stead. He says he knows she'll worry but not to worry, he'll be fine, he always has been, hasn't he? He says he loves her and he'll see us all in a month, on his way south for basic training out of Shilo. He signs, *Yur everlovin son.*

I read it all aloud and Mother sits quiet, shaking her head, face caved in and looking dazed. "Mother, he'll be alright, I'm sure. Mother, you know Kenny, he's… he's tough. He's gonna make it."

"But he don't *hafta*!" she keeps repeating, palms held out like a plea, eyes glassy, face a torment of disbelief and sorrow. "He don't even *hafta*!"

* * *

Well, the days continue crazy with work, work, work getting the gardens harvested. We already been glorying in peas and beans, cucumbers and beautiful corn on the cob, and hills upon hills of new potatoes. Now we're finishing the carrots, dill weed, rhubarb, turnips, radishes and onions, and all that colourful winter squash. The canning and pickling takes over our days, the house sweltering with steam from the canning tubs, the stove kept burning hot. There's clothes to scrub on the washboard, water and wood to bring in, lots of heavy lifting, and Mitch to be put up with. There's no end of kids to be took care of, and lots of noise and commotion, which ain't that bad, kids is kids, and work is work. Apart from that, there's just the sleepless nights and worry.

I can't take a day away to go to town for more pickling spices, so the next time we hear a wagon on the road, I run out and ask Old Sinclair to pick some up for me, and put them on our bill at McKay's. When he drops them off at supper time, he's also picked up our mail and there's a skinny little letter from Culain.

All it says is: *Rose. No visit. I told yuu. Git redy to moov. C Kirk*

Shit! I don't know what the hell is going to happen when he comes home. I'm mad at him for pressing me but I also miss him something terrible. I'm lonesome for him and want him to come, but yet I dread it. I know there's going to be a hullabaloo.

And my nights has gone sour. Trooper Kirk told us before about a silent film he seen of Hitler and his Nazi soldiers. He showed us how ridiculous they look, doing this thing called a goosestep, where they throw their legs out straight and high, looking very serious but not very practical. All the thousands of them swinging on by the Fuhrer, row upon row, with their strange, pointy helmets and all their gear, doing their silly-looking march. It seemed so funny at the time and Trooper looked so comical, we laughed and laughed.

Now I see them in my dreams, Nazi soldiers, with their rifles and their bayonets, going after my brother. He's running and running in some barren place and all them Nazis is after him, marching fast and queer, and they catch him, and he's on the ground, hands out and terrified, and they stick him, they stick him, they stick him over and over . . . I'm so terrified I wake myself, crying in my sleep, and lay there dazed in our dark little shack, heart beating fast, not knowing what is real.

Mother is in a state. Quiet and distractible, yet grouchy as hell, barking orders and smacking the boys anytime they backtalk her. The two of us is sitting by the house one evening, watching the children run, and she says, "He's followin' his daddy, that's what. Gonna follow his daddy to Europe and death."

"No, no," I tell her.

Another time, we're in the kitchen and she's happy as a lark, talking all about when Kenny comes home. He's just coming through, really, on his way to basic training, but yet Mother says *coming home* like he's coming home to stay. She's going to kill that big Tom turkey, she says, bring in all the best from the garden, the new potatoes, the pumpkins, everything, and what a meal we'll have. And how Kenny will sleep in her big bed while she crawls in with the twins, that's no problem. How she's going to fix up fancy collars on the girls' old best dresses, the plaid ones, for going to meet their brother at the train. And how all the folks will come, give him their best regards. The Kirks will come and the Mareses and Lukenbills, everybody will come. The boys will bring their fiddles and guitars. What a lark it will be when Kenny comes home.

And she says she'll tell him, he'll have to listen because she'll tell him. "Kenny!" she'll say, "when yur over there, you mind, that whole war ain't yurs to win or lose. You jist take 'er easy." And "Kenny!" she'll say, "jist, please, son! Jist, don't take chances when ya don't hafta..."

She trails off and when I look, she's disappeared out through the porch. I search all over the yard and finally find her out back of the barn, arse in the dirt up against the wall, shoulders hunched up and her whole self all squeezed tight, trying to hold it in.

I don't say nothing, just go over and sit there with her. Sharing the pain, like. In a while, she sighs and raises her head, wipes her wet cheeks with the heels of her dirty palms, and starts to get up.

I get up too and I tell her, "Everthin's gonna be alright, Mother, I'm sure. He's strong, Mother, and he's smart, and he knows how to fight. He's gonna make it!"

But I ain't sure of that at all. Them dirty Nazis, hundreds upon hundreds of them, goosestepping to beat hell, keep coming for my brother in my dreams.

On the Wednesday night, I wake myself up, crying again. I lay a long time, staring up. Only two more days till Kenny comes home and that is a occasion that cannot end happy. It's only a stopover and then he'll go. That's what he's coming for, just to go away, die in Europe probably, and never be seen no more.

The grey light is beginning in the shack and all I can make out is the lump of Mitch, with his wrong-shaped shoulder, on the other side of my youngest two. There's a ache in me here that these cold tears ain't shaking. A hollow pain at these scary days to come, a wish for hope when there ain't no hope at all, just a terrible feeling of dread that I can't move nor shake.

When I finally sleep again, I dream he's running and running in the strange, ruined land, and the Nazis are marching, the bayonets stabbing, the terror in his eyes. But it ain't Kenny, the man is darker and different than Kenny. And I'm yelling "Poppa!" I'm crying and sobbing, "Poppa! Poppa!"

I come awake and shove my face into the pillow, teeth gritted, got to drive the terror back so the whole house don't hear and think me a scared little kid.

* * *

Well, today is the day, the big day we waited for. The day my brother comes home on his way to the war.

I been over at Mother's helping to get ready since long before the chickens was up. She's killed her best gander and her biggest drake too. We got them stuffed and ready for the oven, we'll get the potatoes and carrots and onions on for supper when we all come back. She's got the matrimonial square and a nice spice cake baked and hidden back somewheres. For Kenny's noon dinner, we done up a big batch of potato salad and sliced three loaves of bread and that beautiful ham she cooked yesterday, and they are wrapped in tea towels and shoved into a clean pail to take along. Mother says that boy will be hungry after the long train ride, so we'll leave the team and rig in that big field down the track aways, the one by Mrs. Lukenbill's. We can all have a nice picnic there together, and Kenny can kind of hold court, she says, visit with all our neighbours that has moved to town since he knew them. Lukenbills, Kirks, Mareses, and such.

My God, the children was crying last night, actual crying, and so was I, damn near, as we could smell all them things cooking, so beautiful and mouthwatering, but knew Mother would slice your fingers off if you tried to sneak a bite. "Never mind," she said, "yuz all will have yur fill tomorrow when Uncle Kenny comes home!"

My little ones is staying with Mitch, but the older ones will come on the wagon with me, Mother, the twins, Mother's Vallee, and my sister Lily. Kenny's train arrives at noon. We got about as gussied up as we ever have, the boys with their hair slicked back, their dungaree britches hitched up, and their cleanest shirts tucked in. We comb out all the girls' hair that we rag curled last night, my three big girls in their best calico dresses, which is mostly too small or too big, a little faded from being handed down and frayed at the hems. Pansy and Tansy's best ain't no better, really, but the new lace collars Mother sewed on is very fancy and they're excited as hell about how pretty they look and how they're going to the train to see their big brother, Kenny.

"Me-me butter do-dur! Me-me butter do-dur!" one of them keeps telling the other children.

"Yes, I know he's a soldier," Margie tells them. "And he might be yur brother, but he's also my uncle, ya know!"

Mother is wearing a dress for the occasion too and it, like most we got, is looking worse for wear. Used to be white with bright red flowers in the skirt, back years ago when she sewed it. Now them flowers is faded. But she has tore some fabric off a old sheet, still white, wove it in with a strip of deep red lace, and sewed it into a kind of scarf, which she has wrapped around her head. Almost looks like fashion. She even lets me put a little lipstick on her.

I stand back to see how she looks. Mother will be fifty next summer and looking every year of it. Her squat little body is thick and square and muscled like a man, yet lumpy and off-seeming where she's a woman. Her skin is wrinkled and dull from all the years of hard work in sun and snow. Lots of laugh lines though, and in them steel blue eyes, the pain of many losses and worries these many years we travelled life together. And now this greatest fear, a deeper shadow yet.

I smile and tell her, "Yur beautiful, Momma." Because she is. To me, like.

Well, the stuff gets loaded, the children are on the wagon, and we get on our way to town. Again, I make a point to be sitting behind the seat on the wrong side as we go past LaRocques' shanty.

We get to town and go park the rig down Railroad Avenue, tether out the horses in Lukenbills' field, and walk up the tracks a ways to the train station. There's folks already there on the boardwalk and me and Mother stake out a bench on the south side where the kids can run around in the grassy lot behind. There's Mr. and Mrs. Cleaver with their son, Harold, seeing him off today. And don't he look smart in his uniform, smiles from ear to ear and with his dark hair all slicked back. Mr. Cleaver is telling anyone who will listen about his son, how smart he was in school, what a hard worker, what a boon he'll be to the army. Going to be artillery, they think, on account of he's a crack shot. Heading down to Portage la Prairie today, where him and all the other men will be collected by the bus for Shilo.

There's a bunch of other folks arriving too. I see two of them well-muscled, blond Gustersons from down our corner is in uniform and surrounded by a gaggle of folks and kids, all quiet and sad-looking. One of the sons keeps stepping out, looking north up the track, then lighting another smoke, which he keeps flick-flicking way more than is needed.

Well, and here comes Crofter Kirk, second oldest boy in Culain's family, looking dapper in his new uniform. He's brought his mom, Elvie, and Trooper and young Calhoun, and all the sisters. There's our Grace, that was born in the caul, must be about nine or ten now, dark hair spilling over with natural curl, pink-lipped and skin like pearl. They come stand with us while old Charles deals with the team, Crofter very serious and proud, Elvie looking worried, and the kids chattering a mile a minute.

I didn't know Crofter had been taken on. I tell him, "Good for you, Croft." He juts out his jaw, smiles, and winks. And don't Trooper Roaring Kirk look like he could die of envy? Elvie says her third boy, Christian, also tried to join up, but was disqualified on account of low I.Q. I don't know what that is, but he don't seem troubled by it. Must be like the Gout or something, comes and goes with the weather.

Well, here's the train finally. Seems like a snail train as it pulls up, very slow, folks crowding forward to meet it. It's finally stopped and we're trying to look above the heads to see who's getting off. Jeez, there's a twenty-minute stopover before the train leaves, do folks have to be so pushy? Where is my brother? No, that's not him. Don't see him, so I step up into the first car but he ain't there. I come out and lean off the steps, hollering across the heads to Mother, "Do ya see him?" She hollers back no, craning her head. I push my way to the second car, get in, and there's soldiers in the aisles and some sleeping in the seats but none of them is my brother. I step off again, jog down the platform, and step up into the next car.

And there he is, my wonderful brother in his uniform, looking so handsome and fine, but he ain't standing. Instead, he's sitting in a family booth with, I guess it's his wife, Vera, though I've only seen her in a picture. Him and the woman seem to be having words, talking low, and she looks mad. When he sees me, he tells her hush and stands up, looking strange and nervous.

"Rosie," he says, coming over, and I throw my arms around him, holding on for dear life, all teary and trying hard not to cry out loud.

"Ah, come on, Rose, don't blubber now," he teases. But his voice is gentle and he hugs me tight. Then he stands me back, takes the white hanky from his pocket, and wipes my cheeks, which makes me laugh through my tears and I go back to hugging him up.

I tell him Mother's on the platform and wait till he sees the twins, all dolled up, and there's going to be a picnic in town with all the neighbours and wait till he sees the spread Mother's laying out at home and oh my, ain't Vera just the prettiest lady? "Hi Vera," I wave, trying to give her a smile, but she's glaring like she hates me and turning away, now huddled to the window like she needs shielding from mortal danger.

I look up at Kenny, confused, and back at the woman, and back at my brother again.

He glances that way, purses his lips, and shakes his head at me. "Rose," he says. "Rosie, um... I gotta talk to Mother."

He gets thronged on the platform. Mother grabs onto him like a drowning man to the pier, laughing and crying and singing Hallelujah. The twins and Vallee and Lily and all my children crowd around, laughing and hugging him, jumping around, asking questions, telling him everything they can think of that's happy. Puppies, school learnings, and what all we'll be eating now that he's home. Kenny smiles and answers their questions, giving hugs and tussles, but there's a sadness and a stillness to him somehow and I know something ain't right.

Soon as there's a break in the chatter, he says, "Mother." He glances at the train car and I see the woman, still frowning and mad-looking, pull back from the window. "Mother," he says again. "I... Mother, I gotta talk to ya."

She blinks. "What is it, son?"

He leads her around the corner of the station and I follow, telling the kids to go play. He says that he had a big fight with Vera before leaving Flin Flon. He says not to worry about it, it'll be alright, but him and Vera ain't been getting along and she's been talking about taking the children away to her folks in Alberta. They got the two little children that I guess must be left with someone up north. But with him enlisting, he says, Vera promised she would wait for him and they'd try to make a go of it. And now she wants to go with him on this trip. But she don't want to stop over in Swan River for three nights, she wants to stay in Portage in a nice hotel and go to the shops instead before he takes the bus to Shilo.

Mother says, "Well, we'll go talk to 'er."

"No!" Kenny jumps, looking very bashful and like he don't know how to say what he's trying to say. "No, no, Mother. Vera... well, as ya know, Vera has her ways and she ain't... too crazy 'bout my fam'ly." He looks so pained. "I'm sorry to say it, Mother, but... I jist don't wanna make her mad right now. I jist... I need to be able to know my fam'ly, my childern, is gonna be there when I come home. Mother, I need it."

Mother's eyes are glassy, like a kid that's just found out there ain't no Santa Claus. "So..." she asks, "so, ya won't be stayin' over then?"

"I'm sorry, Mother," he tells her. "I know I'm bein' a louse. But. I jist... can't chance... her takin' my childern away."

"No, no," Mother says, without missing a beat. "That's alright, son. No, no. That's alright. Don't ya worry. We'll... well, we'll jist have a even bigger party when ya come home, is all."

My own eyes begin to smart, but then I see Mother, how she's taking the blow and keeping on. I think of Kenny and his little children, and I swallow hard.

So we stand together for about five minutes, my handsome brother, so tall and dark, my little short mother holding onto his one arm, and little short me holding the other, the kids running and laughing, the sun shining warm and bright on a Indian summer day, geese winging their way to someplace better.

The conductor calls, "All aboard!" Then, he calls it again, and the second time, I force myself to let go of my brother's arm, though it tears at my insides. I can see that Mother is trying too. She says, "Goodbye, son. Take care a yurself over there. And come back home to us agin, woncha?" Then she says again, "Come back to us agin, woncha, son?"

And she seems to be trying to let go of his arm but yet, her head is down like a bull and she's still holding on. Finally, Kenny has to pry her fingers off, gentle as possible, and hand her over to me so's he can run and jump up onto the train car as it's moving by.

He leans off, waving, black curls dancing on his forehead, and the train steams and hisses and begins to chug its way south, people shouting and waving, children running and yelling, all noise and commotion.

Our kids stop in their fun, gawking. "Uncle!" they start yelling. "Where's uncle goin'? Uncle? You ain't sposta go!"

"Butter! Butter!" the twins call out, jumping, arms waving above their heads.

The children swarm us with questions. "Shush!" I tell them. "He ain't stayin', that's all. I'll tell yuz later." I'm too busy holding onto Mother, whose legs has purely buckled. She feels so wobbly on my arm, I'm scared she's going to fall.

The caboose is down the track but still in sight, some folks still watching and waving, others heading for their rigs or into town, and the train grows smaller and smaller way off in the distance. There's a man in uniform standing at the back rail, but he ain't Kenny.

We all begin our slow walk back to the wagon now, Mother stumbling and unsteady. I feel the heave of her chest begin. She's been holding hard not to let out. She takes a breath and pushes off from me, striding fast ahead so nobody will see. I let her go. The twins run to try and catch up but she motors on, head down and back heaving, and soon one of them, I think it's Tansy, drops back and takes my hand.

We walk along quiet for a time. "Sitty?" she asks.

"Yes, twin," I say.

"Butter go-way? Butter na-na tay?"

"No, twin," I tell her. "Brother cout'n stay after all. He... he got his times wrong and jist cout'n stay."

We're coming up to the jigger shed and Railroad Avenue. "Sitty?" she asks.

"Yes, twin."

"Me-mommy cwy?" She looks very upset and scared.

"No, no," I tell her, slipping my arm over her shoulder. "Mommy ain't cryin'. She jist has somethin' in her eye, mebbee a bug or a bitta dirt."

"Me-mommy no cwy? Gotta dit?"

"Yeah," I say. "She ain't cryin', hun, don't worry. Mother's strong. Everthin's alright." Pretty soon she gets happy again and skips off to range and wrestle with the other children.

My brother has gone to war. My beautiful, strong brother who left home long ago, and yet has always been there for us. Our one bright hope afar. All we got left of who we once was. We thought we would have him for a little time, just a day or two to feed him again, and laugh and have fun and tell stories, sing songs, and forget that he was going. Stave it off, like. But no. We been robbed of that too.

And will he ever come home again?

We get to our rig and give the children the picnic, and when some of the Lukenbills and Mareses and our other old neighbours show up, we feed them too. It's all pretty quiet and sad. The children is excited all the ways up the mountain, though, knowing there's more good food waiting at home.

But me, I feel I'll die if I have to drive into that same dirty little yard without my brother, with Mother so sad and still, and nothing to look forward to in this world but work and dirt and kids and troubles. So I jump off the wagon on the big curve, see if I can go get me some cheering up from Vie LaRocque, enough to make it through another day.

* * *

It's the second of December, Culain Kirk's birthday, that we hear about something happened to Hope Kirk out at the Henry farm. Turns out she had stayed on for harvest. Mitch's sister Edith was driving out to Cleavers' to pick up eggs and stopped by to tell us. Not sure on the details, but I guess Hope was in the milk shed in the broad daylight, but on her own, and one of the men caught her there, a Henry man, and she couldn't get away.

Oh Hopey! Not Hopey, so gentle and kind.

She had went up to the house after, hurt and crying, and they changed her clothes and sent her on the buckboard back to her mother, saying she had fell down and wouldn't be needed to work no more. Edith says Elvie and the family just wants it kept hush-hush, as they ain't dumb enough to think they could bring it to the authorities. You don't want this kind of thing made general knowledge, as it will always come back on the girl. What would be her chances in life then, known to be defiled and not marriage material?

Dirty bastards.

Me and Mother makes up a little spice cake and drives down to Kirks' place, just to show we're with them, but Hopey is staying on the farm out by Renwer for a bit with her cousins. So we wind up having a private woman chat with Elvie. She says Hope is okay, no broken bones or that, just needs time to get over it. She had her periods right away when she come home, so that's a relief.

While we're sitting there, Conan comes in for a drink of water, favouring his ribs and with a bit of a limp on the left side. His eyes is both blacked. Elvie tells us after he goes out that he went crazy mad out at Henrys', trying to fight them all when he figured out why his sister was crying and being took to town, so he come back without a job, too.

She says some of the boys was talking of sending word up to Culain but she told them not to. Elvie sits quiet with her hands in her lap, the light soft and white from the south window. Mother and me exchange glances, knowing Elvie will be scared that Culain would try to do something to Henrys, which would be more danger to him than them. That scares me too, and though I want so bad to hurt them people for what was done to Hope, I also don't want our men getting in trouble. And the best way to help Hope is probably just to do what Elvie says, protect her reputation by keeping it quiet.

There just ain't no justice in this world. That's why we got to hope for some in the next one.

Two days later, I'm on the road to the big curve when I see Old Sinclair driving up from town. He's got big news—a fire out at the Henry's farm early this morning, with that huge work shed burned to the ground, all their new machines and tractor in it, representing a loss of thousands of dollars. He says the Henrys is claiming the fire was set, someone seen the shadows of men out there just before it went up, and the smell of kerosene heavy in the air. Says the Mounties is out there now, though the likelihood they'll be able to pin it on anybody is low.

Good! Sons of bitches. If you can't lose sleep for your wrong-doing, at least you can lose your damn precious money. Seems like strange timing, though. I wonder if our hot-headed young Conan or Trooper Roaring Kirk or someone went and got some come-uppance for Hope after all? Culain couldn't have made it down this quick, I'm sure, even if he had got the news.

Now that the winter shack is up and they've deserted this miners' tent, me and Vie gets to use it for our visiting. He has me down on all fours like a dog and he curves his belly right down into me, bringing his long arms around my waist so his hand can rub that spot for the lady's joy. My God, this man! He makes me mad with heat from the minute we start till it's over and we're laying there trying to get our breath. I surely am going to miss this.

I'm just fading off into a little nap when I hear voices out by the shack. I got to get going anyways, so I jump up, throw my skirt on, slip my feet into my boots, lift the flap, and duck outside. And there is Culain Kirk, talking to Margaret Mary.

I freeze, knowing Vie is ducked down to come out right behind me, and I shove my right hand back, chopping at the air, praying he gets my gist and stays put.

Culain is handing her a package, which she takes, smiling all sweet and shy.

I feel two things at the very same moment. Joy at seeing my man, Culain. Solid and strong, blue and green plaid jacket, worn work boots, grey newsboy cap.

And terror. *Jesus, am I caught?*

He looks over, sees me, and his jaw drops. "Rose?"

"Culain?" I stand perfectly still to block the view inside the tent, eyeing up Margaret Mary. "What? What is you doin' here?"

"Oh!" he says, stepping back, tipping his hat to her. "Me and Trooper happened to be in town this mornin'. McKays knew these folks was livin' up road from Goodales and asked me to drop off a package from the Eaton's counter. So I brung it up on my way to see ya."

Margaret Mary stares from me to Culain to me again, raises her brow and seems very amused. I give her back a sour look and step forward, sweeping the tarp down firm as I do. Thank God, Vie ain't come out nor made a peep.

I'll make it like me and Margaret Mary is friends, we was visiting, and I'm just leaving. I give her a wave, say, "Well, I best be goin'," and go traipsing onto the path. What a relief, but Culain comes hurrying behind me and I clip along fast towards home so he'll follow.

He catches up and takes my hand, and we swing our hands together up onto the road. I feel relieved and right and happy and so glad to see my man. For about two minutes. Then he starts telling me we'll be moving north a little sooner now, asking how long it'll take me to finish packing, and if I told Mother yet, or Mitch, and are the children excited about their new life that's coming? Telling all cheerful about the Sherridon house. The street it's on and how close it is to the grocery store and the dry goods and the Bingo hall and all, and how many rooms and it comes with a table and two beds.

He finally sees that I ain't saying nothing and asks me what's up. Pretty soon, it's a full-on fight.

And I'm saying, "Why? Why ya hafta make me go? Ya know I don't wanna. Why can't I jist stay here, come visit sometimes? Why ya gotta be so pig-headed? Why?"

He's asking why I'm being like this. He been working for years, doing everything he can, just for me, and this is what we need now. This is how it's got to be.

I purse my lips, there ain't no winning, and we walk along in silence for a while. A dust of snow is beginning in the air, but by the sky, it looks to be only the beginning. A long, cold winter is coming.

At the top of the curve, he stops, facing me, and takes ahold of my two hands. And right there on the road with the sky pale blue and the grey valley floor off in the distance, snowflakes light and hanging in air, he gets down on his knees. I stop dead in my tracks.

He says, "Rose, I'm not livin' like this no more. I'm comin' up to thirty years old. I'm tired of livin' like a lonely bachelor when I got a woman I love and childern. I want to settle down and raise our family. Rosie, please, come with me to Sherridon. Nobody knows ya there. Come live with me, together, as man and wife."

He looks so sincere and I do love him. Maybe I should go with him? I can't help but smile, shaking my head. "Ya big lug," I tell him. "How am I s'posta say no to that?"

"So ya will?" He flings his arms around my hips, hugging onto me like a kid to mother.

"I dit'n say that," I tell him, still chuckling in spite of myself.

I bend so that I can hug him back, and with my nose buried in his cap, I can smell the kerosene. Now I know why he come home early! *Oh Culain, ya came and made right for yur sister.* I'm seized with a great sense of gratitude. For my man Culain, how he's brave and faithful and he fights for his family. I do want to make him happy.

But he's yanked back from me and jumped to his feet. "Jesus!" he hollers.

"What?" I giggle, not understanding. "What happened?"

His eyes are hard. "You smell!" he yells at me, jaw jutted.

"What?"

"You smell like stud," he seethes. "The smell of sex is on ya, Rose Kelvey. Ya bin with a man jist now."

Oh shit!

His eyes cast about over his shoulder, searching. "What the hell..."

"Uh-uh! No, Culain, I wasn't!" *Oh God, I can smell myself.*

He gawks at me, and all I can do is gawk back, flubbing my words. "I… No, no! I, uh…" shaking my head like a ninny. My face feels like it will burst into flame. He turns all the way around, staring back down the curve and over the bush tops to where he has a full view of LaRocques' yard. And Margaret Mary is leaning back against the shack. And with her, laughing, is Vie LaRocque.

His eyes come back to me, bugged and accusing, mouth hard. "Rose?"

"No, Culain. I dit'n!"

He grabs my arms, squeezing hard. "Rose? What was you doin' in that tent?"

"I was not doin' nothin', Culain, I swear! I was jist, jist… I had a girl problem, and she let me use somethin' of hers, that woman there, and… *He* was not there, Culain, that guy, whoever he is, I swear!"

"So *this* is what ya got goin' on? All these years, I'm waitin' and waitin' for ya! And here ya are, sluttin' around with other guys!"

"No, Culain!" I try to tell him. "But I dit'n though!"

I keep trying to tell him that it didn't happen, I *am* true to him, I would *never* cheat on him. Snow is coming faster now, becoming sleet, driving sideways.

"Yur a liar, Rose! Yur lyin'!" he yells, thumbs biting into my arms. "I know that God damn smell! Smells like a female that's just been bred! And I can smell it on you!"

He's in a rage, eyes bright and hard and full of rage. *Culain. Oh dear Culain.*

Knowing I'm in danger of bawling, I grit my teeth and clench hard to stave it off. I churn it up, spin it round, and come back fighting.

"So what if I did?" I screech back wrenching my arms away. "What if I felt like it? What if I did? So what?"

"So what?" he blinks, jaw dropped, forehead bunched up. "Jesus, Rose!"

I yell at him that I don't know what he's doing up in Sherridon neither, probably cheating on me I'm sure, and he left me alone here for years, never thinking that I might be lonely, might be needy. I ain't his doormat, to be walked on and kicked aside.

"You don't own me, Culain Kirk!" I screech in his face. "I ain't yur propity! You don't tell me what to do! I can do whatever I feel like!" Boring my eyes into him, jaw clenched, chin stuck out. "You forget, Culain Kirk, I'm a married woman!" I fling my words at him. "Married by law! And I'm not married to *you*! So if I was cheatin' on anybody, you ain't him! And whoever I wanna spread my legs for, it *ain't yurs to kick on*! You ain't got no *hold on me*!"

Puffs of breath jangle the air between us, snow falling thicker by the minute. It's only as I stop seeing red and the world turns back regular that his face really settles in view. Culain Kirk. Some change having darkened his eyes. Beyond the anger. A dullness or something. Like how a powder will change the look of what's beneath.

Oh my God! What did I say? "I mean. I mean," I stammer. "Not that I *did cheat on ya!* I dit'n, Culain... And there ain't no smell. I musta stepped in somethin', is all."

He sneers. "Ya stepped in somethin' alright."

A cold veil has been pulled across between us.

"Culain," I try to say, feel like I'm calling out across a great distance. "Culain, please!"

He begins to turn, begins to walk. I reach out my hand, but he's walking away. "No, no, no, Culain! Culain, I dit'n mean it! What I said! About goin' with other guys! I dit'n do it though! I jist said I *could*! But I dit'n. Culain!"

He yanks around. "Rose Kelvey, yur a God damn liar!" he growls. "Ya know damn well ya was with that man jist now, shaggin' like a bitch in heat! Admit it! Cuz I ain't gonna stand here and listen to yur God damn lies no more!"

His eyes bore into me, seeing my blackest heart.

My head only shakes and he begins to turn again.

"Okay, Culain! Okay, stop!" I holler. *I don't wanta tell him! I don't wanta! But I gotta!* "Stop! Okay, okay, I'll tell ya."

He comes to a stand, back still to me, but head cocked, like he might be listening. *Oh God! I'm scared for him to know.*

"Okay, okay," I tell him. "Look. I... There was somethin', it was jist a accident though, a mistake. And it only happened once. The guy was comin' around me, and I was jist, I was so lonely without ya. I was confused and missin' ya, and then he give me alcohol, and I, jist, done somethin' and it was wrong, but... I'm done with it now, Culain! It was a mistake, jist somethin' crazy that almost happened. And, it *dit'n mean nothin'!* And it will never happen again. Never!"

He stands turned away, the blue and green plaid of his coat excruciatingly familiar, the valley pale and lovely in the distance, snowflakes falling thick and hard, snow coating his cap, his jacket shoulders, the legs of his trousers.

"A accident?" he says. I strain to hear him, facing away as he is and with the muffling snow. "Well, that's some God damn amazin' kind a accident ya had there, Rose."

Then he charges down the road. "Culain!" I'm trying to grab the edge of his sleeve but he barrels on, dragging me by fits and starts, ice and stones flying up, my fingers not strong enough, losing grip. "No, Culain!"

I try to grab again but I'm off-kilter and upset, I trip, lurching down on my knees on the road. I jump up, flesh bleeding and gravel chafing me, trying to limp after him, "Culain!" I'm calling. "Culain!" He's fast disappearing, gravel flying from his heels, mixing with the fall of snow that swirls and eddies and churns behind him.

I'm winded and bawling and he's too far ahead now. "Culain," I say to the snowy air. He's smaller and dimmer in the distance. I stand shivering, bare legs going numb, cheeks burning with frozen tears, flakes like cotton driving down. He swerves off at the path to Goodales' and is gone.

Damn. Damn it. I turn for home and trudge back up the road to where I can take the shortcut through the bush, feet freezing, arms around my wretched self. Can't stop shaking.

* * *

Only a week till Christmas now, two weeks gone and Culain ain't been here. Winter has hit in earnest. It's been snow, snow, snow, till we've had to start keeping the shovel in the porch so's we can dig our way out of the house for chores in the mornings. We been living in Manitoba most my life, so we're used to deep snow. It just don't usually all drop in a couple weeks' time. That's probably why Culain ain't been here.

I don't blame him for being mad. I know I done wrong. Bad wrong. I just need him to come back and let me make it right. I know it will take time for him to let go his anger, though.

But I'm going to tell him, when he comes back, "Culain, that's it, you was right. I *will go with ya*. I will move to Sherridon with ya, settle down together, you and me. And live that happy life. I'm ready now."

That's what I'm going to tell him. And how sorry I am. So, so sorry, and that I won't do bad things no more.

Hopefully the weather will clear up now for a bit so we can get the oxen out and make a track to the road without worry of it being buried again. Then we can load up the children and go down to town for the Duncan School concert or the Christmas carols at the Pentecostal or something. Just for a little break from the boredom and to get some good food in our gullets.

At least we got that package sent to Beatrice last time we got to town. Some hard candies, date square in a tin, a Christmas picture the children coloured for her, and three pairs of nice clean bloomers that mother sewed. So come hell or high water, at least Beatrice will have a present from home. Whether or not we make it in again.

Well, sure enough, by the afternoon, here comes Old Sinclair driving into our yard, just back up from town. He wishes us a Merry Christmas, and out of his pocket comes a big bag of ribbon candy for us all. Holy Moly, is the kids ever excited!

Best of all, he thought to get Mother's mail and there's a letter from Kenny. Real cheerful letter, about his basic training he's taking down at Shilo there. It's pretty hard for some of the fellows, Kenny says, but for men like him, that's tore down rock ceiling for a day's work, it's a picnic. I like that picture I get in my mind's eye. Kenny having a picnic in a pretty meadow. Maybe that will keep them Nazis out of my dreams.

When I walk the old fellow out to his team, I finally get the chance to ask if he happened to bump into any Kirks in town, Culain or anybody? And he says, yeah, he did see a bunch of Kirks at the Orangeman's Hall, where he went for the Christmas luncheon. "There was Elvie, and her two older daughters and young Grace, and that dark-haired girl. And let's see, Trooper was there, and Conan. And

Culain." He says it was for sure the best meal he had in a month. "My goodness, how them Orange ladies can cook!"

Okay, so Culain ain't been here, but at least he's still around. Ain't gone back north yet. I know. I know I done wrong and deserve punishment for it. Still, I do long to see him and get things back to the right way between him and me. And soon as I get a chance to talk to him, I know he'll come around. I'll tell him it was just the once, it didn't mean nothing, and I'm sorry. And he'll get over his mad and we'll get going on the move.

Sinclair has checked his horses and got the lines straight, and now he heaves hisself up into the seat. He gets his coat collar up, ties his fur hat at the chin and wraps his muffler all around, then throws that big wool blanket over his lap and gets his big hide mitts on. "Oh, by the way," he tells me. "Did yuz know ya lost yur neighbours down here on the big curve? Tarp tent is gone, yard all snowed in, jist the little shanty there, near covered over."

"No, we dit'n know," I say as he gives the reins a flick and them huge blacks start to move along. "Oh well. I'll tell Mother."

I suppose I'm relieved. Definitely glad to be shed of Vie's stupid cousin with her knowing eyes, judging my every step. Though I do admit there's certain things I'll miss about Vie LaRocque, some of his finer qualities, maybe I'd say.

*   *   *

Christmas has come and went and still no Culain. Me and Mother was trying to figure out if we could maybe get a orange or something for each of the children for a present, but the winter come on so fierce, with heavy snow all Christmas week. So the only presents they got was Mother's roast goose and fixings on Christmas day, and a turn at the shovel, digging out the house and barn and our roadway. I dearly hope to get into town for the New Year's dance, maybe me and the older kids could go in and stay at Mareses' or Lukenbills'. I just got to see Culain.

I confess, I'm surprised he didn't come up for Christmas day. Even bad weather never stopped him before. Other years, he would just put on the snow shoes and tramp his way up the mountain, always bringing packages, wild meat for the household and some small trinket for me, maybe a bit of fancy fabric or something from the notions department. Last year, he give me a tiny bottle of *Irish Rose* perfume from the ladies' counter at McKay's.

What a bitter cold year it's turning out to be. Baby, Mother's ox, started some sort of cough a couple weeks back and went off her feed. You could see she was weak, which was a worry, and we couldn't no way come up with money for Doc Oliver, the valley vet, even if there was some way to get him word. So my James and Mother's Vallee was out there for two days, rubbing her down with camphor, trying to keep her warm with them old, moth-eaten tack blankets, and Vallee shovelled snow high as he could around the shed, try to give her more shelter. But it didn't matter. Baby gave up the ghost and is laying stiff out in the tree line till it thaws enough to dig a hole.

She was a good ox, really, a hard worker, good partner to Sunshine, and Mother loved her.

So that was our Merry Christmas.

* * *

Tomorrow being New Year's Day, I *will* see Culain Kirk, come hell or high water. He's bound to be heading north again soon and I'm determined to see him before he leaves. He's stayed away too long. And if he won't come to me, then I'll go to him. I got to tell him that I've learned my lesson. I ain't too proud to admit my mistakes and be the first to say sorry. Surely to goodness, he'll listen to reason.

We're just finishing the dinner dishes when the dogs are barking, I look out the window and it's Kirks' rig coming up the lane. *Hallelujah!* I throw on my coat and run out to wave them in. The team has jingle bells still attached to their halter, and I laugh. "Well, that's merry!"

But then I see Culain ain't with them. There's Hope, and her sister Faith, and young Grace, nut brown hair all natural curls framing her face under a big gold hood, cheeks like alabaster. Christian, being the oldest boy left at home, is their driver. The girls all jump down, but then they seem to hesitate, all bunching up over by the rig.

"Well, come on in!" I yell over. "Before we all catch a chill!"

Hope comes first, but instead of going in, she comes to a stand in front of me, the others still holding back. My Gawd, she seems pale and nervous, and I think, maybe something else happened with her troubles out at Henry's farm. But then, why would she make the trip all the way up here?

"What's goin' on?" I ask, joking. "Somebody die?"

She don't even smile, just takes my arms gentle-like, looking very tender in my eyes. "Rose," she says, "ya know how much we love ya. You was our good neighbour for many years. And you're fam'ly. So we wanted to come and tell ya ourselves." Faith and Grace have gathered round a bit, but also seeming nervous, like something's wrong.

"Oh no!" I stare. "What happened? *Did* somebody die? Where's Culain?"

"My brother," Hope says plainly, "got married yesterday."

"What?" I say. "Which brother?" Conan and Trooper's too young, Crofter's gone to war, and Christian is standing right there with the team.

"My brother," she says again. "Yur, yur..." She leaves off, shrugging, and I feel her hands holding firm on the outsides of my arms as the ringing begins in my ears.

"What?" I tell her. "But... but, who got married?"

Who got married?

"My brother. Culain. And Rosie, I want ya to know and never forget that we love ya and we love yur childern, all of 'em, and you're still our fam'ly."

I gawk. Her words don't make sense. And this ringing, ringing in my ears. Her brother did something. But I can't figure out which brother. I know something terrible has happened but I can't figure out what. "What d'ya mean?" I squint, backing away. "Who did?"

"Culain," she says. "Rosie, Culain got married yesterday."

Nooooooo!

Somehow, I seem to be half-laying against the outside window, my legs buckled under me, head against the window sill, hurting, and snow up my back. The sky is far and cold blue above me.

Mother is here and taking charge. "Grab 'er there! Lily, take 'er feet! Watch 'er head now!" My view has changed to the grey slats in the kitchen ceiling, then I'm tipped and sitting, with hands holding me up, at the table. And I sort of come around, sitting on a chair, someone pressing water to my lips.

Culain Kirk got married.

There's commotion all around me, someone patting my hand, Mother giving me tea. And it's so strange, like I'm watching it all from far off, familiar people having a visit, like watching a play. Regular life. Folks chatting about the weather, and how their Christmas was, and who's come down sick, what with all the cold weather, and how we doctored Baby.

I want to ask something but I can't remember what so I just sit, that ringing sound loud in my ears, empty space before me, feeling like I ain't even here.

Culain Kirk got married.

And I wanted to ask something.

At some point, the Kirks start getting up out of chairs, putting their duds on, going towards the door, and I look over slow, finally remembering what I wanted to ask.

"Hopey?" I say.

"Yes, honey?"

"Who did he marry?"

Faith pipes up, all breathless, like she's telling a funny story, "She was kind of a old neighbour a yurs, actually, a while back. She's a Metis girl. Young but she already has the one baby and my brother says she's a great girl. And she's got two first names, can ya imagine? That's a Catholic thing, I guess."

"What?" I tell them, "What?"

The others are trying to shush her but Faith keeps on. "And she's quiet, very good company, Culain says, but then she likes to laugh and dance and have fun. A great girl! Gosh, she makes my brother happy. And ya shoulda seen how pretty she looked in my mother's wedding dress!"

"Faith, shush!" Hope tells her direct. Then to me, "Margaret Mary LaRocque, I guess was her name, but she's our new sister now. Mrs. Culain Kirk."

I'm at the table. Day moves, light changes, and I sit. The north wind picks up, howling and screeching around the house, bringing five more inches of snow. The boys go in and out with their chores, snow caking their faces and coats and pant legs, the girls do dishes and floors and meals and sit together on beds, chattering in play. Mother brings more tea, watching over me, like. She puts butter and a big lardy piece of goose on a thick slab of bread, salt and pepper, and feeds it to me, like nursing a sick child.

"Never mind, my girl," she tells me, patting my hand. "You'll be alright."

But memories and moments go round and round my head, light fading at the window, cold and more cold coming down, that strange ringing in my ears going on and on and on.

Guess there ain't no need to go to town in the morning.

Culain Kirk got married.

* * *

February, 1940. Been cold and snow and howling wind, not relenting, the better part of two months. No relief. So bitter cold last week, the well froze up, couldn't even get water for the animals. Had to wrap ropes around Mother's Vallee and my James and hoist them down there with a pick axe and a hatchet, get them to chip and gouge away at that thick layer of ice cover, just so's we'd be able to keep a patch of water clear again with the pail, like regular.

No wonder our one lonesome ox, Sunshine, started failing. Wouldn't eat, wouldn't rouse, just stood in the dark back of her stall, head drooped, waiting to go. Dying of heartbreak as she's lost her one true love, Mother said, but she made up a big pail of poultice, still steaming, went out, slathered it over her where the liver is, and tore up her oldest cotton sheet to wrap that warm gunky healing on around Sunshine's slats. She slept out there with the old girl the last night, shivering in the straw in her coat and boots and a old blanket threw over.

They're laying out there together now, Sunshine and Baby, on their sides, frozen legs sticking out, like two toppled snow statues, waiting for spring and the thaw. If that ever comes.

Now how are we going to get around? Ride with our neighbours, I suppose.

And Mitch is not good. Coughing up thick phlegm these past months, now with blood in it. Doc figures it's the consumption and has wrote a letter to the sanitarium down at Ninette, saying he needs to be admitted. But where would we find the money to get him there? And then, he does help out with the children a fair bit so if he goes, it'll be more work for the girls. I suppose Mitch is going to be the next to die, just to make things harder for us.

I'm feeling so lost and hopeless, like the wind has been knocked out of my life. I ain't been sleeping, nor eating, don't even feel like yelling at the children, keeping them in line. This baby I'm carrying is due in a couple months, yet I ain't hardly gaining weight.

I seen Culain Kirk twice in town, always with the woman. First time was at McKay's, down the fabric aisle. She was looking through the boxes of cottons and ginghams, him holding her little kid. I almost reached out my hand to touch him, his plaid colours so warm and familiar, but yet, here he was with her. Like a strange hurtful dream. I turned on my heel and ran.

Second time, I walked into the Legion and they was dancing together, Culain smiling proud, and her, cheek against his shoulder, eyes shy. Don't know why that pained me so. But I walked out and went down to the Mares's to wait for Mother. Losing at Solitaire hour upon hour, crying there alone in someone else's empty house.

Me and Culain could never dance together in public.

* * *

March. Supposed to be spring coming, yet it don't feel like spring coming. For a couple days there, it looked like the melt was trying to start, mud and brown grasses showing in patches, but then it froze solid, winds howling, our bones cracking with cold, and again we're buried in snow.

After our dinner at noon one day, I take another tub of clothes from the washboard to the clothesline and I'm fighting with the wind there, trying to get them pinned up before my fingers freeze purely off, and here I see the Mares's rig coming up the lane. Mother Mares goes into the house for a cup of tea with my mom but Norma comes over, helps me finish the pinning, and we sit back in the nook between the porch and the house on straw bales to visit, cuddled in together against the wind.

They've just come back from town and she starts telling about all the goings-on. It's busy, busy in there, store goods selling like hot cakes. Lots of men passing through, what with them in uniform heading south for basic training, and throngs of others heading north for the mines, which, as Old Sinclair said, is part of the war industry. And so many of the union men have enlisted, like my brother did, that there's scads of jobs has opened up. Flin Flon, Sherridon, Lynn Lake. But yet, the towns is hardly developed. Many of the men are just camped out in tents. And there's no women at all to speak of, maybe some of the bosses' wives or cooks and that. She says as soon as she saves enough money for a train ticket to Sherridon, she's going to head up there. Get her a job.

"They say that up north, there's six men for every girl," Norma says. "Like six times as many men as there is women." Then she hee-haws, making her fat chins wiggle merrily. "But I was thinkin' to myself that maybe it could mean each girl up there could have six men. To herself, like."

I chuckle. "Maybe that way, she'd find at least one good one!"

Her and me are joking and giggling away in our cozy spot out of the wind, watching down the lane, how the spruce trees dance and wave and shiver. But we eventually wind ourselves down.

"Did ya hear about Culain?" she asks me, quiet. "Gave up makin' real money at the mine, I guess, and is runnin' a trapline just here in Porcupine Mountain instead."

"Hm," I shake my head.

She says him and his wife stayed up there for the best part of two months over the winter, kind of a honeymoon, I guess you'd say. Apparently, they're going back up for the summer run, though Culain is helping out this month at the lumber yard here in town.

"Must be hard for ya, Rose," she says, laying her big arm over my shoulder. "'Specially now that his wife is expectin'."

"What?"

"Oh, oh dear," she says. "Oh, ya hadn't heard, I'm sorry." She leans in and gives me a squeeze. "Sorry to be the one to tell ya, but... I guess ya knew it was bound to happen."

I sigh, nodding, feeling again how small and sad the hand is I been dealt. But Norma is so big and rolly-polly that I feel for a minute like a kid taking comfort from a momma, and I lay in towards her warmth, glad for the heartening.

I should have gone north with Culain. I shouldn't have fought him on it. I was wrong on that, and wrong on the other thing I done. It was catching me there that made him do crazy things. Marrying that girl. Why would he do it? She don't even know him!

* * *

April. Glorious April. I woke this morning knowing what to do.

I was laying there, thinking, and it just come to me. Oh my God! He got married—but that don't mean he never wants to see me again! I mean, I was married to Mitch all the while me and Culain was together, and that worked out just fine. Married or not, Culain and me could still be friends. Secret friends like, a comfort to each other.

Happy, happy, happy as a lark, in spite of the cold and dreary weather. Because I finally seen the light and I know what to do.

You always been mine, Culain Kirk. It always been you and me, through thick and thin. Ain't no brown little girl with a sly smile can change that.

I heard he was staying with the woman and her cousins out west of town, on the other side of the tracks from CN station. And I know right which way he'll be going home for his supper. He'll come west through town and cut across the tracks between the Pioneer grain elevator and the big one that says Swan River, taking the wide path to the shanties and shacks on the other side.

I see him coming when he turns off Main Street. His blue-green Irish plaid and grey cap, his metal lunch bucket. I duck back against the south wall of the station, heart pounding, peeking out now and then. As he rounds the corner, I jump out and say "Boo!"

"Jesus!" he jumps, and I laugh like crazy and throw my arms around him, and he's laughing too. "Christ, Rose, ya scared the shit outta me!"

"Culain!" I tell him, stepping back. "I come to see ya."

"Crazy girl," he says, still grinning a little, shaking his head. "Jesus! Give a man a heart attack."

"Come and sit on the bench," I tell him, "so we can talk."

"I..." he balks. "Well alright, but I can't stay long." I slip onto the bench and pat his spot, and he stands, looking around. But it's deserted. Next train ain't till nine tonight. He looks ahead to the way he was going, scratching his head, but then he does come over and sit with me.

"What... did ya want, Rose?"

And I tell him. How hard it's been without him, how I know I done wrong, that time when I done wrong, and how I should have gone with him to Sherridon. I was just being ornery, I don't know why, but I should have gone with him, I know that now. And all them things I said to him, well, that was just the anger talking. I didn't mean none of it. And I'm sorry. And I want to know if he can stop hating me, and maybe, forgive me?

He's been sitting stiff, looking straight ahead all this while. Then he stands suddenly, startling me.

"Look, Rosie," he says. "I don't hate ya. I was very damn mad, true enough. And... I don't know if I'd say I forgave ya. But I ain't... holdin' onto it. And I don't hate ya."

"Culain." I stand and step into him, sliding my arms around his waist. "Culain, we don't hafta stay apart."

He jumps and moves my arms off in a hurry.

"Oh come on!" I tell him, aggravated. "As if I'm gonna kill ya, jist to give ya a little hug!"

He's shaking his head, trying to sidestep me. "I gotta go, Rose."

"No!" I tell him, getting back in front. "Culain! Don't ya see? I'm tellin' ya I'm *sorry!* I'm *admittin'* I was wrong! Culain, yur my man. And I'll do *anythin'*. I'll go with ya to Sherridon if ya want. I'll stay home and be a nice wife. I'll never do ya wrong agin. I learnt my lesson. Can't we jist, jist..."

"Rose?" He's got a look on his face like I just sprouted wings or something. "Rose! I'm *married!*"

"I know that!" I purse my lips. "But... okay, we won't go to Sherridon then." I step in again, sliding my arms around him, and this time, I get a good hold. He can't sidestep me, and I let my titties curve into his chest, looking up, all cutesy, into his eyes. I give him that cat-purr look. "Culain... Jist cuz yur married, don't mean we can't still be friends."

I can feel in his body, how he's tense and mad. "Leggo, Rose!" he glares.

I feel the heat begin to come up my throat. "Ahhh!" I tell him, pulling away. "Why ya gotta be so... persnickety."

"Listen to me, Rose!" he says, eyes boring into mine. "I *ain't yur man* no more. And jist like I was true to you all them years," he tells me, "I will be faithful to my wife."

"I know. But we could... We could jist... make each other happy."

"Rose!" He's shaking his head in wide, slow shakes, voice dripping with pity. "No, Rose. It's too late. I'm married now."

He steps around me, and I jump after him. *This can't be it. He can't be walking away.* I grab his sleeve, yanking him around. And I slap him! Just haul off and slap him a good one, right across the face. Smack! "Don't you God damn walk away from me, Culain Kirk!"

His face is red and tight. *Oh shit! Is he gonna hit me back?*

He grabs my wrists, chin out and glaring. "What the hell!" he hollers. Flings my arms down and points his finger at my nose. "No!" he tells me, like telling off a pup that's made a mess. "I'm not some God damn punchin' bag for you to take things out on, like ya done to Mitch!"

"Damn you, Culain Kirk!" I'm screeching. "Walkin' away from me! And yur a liar, Culain Kirk! Claimin' love for me. Then marryin' some other girl! Not even givin' me a chance!"

"Hmph!" he jeers, glancing over his shoulder to the path between the elevators where he's planning to go.

Don't walk away!

"I gave ya my love!" I yell in his face. "I gave ya childern, everthin! And now, ya desert me? Jist over... one little mistake."

He scoffs. "Rose? One time, Rose? Was it one time ya was down on the big curve?"

Damn, damn Margaret Mary with her damn knowing eyes.

"Well, it..." I shake my head, "mighta happened... once or twice."

"Mm hm." His eyes are full of mockery. "I ain't got time for this, Rose. I gotta get home for supper." He turns and takes a step.

Please, please don't walk away!

"You ain't nothin', Culain Kirk!" I shriek at his back. "Yur jist a dirty boy, pokin' it into yur wingy old uncle's soggy leftovers!"

He stops and turns, eyes straight and hard. "My uncle's soggy leftovers," he repeats, and I see the curl of disgust to his lip, "which would be you."

I got to calm down! God! I got to calm down! "I mean... I mean..."

His brows are knit and them fine, deep eyes, troubled. "I suppose I was that, Rose Kelvey, dirty and without pride. For love of you." He turns his back and begins his trek across the lacework of tracks, his words floating back to me through the cold darkening air. "But not no more."

"Culain!" I call after him. "Culain. I'm sorry!" I plead. "Culain, stop!" I beg. "I'm sorry! Culain come back!"

But he has picked his way across all them sets of tracks, entered the dark crevice between the towering grain elevators, and is gone.

Something breaks inside me. "Culain!" I wail into wind and snow and black silent nothing. "Culain, I'm sorry!" I howl. "I shoulda gone, Culain! I shoulda gone with ya! I'm sorry!"

It wains and I find myself trudging, numb and unbelieving, wind screaming in my ears and burning my cheeks, down the long road south towards Mareses' place. And when I reach Railroad Avenue—all that empty road in front of me, withered-up wild rose bushes dead in the ditches—it hits me again, priming up a hundred years of hot tears that flow and freeze and flow again down my icy cheeks, gouging a jagged nest of bottomless sorrow in my guts, my breast, my brain, my sad, sinful, faithless heart.

* * *

End of April, yet there ain't no spring.

My wee, dark baby arrived early. Tiny little thing and born blue. I wasn't sure at first if I should hold her. In case she didn't make it, like, so it wouldn't hurt as much. But then Mother put her in my arms, I held her after all, and she come around and drank my milk, making me laugh through my tears. I said, "Well, sugar, ya done it now! Got yur momma lovin' ya! So ya better not leave us!"

And she didn't. Two weeks old now, and she's doing good, far as we can tell.

I named her April Hope, but we just call her Hope, for short.

Mitch is down at Ninette in the sanitarium, don't know for how long. The children miss him like crazy, wanting to know when he'll be back and forever going on about his cooking, how he made great stew and biscuits, always played cards with them, and sang to them at bedtime. Some of them stories surprise me, but maybe I wasn't paying attention. Strange to say, but I do miss him at times myself, if just to have another body in the bed. For warmth and comfort, like.

That was our final gift from Old Doc True, getting Mitch down to Ninette. He had wrote the letter to the sanitarium before but didn't hear back so I guess he finally made a telephone call. He got Mitch a place, and even threw in some bills of his own to the Orangemen's envelope for Mitch's train ticket.

Doc was found in his surgery, head laid down quiet on his desk. Had a stroke, that's what the new young doctor said. Mrs. Howdle, Doc's nurse, said there'd been drawers and drawers of IOUs, people who owed him for service, hundreds of dollars, yet when they went through his papers, not a bill was found. Nurse remembered the night in his final weeks that Doc was having a lovely bonfire out by the river, and she figured that must have been what he was burning.

He was one of ours, Old Doc, no matter what kind of money he come from. Now, *them* is going to be big shoes to fill.

Mother had a letter from the Sisters of Loving Kindness that it damn near killed me to read to her. They said not to write to Beatrice no more, nor send her gifts. They had threw out all the packages we sent, they said, which were con… contraband? Whatever the hell that is. My God, we could have used the food and clothes ourselves, but they threw them out! And they said that we was not to visit Beatrice neither. "You, her family, can only influence her back to the errant and sinful," the letter said. It said Beatrice was praying for salvation, doing her penance, and had repented her wicked ways.

Mother sat silent a long while. "Repented for what?" she mumbled, getting up to go back to work. "Bein' poor and a girl? Achin' for a bit a fun now and then?"

My letter was from Norma Mares up at Sherridon. She's working at the Hudson Bay Hotel and says there's men, men, men up there. Even though she's in the kitchen, not the dining room, she says fellows ask her out all the time. Maybe she'll get a husband yet! She has a room in a boarding house not far from where she works and says I should come, maybe in the fall when my baby's a little older and one of my girls could watch her while I work. We could maybe get a house together if I do, there's plenty of places I might get work and she will help me.

I tuck the letter away in my drawer, planning to write back after I've figured out how to explain all my reasons for saying no. Which I don't get no closer to, nor farther from.

* * *

If April showers is supposed to bring May flowers, we are failing at that too. May has come in fits and starts, patches of dirty snow crust still laying here and there, sun far off and weak. Still feeling more like winter than anything else.

While baby Hope sleeps, I sit alone on my step, rain dripping off the roof onto the hood of my shawl, not wanting to be in the house with the children jumping around in their games and not wanting to be alone. But I can't go to Mother's on account of the terrible row her and me had last week.

She had made a nice little spice cake, with icing and everything, to have after supper one day and when she brung it out, she told me happy birthday. Thirty years since she brought me into this world, my poppa's mother had been the midwife, and I was born as the sun topped the trees. That was a good birth, she said, and still her favourite to recall.

I'd had another letter from Norma saying she had found a house where only women and children were allowed, and that as soon as I found work, we could try for that and I could probably send for baby Hope and a couple of the children. Pretty exciting. So then, as me and Mother was out stocking up the woodpile, I was just thinking out loud and started telling her about it. And I said maybe in the fall, when the harvest is in, I would leave the children with her for a little while and go see if I could get work at Sherridon after all.

Well, she seemed none too pleased and questioned me a little, saying what would be the point of that? I got too many children too young to be left on their own, she said, so she would have to be the one watching a bunch of young children and still trying to get her own work done.

I was just pitching the wood and giving answers for all the questions she was asking, saying it wouldn't be till after harvest and I would send for Hope soon as I had work of course, not thinking too much about it, when Mother went total crazed on me.

"And who does all this God damn work in the meantime?" she demanded, sweeping her arm out across the two shacks and big yard. "I'm gettin' too damn old to be doin' work that's yurs to do."

"Well, it's jist for a little while," I explained.

"Doncha never learn?" she was yelling, face all red. "Ain't ya learnt nothin' from yur sisters? Ain't ya learnt what happens to women like us out there in the world? What they can do to ya when there's no one's got yur back?"

"I can take care a myself!" I told her, getting miffed.

She'd stopped working, had her fists on her hips, and was just screeching in my face. About how this is what I always do. Never satisfied, always wanting what's out of reach. Just like with Culain. Nobody was kicking about me having Culain for a fancy man, but could I just quit while I was ahead? No! I had to go fooling around down the big curve and throw a wrench into everything.

"And ya still ain't learnt!" she glared. "Can ya not get it through that thick skull a yurs? To be faithful to yur own?"

I frowned. "Well, Mitch can still come back."

"Not Mitch!" she barked. "Me! I'm the one deserves yur loyalty. Me and the childern. Rose, we need ya here! *We need ya!* And yur still actin' like yur fourteen years old, tryin' to run away when the goin' gets tough."

I came home after that, vowing to myself I'd take all the kids and leave for Sherridon tomorrow if I could. But of course, how could I?

I stayed away Tuesday and Wednesday, but it's coming up to the Victoria Day weekend, which is when the seed goes in the ground, and she's out there trying to pull the plow herself in the garden spot, muck clinging to her boots and wind blowing. Just for a minute, I look at Mother and see how really small she is, and the big work in front of her. I sigh and put my coat on, get my rubber boots, go over, and take hold of the plow, which she lets me do. Next time I look, she's got a shovel, breaking up the bigger clods, dragging out rocks and old roots, and I keep on with the plow and the work gets done.

But after, I go back to my place and she goes back to hers.

Next day, we work together again. And when we've done all we can, she says there's pig's feet there at home and potatoes to boil. I say okay, I'll tell the kids to come. We limp along like that together till it feels almost back to normal.

And we don't mention Sherridon no more.

* * *

I cannot seem to sleep these nights, just lay there in my lumpy bed, always too hot or too cold, tossing back and forth. And every damn dream is queer and scary.

I keep having a dream of all my sisters. I'm down low somewheres and there's this steep hillside, lined with all these big ash stumps.

Someone has lopped off the whole tops of them. Coppicing, I think it's called, cutting them back to make them grow again stronger. All gnarly and queer-looking, them trees, like they might just live, or might be dead forever, you wouldn't know. And my sisters is all there, trying to get up that hill, but having a hard time.

Eileen is leading them, beautiful as ever, but yet she seems so wan and full of pain. Holding her hand is little Carly, looking small and sickly, but Eileen is trying to help her on the climb. Next is Beatrice, jumping and raging, not paying attention to nobody else, wearing only a little top and bloomers, dirty and ragged, legs a nasty mess of welts and scars. There's the twins too, seeming lost and confused, flailing in the brambles, cut and hurt and crying. I'm calling out to them, I want to help them all, but they don't seem to hear me. Then I see myself there too, trying to get up that steep hill right along with them, also limping and not whole. Although what my failing is, exactly, what damage has been done to me, I can't really tell.

I lay in the bed, wishing to hell for another hour of sleep, giving milk to my little Hope and keeping her toasty warm. But pretty soon, I'm starting to shiver. The stove is out and the longer I lay here, the colder the house will get. Now that Petunia has run off with the Beaulieu boy and Margie is working at Goodales' farm, it's all on me. So I heave myself up into the grey day and get the porridge going.

Why can't I never have a nice dream, a pretty dream, where the sun shines, people have fun, and happy things happen at the end?

* * *

Deep in summer. Me and Mother is sitting on her step, baby Hope at my breast. I've just read Mother the letter from Kenny. Now that he's done his basic, they'll be heading east for more training on the coast. He should know soon whether he's made it into the Royal Canadian Engineers.

He says a buddy of his at the Flin Flon Herald asked him to do a kind of writeup for the paper, regular-like, that he would send back from whatever different places he winds up going, and he's pretty cheerful on that. That's what the union done for him, he says, the good old union. For years now, they been training up any fellows that wanted to learn reading and writing in the evenings after work and look now. My brother! Writing in the newspaper! Just imagine!

Kenny says he's going to call his writeup Blacky's Tour, on account of how the other fellas always razz him about his daddy's blood, nicknaming him Nigger Workman. I was took aback by that, but anyways... It's usually in good fun, Kenny says, so he just takes up the joke hisself. The odd time, a fella will cross the line and then he'll have to tune them up, but mostly, it's just a joke.

I finish reading and look over at Mother, not sure if I should say something. I mean, Negro, if they said Negro, well, that's respectable. Like just saying Irish or French. But *Nigger*... that's a different thing. "Mother..." I say. "I... well, I feel kinda... mad, what they're sayin' to Kenny. I mean, that don't seem like a funny joke to me."

"No," she says, and spits sideways into the dirt. "It ain't."

Cool wind blows in across the willows, flipping my skirt hem around. I make sure my sweater and that little throw is tucked in good around baby. I'm thinking about my brother, if them Nazis was coming for him and he needed help, I wonder, would them fellows fight for him to the end? The ones that call him that name?

I love my brother so dear. All I want in the world is just for him to make it back home alive. They're saying the war might be over by Christmas, 1940. Wouldn't that be grand? Maybe he wouldn't even see action. And all them other men from the Valley here. Crofter Kirk, Thor Sigurdson, Danny Cleaver, the Gusterson boys, Beau Mitchell, young Art Taylor, there's so many.

Even Trooper Roaring Kirk. Yes, our young Troop had went missing here a while back and a farmer said he picked him up, hitchhiking south, took him as far as Pine Creek. And then someone said they seen him at Dauphin, in line for enlistment. And I guess they must have took him on, because he ain't been heard from since. Little bugger. Well, all I can do is wish him luck. And all of them.

Norma Mares says Sherridon is a boom, there's so many nice people up there. She's got a special beau now, name of Alec McAlec, came all the way from Newfoundland and she can hardly wait for me to meet him. And his brother that came with him. She's got a job lined up for me at the café, long as I'm there before Thanksgiving, and that rooming house room is still open. She says we can always try for a house to share after Christmas. She knows it'll be hard for me to leave Hope behind but it's only for a little while, we're sure to send for her once we're solid.

And don't forget, her letter jokes, about them six men for each of us!

I ain't told Mother nothing more about Sherridon though. I'm scared she's going to be mad again. But yet, I know I got to tell her pretty soon as it's only a month till I go.

Sometimes, I lay in the dark, moon shadows swaying on the walls, Culain Kirk just gentle on my mind. Thinking of times he come to me with smiles or funny comments, always knowing how to cheer me when life was dark and hard. All the times he brung food for my children when we was hungry, wild meat and fish and pheasant, little gifts of cash he always give when he got work. The secret and familiar way he would brush my arm when we met in public, cup his palm around my elbow for a second as he passed. How when I lost my sister and then again when my step-dad died, and when Beatrice was took away too, he come to me in the night, not wanting his own needs met, but just to hold me in my sorrow.

Thinking about the day I first come to him on the bush trail in my skimpy nighty, how the world was dry and dying but the gold hair glinted on his thick muscular arm and my lips was wet with wanting him. How he come up after and took me wild like cool rain in a thunder storm. Times he thrilled me in the woods or the bunkhouse or a backroom in a busy house, nobody knowing. All them endless nights on the trapline, the scent of cedar and pine in the air and the earthy smell of fresh pelts nailed to the cabin wall. Fire cracking in the belly of the stove and raging fire he was pounding into me, filling my arms and my womb and my mouth and every part of me with joy.

I toss to the wall, back towards the empty dark, and back to the wall again. But sleep don't come. There's a feeling gnawing at me here way down, a meaner layer of that old familiar ache. A ache that gapes you open like a black cave you've fell in, sliding down and down on slippery, mean-cutting rock, knowing in your fall that you ain't never getting out. Or the place inside you, when a birth is coming, how it burns and tears and rips you apart till all you want is death to come and end it.

This is what comes of the *seven year ache*, I suppose, but I can't put no bounds on its ending. This here ache, raw and sore and yawning, must be about a seven times *seven year ache*. Shows no sign of letting up anytime soon.

Author's Note:
The Reality of Eugenics in Canada

Many good people are unaware that there was a powerful and thriving eugenics presence here in Canada for much of the early Twentieth Century. I first encountered this dark truth in university course work in sociology and education. Only later did I put this theoretical understanding together with my family's personal experience; several of my very poor aunts and uncles were sterilized during the 1930s and 40s, no doubt by adherents to eugenics philosophy.

This novel's Chapter 5, A Terrible Twinning, centrally involves a run-in with representatives of the eugenics movement. Though fictionalized, it tells one true story involving my aunties and grandmother.

If you would like to research these issues, I can recommend as a starting place Angus McLaren's book *Our Own Master Race: Eugenics in Canada, 1885-1945*. Or, go to the Eugenics Archive online: https://eugenicsarchive.ca/discover/world

Fisher Lavell

Acknowledgements

I am grateful for the many "writer friends" who read and commented on successive chapters of this novel. In particular, I want to thank the members of my writers' groups; in Winnipeg, Hedy Heppenstall, Lesia Shepel, and Dorryce Smelts; and in Swan River, the members of Parkland Writers, Gaylene Dutchyshen, Linda Carpentier, and Julie Bell. Hedy and Gaylene both also gave careful and detailed responses to the entire manuscript, as did my cousin, Melody Abbott, and my niece, Fauna Church. I so appreciate the sweat and toil, the labour of love it was, really, to dedicate those many hours to reading and providing feedback on my work.

I had the unlikely good fortune of connecting with Marjorie Anderson, editor extraordinaire, who told me that this novel needed to be Rosie's story, and in her voice (not in the third person as originally intended), and that it was up to me to get Rosie's story to her readers. Marjorie's professionalism, knowledge, and advice have guided my progress, and my faith in her judgement has buoyed me up through the rough patches, doubts, and discouragement.

Finally, I will acknowledge and ever thank my mother and my father who, although they have left this world, bequeathed to me the priceless gift of family stories, the grist of what has come together here.

CPSIA information can be obtained
at www.ICGtesting.com
Printed in the USA
LVHW100429181022
730945LV00002B/141